THE KINGDOM

A SAM POPE NOVEL

ROBERT ENRIGHT

For my girls,

CHAPTER ONE

Two Years Ago…

The summer evening spread a welcoming warmth through the estate in Toxteth. As part of the Metropolitan Borough of Liverpool, the area had long since held a reputation as a haven for crime and violence. While many areas have their skeletons, Toxteth had become synonymous with a crime hot spot, especially after the town was subjected to riots in the early eighties.

Hundred of arrests were made, numerous buildings had been criminally damaged and hundreds of police officers had been injured.

Including Jack Townsend's father.

As proud a police officer as one could imagine, Sergeant Malcolm Townsend had served with honour and distinction throughout his tenure walking the beat. Respected by his peers and his public alike, his career had taken a different path due to a spinal injury caused during those ill-fated riots.

The man had never been the same again and although he served for another eighteen years after the injury, Townsend grew up watching his father resent what had been taken from him. As he finally succumbed to cancer when Townsend was seventeen, he died unful-filled, and it was something that his son wanted to put right.

Now, stood with his hands firmly in his pockets, looking out at the graffiti covered overpass that cut through the estate, Jack Townsend wondered what would happen if the locals knew he was a police officer.

Worse still, that he'd been successful working undercover in the estate's gang for over a year.

It had been a rough assignment. The Bell View Estate had been built on the promise of a fresh start for the area, with lavish promises of gentrification and a stimulating, local economy. As the flats were erected, most of the scepticism was eradicated by the arrival of a few fancy eateries, but soon, the money dried up.

No matter how hard the town tried, Toxteth just couldn't outrun its reputation.

But where there was dissension and poverty, there was opportunity and slowly but surely, drugs began to flood the estate and the Bell View Gang took a stranglehold on the area. With the rise in class A drugs hitting the streets and any resistance met with extreme violence, the Merseyside Police needed a more subtle approach. Banging down doors and raiding buildings wouldn't endear them to the locals, many of whom distrusted the badge more than their local dealer.

They needed to work from the inside out.

Townsend took the job.

A few teenage boys cycled past, trash talking each other with vile banter and as they approached Townsend, they slowed down.

They lowered their voices.

Townsend knew his reputation proceeded him, and the boys offered him a respectful nod before cycling away into the cool evening.

It was a reputation he'd earnt the hard way.

Despite being thirty-five years of age, Townsend knew he looked younger. His inability to grow a complete beard had been a frequent source of amusement among his fellow officers. Having grown up in the neighbouring town of Edge Hill, he knew the area well enough.

Coupled with his youthful looks he made the perfect candidate to infiltrate the gang.

It was the chance of a lifetime, knowing full well that playing a leading role in disbanding such a renowned crime entity would see his career fast tracked.

A promotion. A big pay rise.

A better future for his wife and little girl, Eve.

Six months they'd told him, which was a long time to leave them, but the spoils were worth the heartache. Mandy, his wife, had vehemently protested the mission.

But he knew he had to take it.

Not just for his own family, but to honour his father's legacy.

The Merseyside Police had worked alongside the local council to procure a flat within one of the estate blocks, moving Townsend in under his pseudonym. With his strong, well-toned physique and penchant for kickboxing, Townsend knew how to handle himself and within the first month of his new life, he'd confronted one of the dealers who'd tried to take a liberty with him.

Townsend broke the man's nose and a few ribs before sending him back to the gang as a message.

They retaliated not with violence, but with an offer to join them. Considering his alias, Danny Miller, had a rap sheet as long as his forearm, it made sense for him to accept their offer.

But running with the gang for six months proved futile. The guys running the estate were kept away from the big boy's table, with their drugs, money, and weapons specially delivered by very rich people who knew how to cover their tracks.

As the mission trundled on, Townsend found it harder to keep his cover, having to go to lengths he'd never wanted to to remain hidden.

It meant hurting people. Badly.

It meant taking drugs he despised.

But he never cheated on his wife. His loyalty to her was iron clad and at a few parties, where the combination of his good looks and mystique turned many a female head, Townsend ensured he made his

3

exit. When one of the lads questioned his manhood in front of the rest of the members, he was resigned to teaching him a lesson.

He'd broken the man's jaw and put him in hospital.

Now, his handler, Inspector Reece Sanders, had communicated with him that they needed to meet. There was every chance Townsend had gone too far and would be pulled from the mission.

It would be easy enough.

There was nothing stopping them sending a squadron of police cars to the estate one morning and kicking his door down. The show would be for the rest of the gang, who would watch as he was dragged from his bed, furiously struggling against his cuffs as he was thrown in the back of the car and driven away for good.

They'd assume he had the book thrown at him and sent to rot in HMP Liverpool.

But then it would all have been for nothing. All the violence and pain that he'd dished out, all the drugs he'd pumped into his body.

All the time spent away from his girls, which broke a little piece of his heart every day.

As Townsend checked his watch again, the bus he was waiting for jolted round the corner and approached the stop. As the doors hissed open, he watched a few local girls step off, one of them offering an inappropriate smile that he didn't reciprocate. He beeped his card on the reader to pay his fare and then marched to the back, staring out anyone who dared look at him.

He had to keep up the act.

He never knew who might be watching.

The sun began to set beyond the backdrop of the vibrant city of Liverpool, and Townsend pressed his head against the window, looking out to a world that he should be a part of. His mind raced to Mandy and Eve, wondering what wonderful stories his little girl was conjuring up as her mother bathed her. It had been just over a month since she'd turned five, and despite it breaking every rule of his assignment, he'd watched Mandy push her on the swings in their local park.

His heart yearned to be back with them.

He should have been by now.

4

But bringing down the people funding and supplying the Bell View Gang was the chance to make the city a safer place for her. As the bus passed Crown Street Park, he watched with envious eyes as a few parents played with their kids. Annoyed by his jealousy, Townsend pulled his hood up, switched on his EarPods, and closed his eyes, losing himself in the music.

Eventually, the bus ground to a halt and when he opened his eyes, he saw the other buses that comprised the terminal garage. The other passengers had long since departed, and the driver gave him a respectful nod as he ambled out from his compartment and exited through the doors. Townsend sighed, removed his EarPods, and waited the few minutes it took for Inspector Sanders to join him on-board.

At six foot two, the man was a wiry concoction of limbs and grey hair, the thinning strands on his head offset by the neat beard that ran the edges of his gaunt face. Approaching his fiftieth birthday, Sanders was a wise hand in the Merseyside Police and had been one of its guiding lights on battling organised crime. His dedication to the job had cost him his marriage, and when he wasn't working obscene hours, he was either on the golf course or spending time with his teenage sons, depending on the weekend.

The man was a walking cliché of a policeman but considering he'd been Townsend's only tether to the real world, there was nobody he trusted more.

As Sanders walked down the aisle, he held two coffees in his hand. With a wry smile, he handed one to Townsend before raising his eyebrows.

'Well, you look like shit.' Sanders chuckled, his Scouse accent thick and proud.

'I feel it,' Townsend said, accepting the coffee.

'What happened?' Sanders asked, nodding towards Townsend's knuckles. The skin was a faded yellow, surrounding a few slight cuts across the bone.

'I had to keep my cover,' Townsend replied grimly, taking a sip from his cup. 'Any update?'

'On?' Sanders sat back, straightening his tie.

'Fuck's sake, sir,' Townsend snapped. 'Six months you said. Six months and we would have everything we needed. It's been a fucking year and I'm still in this shit-hole, having to beat down a fucking drug addict for money. It's not who I am.'

'I know, son.' Sanders gently rested a hand on Townsend's shoulder. 'I know it's been tough. But it hasn't been for nottin'. Because of you, we've made over thirteen arrests and shut down four drug dens. All of it watertight, because of you. That's more in a year than the last four.'

'But it's not enough, is it?' Townsend turned to his boss, who looked solemnly at his coffee cup. The silence said enough, and Townsend shook his head and rested his arms on the chair ahead of him. 'I just want to go home.'

'Say the word and I'll pull you out. It's the way it's always been.'

It was a dirty tactic to put the decision on Townsend's shoulders, and Sanders hated playing it. The man was yearning to return to his old life, to be in the comfort of his own home and feel the touch of his family. It was understandable, but there was a reason Sanders had selected Townsend for the job. Sure, he fit the physical profile and had the local upbringing to make it work, but it went deeper than that.

Townsend was a fighter.

The man had ruthlessly attacked his cases with a dedication that turned heads, and Sanders' undercover unit wasn't the only one snooping around. He knew that even with the likelihood of the assignment lasting years, there was no quit in the young detective. He had a burning desire to do the right thing, a flame stoked by the injustice his father had suffered.

Sanders could pull the plug with one phone call.

But now wasn't the time. Not with what had come up.

'How are my girls?' Townsend broke the silence, his voice heavy with regret.

'They're good. Mandy makes our meetings every week. She sends her love. As does Eve.' Townsend felt the lump in his throat, and he swallowed it back, forcing his body to withhold its tears. Sanders continued. 'Something's come up. Something big.'

'What are you talking about?'

'They confirmed the death of Sam Pope earlier today.'

Townsend sat up.

'Jesus. Really?' Sanders nodded his response. 'How?'

'They found his body mutilated and burnt to a crisp in some abandoned shack in South Carolina. Could only identify him through DNA tests. Nasty stuff.'

'In America?'

'The man had made a lot of enemies.' Sanders shrugged. 'But with his spectre no longer looming, we're expecting some major moves to be made, especially since Harry Chapman is no longer running most of the import/export in this fucking country.'

'Opportunity is an attractive mistress.'

'You're telling me. We'll have no fucking woodwork left with the amount of vermin crawling out looking for their slice.' Sanders pulled an envelope from the inside of his blazer and dropped it onto Townsend's lap. 'Which is why we've been called.'

'What's this?' Townsend asked, lifting the envelope with intrigue.

'Opportunity.'

Townsend pulled it open and removed the briefing within. As he did, his eyebrows raised with a mixture of surprise and concern. He turned to his superior officer, whose grim expression told him it was legit.

'How long is this one for?'

Townsend could feel his heart cracking down the middle, knowing that this would leave a scar that would likely never heal. It had been a long time since he'd felt anything even resembling his old self.

Since he'd felt like a police officer.

A husband.

A father.

He ached to walk through the front door of his house, wrap both of his girls in his powerful grip, and never let them go. But the distance between them had grown considerably and what was written on the sheet in his hands would most likely make that distance permanent.

But if it was true, and he and Sanders could make it happen, then the pride his girls would feel for what he accomplished with his sacrifice would hopefully bring them back together.

He already knew the answer to his question, but he stared at Sanders with a pointless modicum of hope in his eyes.

With his jaw pulled tight, Sanders quashed it instantly.

'As long as it takes.'

CHAPTER TWO

With the wondrous sound of the waves lapping at the shore, Sam Pope gradually opened his eyes, waking from another night of disturbed sleep. The sun was peeking through the gap in the curtain, sending a slither of sunlight across his adequate bed. Somewhere in the sky, a seagull squawked without regard. He turned his head to the side and lifted his watch, sighing at the early rise on another spring morning, his body desperate for a decent night of rest.

But the dream was always the same.

It was as vivid as the memory that had been burnt into his mind and the catalyst for everything he'd been through since.

The flashing lights of the police car.

The mild panic from the passers-by, all of them gasping at the horror that had unfolded before them.

Police officers doing their best to control the scene, his brain distorting their movements and rendering them as faceless, blurry oddities.

The bone-chilling scream of anguish that echoed from

his ex-wife's throat as she collapsed to her knees in shock and despair.

Then the motionless body of his son.

Jamie.

His body had crumpled to the floor, and a stream of blood was slithering from his ear. His eyes were wide open.

He was dead.

Killed by a drunk driver Sam should, and could, have stopped. But his failure to do the right thing had cost him the thing he treasured most in the world, and while his memory of that night was as clear as the blue morning sky, his dreams had a way of emphasising the blame.

Every night, the broken image of his son would contort further, his bones snapping until he was looking Sam dead in the eye.

Then Jamie would speak.

'You killed me.'

Without fail, Sam would shudder awake, allowing his guilt to manifest in a punishing lack of sleep. Without fail, Sam would sit up in his bed, his T-shirt drenched with sweat and stuck to his muscular frame. Some nights, he would resist the urge to return to the nightmare, but when his body was running on empty, he would turn the pillow over, bury his head within it, and try his best to keep the haunting images from his mind.

Outside his window, he could hear the gentle rumble of the morning traffic as the seaside town of Lowestoft in Suffolk began its busy day. The Easter holidays meant a surge of tourism to the town, the sandy beaches a magnet for families with young kids or those who just fancy a change from city life.

On the few occasions Sam had mingled with the locals when buying a coffee, he detected a sense of resentment from the born and bred inhabitants of the town, although the influx of *outsiders* such as himself did mean a sharp uptick in the local economy.

Sam had only been there for a few days, doing his best to lie low in the aftermath of his encounter with Daniel Bowker and his crew. As he rose from his bed and shuffled to the bathroom, he took a glance at the small mirror affixed to the front of the cabinet and sighed. For two years, the world had thought him dead.

His war against crime had made him a folk legend, but had also put him at the top of the UK's most wanted list.

Deservedly so.

From taking down Frank Jackson and the High Rise, to disbanding the Kovalenko human-trafficking empire, Sam had put dozens of criminals in the ground. With every life he took, Sam knew he was breaking a promise to his son, as well as the law itself. Yet had he not picked up his rifle and put those who deserved it in his crosshairs, then good people would have died.

In the case of young Jasmine Hill, who had been kidnapped by the Kovalenkos: worse.

His fight eventually led him to cross paths with his old mentor, Sergeant Carl Marsden, who had been marked as a terrorist and an enemy against the country. With the relentless General Ervin Wallace hunting him, Marsden eventually gave his life to provide Sam with a devastating truth.

The truth being that his career as an elite sniper for the UK Armed Forces had been a lie.

Recruited into an "off the books" unit, known only as Project Hailstorm, Sam had always thought he was carrying out missions for the protection of his country and countless others.

In reality, he was merely a supremely efficient hitman, picking off targets for Wallace to keep him and his associates in power. Under the false pretences, Sam had come close to death, and seen many a good man lose their life for a cause that was never their own.

Men like Vargas.

Like Mac.

Faces and names that were seared into his memory, scarring it worse than the litany of physical ones that adorned his chiselled body.

Armed with the truth, Sam, with the help of his friends Paul Etheridge and Detective Inspector Amara Singh, eventually took down Wallace. Their battle ending with Wallace's own soldier killing him. Farukh, the *Hangman of Baghdad*, hurled Wallace from the top of a building, before fighting Sam to the death moments after. Somehow, through sheer force of will, Sam managed to slit the man's throat and survive.

But it had cost him his freedom.

Offering up his liberty to spare Singh a portion of the blame, he allowed her to walk him out in cuffs and send him to the deepest, darkest prison that didn't exist in any penal system.

The Grid.

Buried under ground and manned by a sadistic group of guards, Ashcroft was a fortress designed to lock away the most brutal of the UK's criminals.

Sam knew he belonged there.

But it also housed Harry Chapman, one of the most powerful criminals to have graced the UK and a man who was still operating his empire from behind bars. The man who funded and supplied the High Rise, and who had opened the Port of Tilbury for the Kovalenkos to traffic young women in and out of the country.

All roads led to him.

And Sam was happy to walk them.

Utilising Etheridge's unrivalled hacking skills, Sam had

been transferred to the prison unbeknownst to the Metropolitan Police, in order to shut Chapman down for good. Once he'd located Chapman's base of operations, Sam gave the information to Singh. Chapman got to live long enough to see his empire crumble to dust, before Sam made a daring escape.

A heartbreaking confrontation with his old friend, Mac, almost cost him his freedom again, only for Etheridge to compromise his own to let Sam run free.

Both men went on the run, and Sam headed to America to fulfil one final promise before he ended his war on crime for good.

Alex Stone had saved his life when a gun had been pressed against his head, and in doing so, had drawn a promise from Sam to help her get her family back. With her life a horrifying mess of street crimes and government manipulation, he found her in the midst of an escalating drug war between a Colombian Cartel and a dangerous Motorcycle Gang. Inserted in by a treacherous DEA agent, Sam went to war in South Carolina to get her back to her family.

In doing so, he'd been able to fake his death and return to the UK under a new name and with a clean slate. That had been almost two years ago.

The fight was over.

There was no need to fight back anymore, and he'd dedicated those years to working alongside one of the best men he'd ever known.

Adrian Pearce.

It had been over three years since Pearce and Sam had met, with Pearce at the time working in the Met's Department of Professional Standards and investigating Sam for his involvement in a few violent crimes.

Through their shared belief in doing the right thing, a kinship was born, and although Pearce never condoned

Sam's actions, he understood the motive behind it. There were places Sam could go that the law couldn't and when both men stepped away from their respective paths, they were drawn back towards each other through their devotion to helping others.

For nearly two years, that's what they did. Working at the Bethnal Green Youth Centre in honour of Sam's fallen friend, Theo Hunter, it had been two of the most peaceful years of Sam's life.

No violence.

No alcohol.

Even the relentless guilt of his son's death subsided a little.

Sam had been searching for redemption and came within an inch of it.

Then Bowker and his crew, under orders from a wealthy CEO who wanted to keep her image clean, violently assaulted one of his friends. Sean Wiseman, a young man Sam had put back on the right track, was beaten into a coma for being associated with a reporter who'd rattled the wrong cage.

Left for dead in an alleyway a stone's throw from his mother's house, Sam had no idea whether Sean would survive.

But he made damn sure those who hurt him didn't.

After nearly two years of peace, Sam had stepped back into the war zone, and as he stared at his reflection in the mirror, he was comfortable with the man that he saw.

Gone was the long, lightly coloured hair and thick beard he'd used to obscure his face. The cropped hair had flecks of grey around the sides, as well as the thick stubble that adorned his powerful jawline.

Sam looked like the soldier he'd always been.

It was who he was, and despite doing his best to walk a lighter path, fate had a cruel way of showing its hand.

Everitt Park. The vast field was home to a number of different activities, such as mini golf, a park, an arcade, and even a museum. Undoubtedly, the place would have been packed on the weekend, but Sam's midweek stroll had found it almost empty, barring a few new parents pushing their newborn babies in their prams and an elderly couple who were feeding the ducks. The edge of the park tapered off into a river from which Oulton Broad found its name, with a number of expensive private boats lined up in the small marina that arched its way around the park. Beyond that was a vertical lift bridge, which was intermittently activated to permit the boats a safe passage through.

As Sam stood and took in his beautiful surroundings, his eyes eventually fell upon the large pub that sat across the bridge and overlooked the expanse of water.

That was the place.

Smithy, the drug dealer who Sam had extracted the information from, had been reluctant to give up his boss at first. It was admirable yet misguided. Having cornered Smithy in an alleyway, Sam had hammered the young man with a precision shot to the kidney. In a blind rage, the man tried to fight through the pain and pull a knife on Sam.

It was a big mistake.

Sam deflected the blow with his forearm, drove a vicious punch into the man's throat, and then snatched the knife from him. Retracting the blade, Sam then jovially whacked the man on the forehead with it, admonishing the man for carrying it in the first place.

A few well-placed punches later, and Sam had the information he needed.

Ryan Marsh was the man in charge of all cocaine supply and distribution in the Suffolk area. He was well protected by a few henchmen at all times, had a wife who enjoyed the finer things in life, and friends in the police.

Smithy didn't know much beyond that, except that Marsh was always armed with a gun.

Which made him dangerous.

Which made him a target.

As Sam looked out from the park, across the beautiful water, and at the gastropub where he'd been directed, Pearce's words filtered through his mind.

'If you go looking for the devil, one day, you will find him.'

Sam was well aware that the path he'd rejoined probably only had one outcome. Despite the movies he'd seen or the action novels he'd read, people don't just get caught in the wrong place at the wrong time and then put the world to rights. To find the true evil that plagued the world, you had to go digging yourself.

And the further into the mud you dig, the dirtier your hands get.

Without the support of Etheridge, who Sam hadn't heard from in two years, there was no way of knowing what he was walking into. Etheridge would have undoubtedly baffled Sam with his expertise, drawing up all the information he could on Marsh and feeding Sam enough of it for him to draw up a tactical plan.

But Sam was on his own.

All he had was his gun and his instincts.

Instincts that had kept him alive under heavy fire in the Amazon jungle and had helped him to bring down some of the most dangerous and notorious criminals on both sides of the Atlantic. There was every chance Ryan Marsh could be the person to put Sam in the ground and reunite him with Jamie.

But until that moment became a reality, Sam would make sure he not only shut down the drug empire the man was amassing but also find out where he procured his firearm.

Sam tried, but failed, to suppress a yawn. The night of

try to wrestle back control from the sudden jolt of pleasure. The house was a wreck, with both he and Carly giving up on it a few years ago, along with a lot of things.

There had been a time when they were happy together, but in the decade since, as Marsh's drug intake grew, so did the distance between them and with her chances of starting a family gone, Carly had found her solace in alcohol. There was no intimacy in their life, no love to bind them, but Marsh still forced himself upon her with a horrifying regularity and she drank to hide the pain of what her life had become.

When she said no, he got violent, and while he wasn't a muscular man, he was still over seventeen stone of tattooed fury and the current swelling on her face was a testament to what one strike from him could do.

There had been broken bones. Stitches. Even an extended spell in a hospital bed.

As she shivered with fear, Marsh shook his head in disgust.

She was just another part of his life that had failed him, and he resented that she was now the best he could do. There had been a time when the two of them were attractive and vibrant, when they connected in a way that would make most porn stars blush.

But now, he couldn't give a shit about her.

'I'm off to work,' Marsh said, sliding his bulky frame into his ill-fitting leather jacket. He didn't even try to use the zip. 'When I get back tonight, don't say no this time. I'm not sure my knuckles can take it.'

Carly turned further in her chair, wishing for the fabric to open up and swallow her. Marsh smirked at the reaction, enjoying the power and control he still commanded over her.

Over everyone.

The afternoon was bleeding into another pleasant

spring evening and he couldn't wait to take his usual seat in the beer garden of the pub, watching the football on the outdoor screen and working his way through several pints and a twenty deck. At the benches nearer the back of the garden, which overlooked the Oulton Broad, two of his dealers would be on hand, raking in a fortune as the evening wore on.

The landlord would stay silent. The monthly envelope of cash he received from Marsh was effectively a rent payment.

That and the very real threat that Marsh would put him in a wheelchair.

Checking the watch that was framed by his tattoos, Marsh realised he had two hours before kick-off and decided to head towards the town centre, hoping to grab himself a delicious dinner. The thought of inviting Carly flashed through his mind for a few seconds, before he dismissed it with a chuckle.

He'd made damn sure she wouldn't want to be seen in public for a while.

As he walked down the garden path to the street ahead, Marsh sprinkled a little more cocaine on his key and lifted it to his nose. Another enjoyable hit put a spring in his step, and he headed off for another night's work, knowing there was nobody in the town who could stop him.

An illusion he would have to wait three more hours to have shattered.

prayed that the night would never end, knowing that in the morning he would have to leave again.

With no idea of when he would be coming back.

———

Townsend barely recognised the man staring back at him from the mirror.

His hair, now tinged with flecks of grey, was cut neatly into a side parting, with his thick beard clinging to his jaw. With plenty of spare time, he'd built an impressive physique, ensuring that he didn't look out of place with the other gang members. Their mistrust of him was understandable, considering they weren't English themselves, but he'd earnt their trust after what he'd done in prison.

It had been two long years.

Two years since he'd gone by the name Jack. Two years since he was taken out of Bell View and, after one glorious night with his wife, thrust into a prison van and put on a dangerous road.

All in the name of justice.

Thrust nearly three hundred miles away from his home, Townsend had done unspeakable things to get to the place he was today.

To get so close.

Every step of his journey had been calculated, with Sanders making sure Townsend kept a closed grip on who he truly was. There were times when it would have been easy to truly cross the line. But he never could.

Not when Mandy and Eve were waiting for him.

Sanders had worked tirelessly to keep them in contact, arranging for police protected visits for his wife and child, where Townsend could spend some time remembering who he was and what he was doing it for. It was a risk, one that Mandy seemed more willing to take than Townsend himself, but Sanders knew that without a connection to the man he was, there was a strong chance that Townsend wouldn't make it back.

But today, he was struggling.

The urge to drink was becoming stronger and stronger, with the sweet release of inebriation a potent tool in helping him deal with things. Townsend only drank in the small flat where he lived.

Doing so in front of the others was too dangerous.

If his guard was to ever slip or his cover blown, it would be fatal. Not just for him, but for his family as well.

It was why today he couldn't drink.

That evening, he could potentially bust the case wide open and step back into the world he longed for every day. He needed his head clear, and he needed to make sure it counted.

Otherwise, all of it, the two years of struggle and questionable actions would be for nothing.

Knock knock.

Townsend turned from the mirror and slid a black T-shirt over his muscular frame and moved to the door cautiously. As he approached it, he retrieved the Glock 17 from the side table, and holding it in one hand, he peered through the peephole.

It was Sanders.

Townsend opened the door and ushered him in. His superior officer stepped in, trying his best to hide the disdain at the dank smell that dominated the flat, and then turned to him with a grin.

'Jesus, Jack,' Sanders exclaimed. 'You mind lowering that thing?'

Townsend placed the gun back on the table as he shut the door, and as had become routine, he gratefully accepted the fresh coffee Sanders had picked up on journey.

'I have to be careful.'

'I know.' Sanders nodded apologetically. 'How you holding up?'

Townsend scoffed and reached for the cigarettes and lighter that adorned the tiny coffee table in the middle of the front room. Sanders tutted in disappointment at the unhealthy habit Townsend had picked up and then cast his eyes over the rest of the table. Empty beer bottles and an overflowing ashtray.

The evidence answered the question for him.

'I'm worried, sir.' Townsend was clearly on edge. 'I think they're on to me.'

'Impossible.' Sanders shook his head. 'Everything has been watertight. Your records, your links to organised crime. It's bulletproof.'

Townsend took a long drag on the cigarette, knowing his wife would admonish him if she saw him smoking.

'I think there's a rat in the team.'

Sanders nearly spat out his coffee. One of the defining traits of his well-respected career within the police was his judge of character. There hadn't been a person he couldn't read, nor an interrogation he couldn't handle.

Nothing got by Sanders.

Nothing.

'That can't be. You know the team. They're good officers.'

'The fuck I do,' Townsend angrily remonstrated. 'You stuck me in a fuckin' prison cell and then told me who the team was when I got out. I don't know your guys anymore than the people I'm working for.'

'I do. And I trust them.' Sanders was aware his judgement held considerable weight. 'I know you're frustrated, son. And I know this has gone further than we ever imagined. But we are this close.' He held his hand up, the thumb and forefinger tips a millimetre apart.

'I'm telling you, sir. They know something's up. On the last two potential busts, he knew you guys were coming. He even said as much. Told us we needed to change the shipment route and the distribution chains. Which meant everything I gave you was bullshit. It's why he doesn't tell us the locations until the moment we're leaving now.'

'Look at me, Jack.' Sanders raised his voice, exuding complete authority. 'The man is one of the most powerful criminals to have risen up since Chapman was killed. We knew this going in. You don't build a multimillion-pound export empire without being several moves ahead of everyone else on the board.'

'Something feels off.' Townsend finished his cigarette, took a sip of his coffee and then lit another. 'I can't risk my girls, sir. You know that.'

'They couldn't be safer,' Sanders assured him. 'Police protection. If tonight goes as planned, then I'm pulling you out.'

Townsend took a long, deep drag of the cigarette, staring into space. Eventually, he turned his head to his boss and looked at him with pain in his eyes.

'I just want to be me again.'

Sanders stepped towards him, wrapped his hand around the back of his head, and pulled him in for a hug. Townsend accepted, burying his head in the man's coat and doing his best not to sob.

'I know, son.' Sanders patted him on the back. 'You give us Slaven Kovac and his boss, and I'll get you home.'

After a few more moments of comfort, Townsend pulled away from his handler and stepped back into the flat, lifting a picture of Mandy and Eve that he'd stuffed into the frame of the mirror.

His entire world captured in one frame.

His reason for everything.

Ash fell from his cigarette as he took the final puff and

he pressed it against the wall. This wasn't his home, and he held little love or regard for its upkeep.

Sanders stood patiently waiting for his undercover officer to bring himself together. It was a hard gig, and Sanders appreciated that. It wasn't just the separation from his family and the police service that was taking its toll on Townsend.

It was the separation from himself.

From the man he was and had proudly been. The things he'd done just to get close to Kovac's operation were enough to put him away for a few years, and the things since would have seen them throw the book at him.

But it was necessary.

Sanders needed Townsend deep inside Kovac's operation. That was the request two years ago, and Sanders couldn't have been prouder of the man.

After a few more moments of reflection, Townsend slid the photo back into the mirror frame with a renewed sense of purpose.

It would all be over soon.

He turned to his boss, thankful for the support he'd given him throughout it all.

'I'll give him to you. Tonight.'

CHAPTER SIX

The entrance to Top Pocket was through a side gate behind a row of shops, opening up onto a derelict court-yard that had long since been forgotten. The entire wall was caked in graffiti. Sam admired some of the artwork as he ventured towards the door, already drawing the gaze of the large, unkempt man who was smoking by the door.

'You a member?' the man said gruffly, sending a plume of smoke in Sam's direction. He stared at Sam with his dark, sunken eyes, and the wind carried the smoke up into the grey sky. Unlike the pleasant day before, the weather was overcast, and Sam was grateful for the need to wear his jacket.

It concealed the Glock tucked against the base of his spine. The one he'd taken from Ryan Marsh the previous night. Turning to face the man, Sam offered him his best smile.

'Not yet.'

'Then fuck off.'

'Where can I sign up?'

'Invite only,' the man replied dismissively. He took one

final drag on his cigarette and then flicked it towards Sam's feet. 'Like I said, fuck off.'

'I'm here to see Luka.'

The man, who had reached out for the door, stopped and turned back to Sam, his brow furrowed.

'There ain't no Luka here. And word to the wise, if there was, I'd be real fuckin' quiet about it.'

'Tell him his friend, Ryan Marsh, sent me. Told me he'd be up for a game of pool.' Sam shrugged. It was just after one o'clock and Sam was banking on Marsh being right. The large man grunted and then heaved the door open.

'Wait here.'

The man disappeared into the building and pulled the door firmly behind him. Sam stepped forward and inspected it. The lock was hooked up to a metal keypad, which was drilled into the wall. Sam was skilled in many things, but hacking a security lock wasn't one of them.

Sometimes, he really did miss Etheridge.

It was fast approaching the two-year anniversary of the last time he'd seen or heard from his friend.

Paul Etheridge had served with Sam during his first tour, but soon found that the life of a soldier wasn't the right fit. A bomb disposal expert, Etheridge turned his attention to internet and database security, eventually building BlackOut Software, a multimillion-pound business that offered cyber security to the biggest companies in the world. Living the life of a middle-aged millionaire, Etheridge seemed to have everything he'd ever wanted.

Limitless money.

Expensive cars.

Young trophy wife.

But when Sam had reached out for help in the pursuit of Jasmine Hill and unintentionally pulled Etheridge into his world, everything changed. Despite being beaten and tortured, Etheridge found what he was looking for.

Purpose.

And up until Sam set off to America to find Alex Stone, Etheridge had worked tirelessly to support Sam's crusade on crime, using his expertise to source information, track criminals, locate weapons, and even hack an underground prison.

All in the aid of the fight.

Successfully pulling off an armed raid on a police convoy to free Sam from custody put Etheridge firmly on the Met's radar, and with the resources the man had, he'd disappeared. Sam had said goodbye to him at the airport, and since then, nothing.

Etheridge had left a bank account for Sam, with an eye watering amount of funds secured inside, for Sam to use however he saw fit.

He hadn't touched it, living just above the poverty line and dedicated his time to the youth centre.

But now, with his path chosen and his fight against crime the only future available to him, Sam had already dipped into it a few times.

Deep down, all he wanted was for Etheridge to reach out. Just to let Sam know that he was okay.

The door opened and the large man reappeared, this time with another burly man who looked just as world-weary. Despite ushering Sam in, their faces betrayed how unwelcome he was. Sam nodded politely and stepped through, pleased that their arrogance meant they ignored patting him down. As soon as he entered, Sam was immediately hit by the stench of stale smoke and alcohol. Despite the flashy website, Top Pocket was anything but. The well-worn carpet on the stairs led Sam up towards the dark, dingy main floor, where twelve pool tables were spaced out, all of them glowing under the hanging lights above. The cushioned edges had lost their colour, and the cloth that covered the tables was ripped in places. The hall had certainly seen better days, but judging from the two men who shadowed Sam's ascent to the floor, they were hardly attracting the town's best or brightest.

A game of pool was taking place in the far corner, where one man was arched over the table, clinically striking the white ball into the mass of colour at the other end, as a few others watched on, surrounded by bottles of beer and the thick cloud of cigar smoke.

On the speakers above, nondescript jazz music was crackling through the sound system, trying its best to add a little class to the atmosphere.

It failed.

As Sam walked, he realised the two men had stepped to either side of him, as if they were leading him down the green mile to the executioner's chair. Running along the left-hand side of the room was a brightly lit bar, the shelves filled with multiple bottles of spirts and mixers. A blonde woman sat on the other side, phone in one hand and a cigarette in the other, and she stared at Sam with venom as he passed. Although he assumed it wasn't the best idea, Sam offered her a smile and carried on. As they approached the table, the large man who had snarled at him at the front door shoved Sam in the back, nudging him forward a few paces.

It was a poor attempt at intimidation.

The voices ahead mumbled something in Croatian, and one of the audience turned and looked at Sam, before taking a long puff on his cigar and bellowing the thick smoke in his direction. Sam waved it away, mildly irritated.

'You know it's illegal to smoke inside, right?' Sam said, shaking his head.

'There are many illegal things in here.' The voice boomed from the other side of the table, where Luka leant forward, lined up his shot, and then struck the ball with powerful conviction. Moments later, a red ball nestled in the far pocket and drew a few grunts of approval. 'Like the gun I have in my jacket, or the drugs my good friend, Jacob, has been enjoying. You policeman?'

'Do I look like a policeman?' Sam shrugged.

'If you policeman, you know that you are not welcome here.' Luka casually began to chalk the tip of his cue as he meandered around the table, stopping a few feet from Sam, before arrogantly blowing the excess chalk in his direction. 'So I think not. Which means you're the fool who attacked Marsh last night. Am I correct?'

'He started it.'

Luka chuckled.

'Maybe. The man is a fat prick. Lazy. But he sell a lot of drugs for me. Drugs that he tells me you threw into the lake. Which means you owe me money. Which means you owe my boss money.'

'Slaven Kovac?'

The uttering of the name drew a panicked hush throughout the room. Sam could feel the tension rise, and he noticed the little twitch at the side of Luka's eye. Despite the whole show the man was putting on, he was still just a foot soldier. In the eyes of those who surrounded them, Luka was obviously the alpha male. But in the grand scheme of things, he was just another dog in the pack, and Sam could sense the man's ego was fragile.

It was a skill he had.

His attention to detail.

It was what had made him the deadliest man to ever lie behind the scope of a sniper rifle.

Not only could he search and find the details, but he committed them to memory. It allowed his mind to formulate plans or devise escape routes without even trying and then execute them when needed on muscle memory alone. He'd done it the moment he'd walked in.

They had climbed seventeen steps to reach the floor and passed two doors on the way to the main hall, both leading to toilets. The fire escape in the opposite corner to them was padlocked, and there were three other men besides Luka and the two standing guard behind him.

Neither of them were armed, but judging by the way another of the men was sitting slightly forward on his stool, it told Sam that like himself, he had a gun resting against the base of his spine.

It meant Sam knew who to disarm first, how quickly he could exit the place, and which way he needed to run to get out.

But he had no intention of running.

His mind hadn't been devising an exit strategy.

It had been building a plan of attack.

Sam's mention of Kovac's name still hung in the air alongside the stifling cigar smoke, and he fixed Luka with a stare. Seemingly caught a little off-guard, Luka chuckled and then pulled a cigarette from his pocket and lit it.

'You know how dangerous it is to say that name?'

'I think I'm starting to figure it out,' Sam said sternly, realising the crowd was beginning to feel uneasy. 'What I would like to know is where I can find him.'

'Find him?' Luka laughed. 'You do not find him. He find you.'

'Give him a call, then. Tell him I'm here.'

Luka took a considered puff on his cigarette and regarded Sam with a raised eyebrow. If Sam's bullish insistence had rattled him, Luka did a good job of disguising it for nonchalance.

'Who are you?'

'My name is Sam Pope.' Sam stood tall. He could see a

few bemused gazes aimed in his direction. 'And I would very much like to meet your boss.'

'Sam Pope is a dead man.' Luka dismissed. 'He died a few years ago.'

'I did. But now I'm back and I'll be honest with you, Luka, I'm starting to lose my patience.'

'Your patience? You walk in here, into my sister's business…' Luka gestured to the woman behind the bar, who scowled at Sam. 'You speak of a man you do not know and now you make threats to me. Now, I could take you to Kovac and let him deal with you himself, but then that would make me bad employee. So instead, how about I have my friends hold you still while I take a knife from your belly to your balls and make Sam Pope a dead man once again?'

Sensing movement behind him, Sam glanced around at the other men who surrounded the table. The one he suspected was armed had shuffled further off his seat, his hand resting at the base of his spine and clearly ready to pull his gun at a moment's notice. Sam resisted the urge to do likewise. The other man, who'd been playing Luka at pool, had positioned himself to Sam's left, with both hands affixed to the cue and ready to use it as a club.

Luka calmly finished his cigarette, revelling in the control he had just asserted. Sam had no other option but to raise his hands in surrender.

'While I would prefer you just took me to see Kovac himself, there are two more options you've missed. One, you let your men quietly leave the building and you and I go to see Kovac like gentlemen.'

A few snickers of laughter echoed from around Sam, as if mocking him in stereo. Luka took his final drag of his cigarette before stubbing it out in the full ashtray on the side table.

His words danced out of his mouth on a cloud of smoke.

'And the other option?'

'I shut you all down. One by one.' Sam's voice carried a serious menace as he shot meaningful glances at the nervous group. 'Piece by piece. And when I'm done, you'll be begging to tell me where Kovac is.'

Luka grit his teeth and snarled, clearly not used to being threatened. Especially not in front of his crew. He looked beyond Sam and nodded, signalling them to jump into action.

Behind him, Sam could hear the two larger men approaching, and the armed man stepped off his chair, his hand returning from the belt of his jeans and ready to put a bullet in his skull.

The details of the situation raced through Sam's head like the credits at the end of a movie, arriving at his best plan of attack.

Instinct then took over, and his hand shot to the pool table, his fingers clasping on to the solid, ceramic black ball.

Five against one.

Unfortunately for Luka and his crew, that one was built to survive.

And trained to do much, much worse.

CHAPTER SEVEN

Ryan Marsh hadn't slept a wink.

After the humiliation and agonising pain he'd been put through by Sam Pope, the police and ambulance arrived not long after the man had left. Knowing full well who he was, the police were soon scouring the premises for drugs. Momentarily, Marsh had been thankful that Sam had thrown them into the Oulton Broad, but then was side-swiped by the horrifying realisation of what was to come.

He would need to tell Luka.

Who, in turn, would need to tell Kovac.

An ambulance had been quickly on the scene, treating Marsh both for his foot wound and the resulting shock due to blood loss. As soon as he'd been loaded up into the van, a police officer quietly informed him that Luka would be informed of what had happened. The officer was clearly on Kovac's payroll, and his boss's reach suddenly became a little too real for Marsh.

There were certain luxuries that came with being a drug dealer for one of the biggest criminals in the UK.

Money. Drugs. Women.

Despite his long-term relationship with Carly, Marsh

had enjoyed what his misogynistic mind thought was his *fair share* of *loose women.* Whether they wanted him for his money or supply line, he didn't care, and he never turned down sexual gratification when it was offered. Whenever Carly spoke out against his adulterous ways, she was treated to the back of Marsh's hand, or at times, worse.

Sometimes, Marsh would assert his authority by forcing himself upon her, he being small-minded enough to still think he was entitled to her body regardless of her wants.

Now, lying in a hospital bed, having endured a sleepless night, Marsh regretted all his choices.

A police officer had been standing watch at the door to his room all night. The bullet that had been sent through his foot had shattered his metatarsal, the bone collapsing into a number of pieces and slicing his cartilage to shreds. The paramedics had stopped the bleeding on the way to Lothlingland Hospital, and upon arrival, doctors went to work to help ease his pain and save his foot.

They had. Just.

Discussions had begun about surgery, which could require Marsh to have a metal plate inserted into the top of his foot to hold it together. That alone would see him cut off by Kovac, as his inability to make it through a security scanner without drawing attention would make him redundant for any international collections. Marsh had never been on a drug run before but being unable to would work against him.

But it was the least of his problems.

Kovac was a careful man.

Building such a profitable criminal empire didn't happen by accident, and Marsh knew that Kovac took his privacy very seriously. It was why he had his foot soldiers such as Luka deal with the dealers.

It was why Marsh had never met the man.

With a deep sigh, Marsh looked down at the bandages

that had been wrapped around his obliterated foot, which had now been suspended slightly above the bed. It was inevitable that he would lose his job within Kovac's empire, but the very real possibility of losing his foot hung over him.

All because of one man.

Who was he?

Marsh had tried racking his brain, trying his best to recall the man from some point in time. Perhaps it was someone he had wronged? A relative of one of his customers who'd chased the dragon too far into the abyss?

Whoever he was, the way he took out Marsh and his boys showed that he was exceptionally dangerous, and was certainly a threat to Luka. Despite his best efforts to retrieve his phone from his belongings, Marsh was bed bound and, as he was also a known criminal, the nurse in charge of his care was under strict instructions not to communicate with him unless it was on medical grounds.

He had no way to inform Luka of who was heading his way.

No chance to try to win back some trust from a very dangerous crime organisation.

Marsh closed his eyes, tried to block out the relentless hum of activity from the hospital beyond, and did his best to sleep. Just as he felt himself finally nodding off, the door to his room flew open, immediately followed by a number of footsteps. Marsh opened his eyes, and they quickly widened with fear at the man who stood at the end of his bed.

The man's thick, brown hair was neatly brushed back, flowing in slight curls to the bottom of his neck. His strong jaw was covered in stubble, and his green eyes had locked onto Marsh like a sniper scope.

His clothes were pristine, with a navy blazer fitting snuggly to a soldier's physique.

Marsh had never met the man before, but the sheer fury that emanated from his eyes told Marsh who he was.

Slaven Kovac.

Behind Kovac, a muscular man about a decade younger, followed. The henchman closed the door quietly and then turned to glare at Marsh, the light causing the grey flecks in his beard to shimmer. He was an imposing figure and Marsh understood immediately the trouble he was in. As the tension in the room grew, Kovac picked up the clipboard that was tucked into the holder at the end of the bed and faked understanding it, even nodding his head as if in agreement.

'How are you feeling?' Kovac eventually spoke, his Croatian accent adding an element of threat to his words. Marsh looked towards Kovac, and then to the henchman guarding the door.

'Is the police officer outside—'

'Gone? Yes.' Kovac offered a sinister smile. 'Incredible how little you have to pay to get five minutes alone in here.'

Marsh audibly gulped.

'Look, Mr Kovac, I—'

'Please, just call me *sir,*' Kovac interrupted, before handing the clipboard to his henchman. Marsh nodded.

'Sir. I'm sorry for what happened. The man attacked us and, well, look at what he's done to my fucking foot.'

'And what did he want?'

Kovac stared a hole through Marsh, who sunk further into his pillow.

'You, sir. He wanted you.'

'I am flattered. To what do I owe such attention?' Kovac's smile instantly vanished from his face, his sharp features pulled tight as his entire demeanour changed. The room suddenly felt cold, and Marsh felt his sizable gut flip with fear. 'What did you tell him?'

'I…err…' Marsh stammered. Kovac stepped to the side of the bed and lowered himself onto the edge of the mattress.

'It's okay. Just tell me.'

'He had my gun. He had it pointed at my head.' Marsh pleaded, shooting a glance at the unmoved henchman and then back to a terrifying Kovac.

'Did he? Is that what it takes to make you talk?' Marsh nodded, and quick as a flash, Kovac pulled a Glock 17 from the inside of his jacket and pointed it directly at Marsh's forehead. Marsh squealed in fear, and Kovac snarled. 'There you go. Now tell me what the fuck you told him.'

'Oh God. I told him your name. I told him about Luka.' Marsh spoke frantically, beads of sweat sliding down his chubby face. 'Where he could find him. I'm so sorry. Please don't kill me.'

Kovac held the gun in place for a few moments, revelling in the terror of the slobbish man before him. With a firm nod, he withdrew his weapon and lifted himself from the mattress and began heading to the door. His henchman leant across and yanked the handle, allowing the bright lights of the corridor to invade the room. Kovac stopped, adjusted his expensive looking jacket, and ran a hand through his hair.

'You have two days to disappear, you understand?' Kovac didn't look back. 'Two days, otherwise I'll have my boys take you apart while you're still alive. Do you understand?'

'Yes, sir.' Marsh nodded readily. 'Thank you, sir.'

Kovac nodded and then turned to his henchman.

'Make it quick, Danny.'

The door slammed shut and Marsh squirmed in terror as the silent henchman marched towards the bed and roughly stuffed a towel into Marsh's mouth.

'You'll need this. Trust me.'

The man's Scouse accent caught him off-guard, but as the man lifted the clipboard above his head, Marsh's eyes widened in horrified realisation. With all his might, the man drove the clipboard down, edge first, onto Marsh's already obliterated foot, sending shock waves of agony coursing through his body. After a few more venomous slams, Marsh passed out from the pain, and Danny tossed the clipboard onto the bed, straightened his jacket, and marched out of the room. As he shut the door behind him, he was greeted by a frustrated looking Kovac.

'Everything okay, boss?'

'No.' Kovac frowned. 'I cannot get hold of Luka.'

———

As his fingers clutched the solid, black eight ball from the pool table, Sam was already a few steps ahead of everyone else in the room. With the thudding of heavy feet closing in behind him, he lifted the ball and in one fluid motion he hurled it as hard as he could across the table.

The henchman, who was clearly reaching for a firearm, didn't see it coming until it was too late.

The impact was sickening.

The audible crack of his nose, as the ball decimated it, echoed over the music that was echoing from the speakers and the man spiralled to the ground, motionless, with blood pumping from the shattered remains of his nose.

'Get him!' Luka yelled, pointing his finger at Sam, as if unleashing his hounds.

Before Sam had the chance to move again, he felt both of the larger men grab him from behind, each one clamping their powerful grips around his muscular arms and digging their fingernails in. Sam grimaced through the pain, aware that being restricted would no doubt end in his immediate death. The man who was playing pool with Luka was marching round the table, spinning the cue so he was holding it by the thinner end, and he mockingly tapped the club of it in his hand.

Sam struggled against the sheer power of the two men, but they wouldn't budge.

The pool cue swung at Sam, as if the man was hitting a home run at a baseball game.

But Sam ducked.

The cue clattered into the meaty, flabby neck of one of his captors, slightly loosening the grip and allowing Sam to take one step forward.

That was enough.

With his arms locked in place, Sam lifted both feet off the ground and pushed them against the pool table with as much force as he could muster, sending all three of them tumbling backwards. The large men lost their balance under Sam's weight, and as they crashed to the floor, Sam rolled backwards, his handgun pressing deeply into his spine. Sam shrugged off the pain and continued his roll, freeing himself from their grasp.

The furious man who had greeted him at the door turned on his knees to Sam, who had already sprung to his feet. As quick as he could, Sam leapt forward, driving his knee straight into the man's jaw. As soon as he connected, Sam felt the man's jaw dislocate, taking him out of the fight, but as Sam tried to regain his balance, the solid oak pool cue connected with his rib cage.

The attacker drew it back again, swinging with all his might, and Sam absorbed the blow once more in the ribs, but this time locked the cue under his arm. Overpowering the attacker, Sam drove a foot forward into the man's standing leg, the full force of his boot snapping the man's shin backwards and drawing a blood-curdling scream of agony as rolled over in anguish.

Sam shut him up with a clubbing blow of the pool cue, before following it up with another one to the large man who had accidentally taken one to the throat a moment before.

This one was to the skull.

This one sent the man straight to sleep.

It was over in a minute at most, and Sam let the pool cue lazily hang by his side as he turned his attention to Luka, who, in the midst of Sam's impressive display, had taken the opportunity to light a cigarette. While Sam had expected to see fear etched across his face, Luka had a smirk as he took a long puff on the cigarette and then slowly applauded.

'Very impressive.' Luka tapped the ash on the floor. 'Slaven would find use for you.'

'I'm not looking for a job.'

'You should be. Will be less painful for you.' Luka reached into his pocket and pulled out a flick knife, which he made a show of revealing. As he did, Luka flashed a look over Sam's shoulder. Sam clocked it, but kept his eyes on Luka, who offered him a dry grin as he raised the knife. 'Like I said, from your belly to your balls.'

Behind him, Sam heard the gentle footsteps and spun round, just in time to see Luka's sister, her arm held high, another knife lunging dangerously towards him. Sam deflected the blow, snatching her by her wrist, before driving her face down onto the green felt of the pool table. Luka yelled with fury, and began to charge towards Sam, only for Sam to reach to the back of his jeans and pull out his Glock 17.

Luka stopped in his tracks, his eyes wide with worry.

'Okay. Okay.' Luka begged, dropping the knife and holding his hands up. 'Just put the gun down.'

The gun wasn't pointed at Luka.

Sam had it pressed to the back of his sister's skull.

'You have five seconds to tell me where to find Slaven Kovac.' Sam said coldly, his eyes locked on Luka. 'Five.'

'You are making a big mistake—'

'Four.'

'Misha, I promise you, he will not pull trigger.'

'Three.'

Misha yelled something in Croatian, her voice trembling under the very real threat of having a bullet put through her skull. Sam held her in place and kept his eyes fixed on Luka.

'Two.'

'Okay. Okay.' Luka lowered himself to his knees. 'I am begging you to take the gun away from her.'

'One.'

'I'll tell you. Fuck,' Luka screamed. 'I'll tell you.'

It was at that moment, with the desperation in Luka's eyes, that Sam realised the true legacy he had had within the criminal underworld. Despite the man before him being a dangerous, violent criminal, he still cowered under the threat of Sam's promise. It had been two years since Sam had walked away from it all, given a second chance with a new identity.

But this was just another reminder, on a path strewn with them, that he was very much a necessity in the world.

Someone who would fight back.

Someone who fought for the right reasons.

For two years, the world thought him dead, but even still, the echoes of his war on crime still rung loudly among those he targeted.

It was a lonely path to take, and the only one he had left before him.

The road less travelled.

With his eyes watering, Luka looked to Sam to release his sister. The man had been broken, and Sam knew that once he released her, there would be no repercussions.

He would get what he wanted.

The scattered, broken remains of Luka's crew were lying motionless around the tables.

Misha ran to Luka once she was released.

Luka told Sam everything.

And when Sam marched out of Top Pocket fifteen minutes later, he'd left them with their hands, feet, and mouths taped and their phones smashed.

He had his location.

Which meant he needed to get moving.

CHAPTER EIGHT

TWO YEARS EARLIER...

'We need to make the moves. Now.'

The sharp, angry voice cackled over the speaker of his mobile phone before abruptly hanging up, leaving Slaven Kovac with a wry smirk across his face. Despite his years within the BSD, Kovac's face didn't hold the war-torn scars that the rest of his crew did. Leading his battalion through countless CSAR and Direct-Action missions, Kovac had built up a reputation as the Man of Stone.

Cold.

Calculating.

Without prejudice.

The higher-ups likened him to a heat-seeking missile, where it didn't matter the target or the requirement, Kovac would lead his crew without hesitation. But as the fighting took its toll on his crew's bodies, the weight of responsibility took its toll on Kovac's mind.

Watching good men get killed or maimed, fighting for the orders of others, soon led him to despise the very emblem he'd worn with such pride and when the chance came to hang up his M4 Carbine, he took it took with both hands.

It was an opportunity too good to pass up, and as he'd never given his life to another person and settled down for the family life, Kovac saw the opportunity to get rich by using his expertise.

Guns.

War.

Bloodshed.

After being approached by a general within a wealthy Ukrainian crime syndicate, Kovac became their chief gun runner through Eastern Europe. With his reputation as the Man of Stone *preceding him, he soon learnt that his reputation commanded either fear or respect.*

Either currency was worth its weight in gold and he was handsomely rewarded for helping the Ukrainians smuggle millions of pounds' worth of weaponry across Europe. When the Crimea crisis hit, Kovac was first in line to profit.

It all went so well.

Until Sam Pope intervened.

The man took down the English arm of the operation, shutting down a trafficking empire that saw the Ukrainians abduct English teenage girls and sell them into sex slavery. It was a nasty business, and one Kovac made clear he wanted little to do with. When the empire crumbled, Kovac pushed for their product to change.

No longer would they profit from the butchering of innocence.

Instead, along with the firearms his connections allowed him to procure, he used the Ukrainian's long-standing partnership with the British gangster, Harry Chapman, to import copious amounts of class A drugs. It was cleaner than snatching young girls away from loved ones, as it didn't leave any ripples. No one was running to the police.

No was one looking for them.

With the remnants of the Ukrainian's empire hanging off Kovac's operation, they spent a year working to build a distribution network through the east of England. Despite the calls to take the drugs and guns into the country's capital city, Kovac made it clear that the last thing they wanted to do was enter Sam Pope's hunting grounds.

Chapman agreed.

Instead, just like a number of the missions he'd led his battalion bravely through, they snuck in the back door, infecting the country without it even knowing.

Then Chapman was killed.

Rumours swirled of a prison riot that had got out of hand, but a few disgraced prison guards eventually told Kovac's right-hand man, Luka, the truth under intense torture.

Their prison had been infiltrated by Sam Pope.

Which meant he would soon come looking for the rest of Chapman's operations. With the Ukrainian demanding Kovac press on, he readied his men for war, refusing to underestimate the man like so many others had done before him.

Then the word spread through the country like a ghostly whisper, snatching the breath from every criminal who had ever looked over their shoulder.

Sam Pope was dead.

His body had been discovered, tortured and burnt to a crisp in an abandoned warehouse in South Carolina.

Within minutes of the news breaking across the news channels, Kovac had felt his phone vibrate. He reached into the inside of his blazer and smirked at the number.

It was the Ukrainian.

Upon first meeting her, she hadn't even given him her name, but there was a cold, evil desperation behind her eyes. She was out of her depth, doing her best to piece together the ashes of the crumbling empire and without the military or logistics knowledge Kovac had, she would soon lose it all.

It put him in a position of power.

Eventually, that position would supersede her, but for now, he needed the collateral she'd inherited from the wreckage and the doors her name could still open.

She demanded he continue to build the operation, even going as far as to assert her power over him by drawing him to her bed on a number of occasions. Their meetings became a strange, physical encounter, which usually involved her barking out orders of dominance

64

before succumbing to him, usually in an awkward, aggressive sexual episode. When they finished, she would make it clear to him that it was nothing more than a need that had to be satisfied.

Just another responsibility he had to fulfil.

But with Sam Pope being declared dead, there was a twinkle to every word she spoke and an excitement behind her voice.

'Have you seen the news?' Her voice was shaking with excitement.

'I have,' Kovac responded calmly. 'You must be pleased?'

'My only regret is that I was not the one to put him through such pain.' She sighed. 'Yet, when I get the chance, I will spit on his grave.'

Kovac let that hang for a moment, resting his phone on the desk and sitting back in his chair.

'Now what?' he eventually asked.

The Ukrainian continued to babble, talking about the clear pathway ahead and how she wanted to expand towards London as soon as possible. Despite Kovac's objections, she demanded he yield, only drawing a shake of the head.

Eventually, she would swim too far off shore and he would let her drown. With no Chapman or Sam Pope, the country was begging for someone to take control of the underworld, and there was no one as well-trained or as cold as Slaven Kovac.

The Man of Stone.

But for now, he still needed the doors to be opened and he grit his teeth and told her he would make it happen. It was time to expand, to take out any potential rival to the throne and sit her in it, albeit for a short while.

Then, when they were so deep in the underbelly of the country, when their reach and control was untouchable from both sides of the law, he would dispose of her and take his rightful place at its helm.

The Kingdom would be his.

With a wry smile, he hung up the phone, placed it back into his pocket, and wondered how long it would take before the country cowered at his name.

As Kovac approached the door to Top Pocket, he pressed the buzzer with a gloved finger. Fastidious with every detail, he refused to leave even one fingerprint on anywhere that might be searched. Despite masquerading as a pool club, and for the most part, being a legitimate business, Kovac knew that Luka and his sister, Misha, used it as a drop off point for a few of their other schemes. Usually, such infringements on Kovac's patch would result in the removal of fingers, but Luka was as loyal as a dog, and as vicious as one too.

He'd been with Kovac through every mission and had saved his life on numerous occasions.

If Luka wanted to skim a little off the top or run his own little drug racket in a vile pyramid scheme, Kovac would allow it.

But one thing he didn't abide was being made to wait.

A few more seconds passed before he impatiently pressed the buzzer again.

Kovac frowned.

Danny stepped forward, pressing his hand to the glass and peered through, seeing nothing but the worn carpet on the stairs.

'What do you wanna do, boss?'

'Smash it,' Kovac replied nonchalantly, taking a step back as Danny drove his elbow through the glass pane on the door and reached inside to unlatch it manually. He yanked it open and then stepped through, oblivious to any potential danger that lay ahead. It was a trait that Kovac appreciated.

There was no fear in Danny. Although some of the other crew were sceptical of bringing in someone from outside their military past, Kovac had seen sense in bringing in someone from the very country they were infiltrating. Over the few years Danny had been by his side, he'd seen the young man harden, much like the soldiers had under his command all those years ago.

Danny was a soldier now.

As Danny disappeared up the staircase, Kovac slowly followed behind, adjusting the lapel of his blazer he'd thrown on over the white button-up shirt which was tucked into his dark jeans. After years of scrambling around in the muck, Kovac had acclimatised nicely to life as a criminal overlord and he enjoyed the expensive clothes his tastes and, most importantly, his money afforded him.

Halfway up the staircase, Danny's voice rang out.

'Jesus Christ. Boss, get up here.'

Kovac quickened his pace, bounding up the stairs two at a time until he stepped onto the main floor of the pool hall.

Lying prone among the tables were four of Luka's men, all in different states of consciousness and pain. As a few groans of pain echoed from them, Kovac walk towards Danny, who was crouched over Luka who'd been bound and gagged on the floor. As he approached, Kovac noticed a flicker of emotion in the usually cold eyes of his friend.

It wasn't pain.

It wasn't anger.

It was embarrassment.

As Danny sliced through the layers of thick gaffer tape that bound Luka's wrists, the burly Croatian shoved him away, rejecting his help. With his hands free, he pulled the tape that had been plastered over his mouth and nodded to his sister.

'Leave me. Help her.'

Danny shot a glance to Kovac who gently nodded, and the young man rolled his eyes and obliged. Luka angrily peeled the tape from around his ankles and as he began to scramble to his feet, Kovac reached out a hand. Luka took it.

Both of them had the same skull tattoo between their thumb and their index finger.

'*Što se dogodilo?*' Kovac demanded, drawing a quick glance from Danny who had made it clear that he did not appreciate it when they spoke in their native tongue. Ever the diplomat, Kovac spoke again, his thick accent smothering his words. 'What happened?'

'We were attacked.' Luka scowled. 'Ambushed.'

'One man ain't an ambush,' Danny piped up as he helped Misha to her feet. Luka stepped forward and shoved him powerfully in the shoulder.

'Take your filthy English hand off her.'

'Fuck you.' Danny's eyes bulged in anger, and he stepped towards Luka, their foreheads pressed against each other as the animosity between them threatened to explode.

'Enough!' Kovac slammed his fist on one of the pool tables, drawing their attention to him. Behind Kovac, a couple of Luka's men had made a pitiful attempt to get to their feet, but Kovac ignored them.

'This attacker. This man. He was the one who took out Marsh, correct?'

'Yes.' Luka nodded, looking at the floor.

'One man. He did all this. To you and these pathetic men?' Luka took a deep breath and straightened his shoulders, standing to attention for a man he'd served so diligently for over a decade.

'Yes.'

Kovac shook his head. As he did, one of the men on the ground murmured in pain, his hands grasping at a shattered shin bone. Allowing his usual, dignified etiquette to slip for one moment, Kovac turned and stamped as hard as he could on the broken remnants of the man's leg, drawing an anguished howl before the pain stole the man's consciousness. Both Luka and Danny tried not to react.

Despite his demeanour, and his unrelenting grip of control, underneath, Kovac was still a brutal man.

The Man of Stone.

Kovac ran a hand through his hair, flattening it back over his head and he looked at Luka with a shake of the head.

'Did you tell him what he wanted to know?' Luka flashed a nervous glance at his sister. 'Ah, your weakness.'

'He had a gun to her head.'

Kovac reached into his blazer and pulled out a HS2000 semi-automatic pistol, the same one he'd had strapped to his waist through his years of service in the BSD. Without even batting an eyelid, he aimed it directly at Misha, who raised her hands in horror.

'So do I,' Kovac said with no emotion. 'So, tell me exactly what you told him.'

'Slaven, please…'

Dramatically, Kovac disengaged the safety lever on the rear of the grip.

'Tell me.'

'I told him what he asked for. Where the drop was tonight. That you would be there.' Luka looked at his sister reassuringly. 'He asked for you by name. Marsh must have spoken.'

'Like you did.'

'I had to, Slaven. I beg you. Lower the weapon.'

Kovac took a deep breath and then clicked the safety back on and slid the weapon away.

'What else?'

'I told him the boss was going to be there, too. And—'

'Not anymore,' he interrupted. Before Luka could continue, Kovac pulled his phone from his pocket.

Danny shot a confused glance at his boss. 'The police

are watching the drop tonight, but they won't move until they see her. So we have that, at least. As for who this rat is, we will need to extinguish him first before she can see what we've been building. I've worked too hard for this for some junkie with a death wish to ruin it.'

'He is not a junkie.'

'Look, Luka, just because he kicked your arse doesn't mean he isn't a junkie.' Danny negged Luka, drawing another rage fuelled scowl.

Kovac lifted the phone to his ear, but the next four words from Luka's mouth caused him to hang up immediately.

'It was Sam Pope.' All eyes turned to Luka. 'He's alive.'

'Bollocks,' Danny scoffed.

Kovac took a moment, ingesting the information and running his tongue along the inside of his lip.

Sam Pope was alive and was coming for them.

When faced with the very real threat of death, most men cave. Kovac had seen it countless times, whether during his days in the BSD or moments before he executed a rival gang member. Without question, when all men were out of options, they begged.

Kovac and his crew had been targeted by a resurrected Sam Pope and judging from the carnage of the last twenty-four hours, he wasn't playing any games.

But Kovac didn't care.

He didn't even register it as a threat.

To the horror of Luka, Misha, and Danny, Kovac's handsome face pulled into a smile, and he let out a laugh of joy. After a few moments, he collected himself and straightened his jacket. Danny stepped forward; his brow furrowed in confusion.

'What's so funny, boss?'

Kovac flashed him a grin.

'It has been too long since I have been to war.'

CHAPTER NINE

Sam carefully slid his hand across the SA80 Assault Rifle that was laid on the table before him. Part of him wondered what would happen if the owner of the Airbnb he'd hired for the week suddenly walked in, to witness Sam inspecting such a deadly weapon. Although Sam would never hurt an innocent person, he was certain that the intimidation factor alone would keep them quiet.

Beside the SA80, were two Glock 17s, both cleaned and fully loaded. One of them he'd kept after bringing down Daniel Bowker and his crew a few weeks earlier. The other, he'd confiscated from Ryan Marsh the day before and had added to his rather meagre arsenal.

That was what made this next target so important.

Although Etheridge had left Sam a vast fortune to fund his war against crime, the one thing he couldn't provide Sam with any longer was access. The newspapers were already swirling with stories that Sam Pope was back in action, sensationalising his rise from the dead to seek vengeance upon the criminal underworld.

That meant a lot of people were on high alert, and

without Etheridge's connections and considerable hacking skills, getting access to guns was difficult.

Slaven Kovac ticked that box.

The Glock he'd taken from Marsh was a new model, kept in pristine condition, and Sam was certain the rotund drug dealer had never had to pull the trigger. Considering the pathetic fight the man put up, Sam doubted Marsh ever had the stones to.

But not only was Kovac a dangerous man, flooding the streets with drugs and military grade weapons, he also offered Sam the chance to arm himself properly. He'd already made the decision that there was no going back to a quiet life, that his only path ahead was to continue the fight.

He needed guns.

The assault rifle and two handguns were enough for now, but Sam knew there were only so many bullets in the magazines he had and that getting his hands on a wider variety of weapons was paramount to the cause.

Having extracted the information from Kovac's soldier at Top Pocket, Sam knew were the drop off was happening. It was a pretty impressive system Kovac used.

Shipping containers were brought into the Port of Felixstowe from various parts of Europe, each containing high-calibre weapons. Packed away inside empty shells of computers and boxed up, they were made to look like they were heading to the high street.

The right people were paid off to ensure the boxes were ticked and the red tape was removed. Once the products were loaded onto a haulage truck, a driver would then park the nondescript truck among others in one of three different quarries that scattered East Anglia. There, they would be unloaded, the weapons removed and taken back to Kovac's factory where they would be assembled and then sold into the country at a high cost. To keep the gun parts securely packaged during the transit, the boxes were also packed tightly with double wrapped bags of class A drugs.

The shipping manifest was changed on a weekly basis.

The drivers were circulated in and out.

The only people who knew what was coming in, when and where, were Kovac and his crew.

And now, Sam.

He knew where the destination was tonight, and although he felt uneasy at not having scouted the area beforehand, he knew there would never be another opportunity to shut the operation down and upgrade his armoury. Especially now that Kovac was likely to have discovered his handiwork and would be taking precautions.

They would be waiting for Sam, and he was certain they would have no problem putting a bullet through his skull.

Sam had a plan, but it was a risky one.

But heading guns blazing into an unknown situation against violent, well-trained men wasn't the way to go.

Getting to the guns would be the easiest part of the plan.

Getting out with them was a different story altogether.

After carefully engaging the safety of his rifle, he packed the weapons away in his sports bag and slid them under the pristine bed. The ritual of making his bed had been instilled by his military father and was only enforced further during his time with the army. Throughout his entire war on crime, Sam had constantly battled with his own demons, knowing full well he'd broken the promise he'd made to his son that he would never kill again.

Jamie had made him promise, and although Sam knew that the violence had been necessary, every person he put in the ground only added to his guilt.

Not that he'd killed another human being.

But that he'd failed his son.

It had been a recurring feeling that had snapped his heart in two. Sam should have been there to protect Jamie, but he'd failed him.

One thing Sam had never thought about, was what his father would have thought about the path he'd taken. General William Pope had been a strong, caring man, who had commanded an insurmountable amount of respect during his service for the British Armed Forces. Despite stepping away from battle at an early age, his tactical brain and caring demeanour had made him a cherished senior figure among the ranks. As a military kid, Sam had flourished. Despite moving from school to school, Sam had idolised his father, and it didn't take long for him to realise that he wanted to follow in his father's footsteps.

Sam's mother, however, never enamoured to life on the road, and she left them both when Sam was too young to remember. Fuzzy memories of her often tried to infiltrate his mind and while he tried to piece the fragments together, even just to remember her smile, the image never quite came together. He should have hated her for leaving, but as he got older, all he felt was a sadness.

A sadness that he'd never really cared.

Sam's father died when Sam was just seventeen years old, meaning he never witnessed Sam's ascension to the elite soldier he became. It was a fact that broke whatever was left of Sam's heart.

But now, would he want his father to see what he'd become?

Sam knew he was fighting for the right reasons, pushing back against those who defied the law without consequence. But his father practically drew the line between right and wrong and was a stout believer in justice. Undoubtedly, he would see his son as a criminal, and similar to the pain of his son thinking him a killer, the notion that the dearly departed wouldn't look upon him with pride prodded at Sam's mind like a woodpecker.

Shaking away the potentially dangerous train of through, Sam lifted his bomber jacket from the chair in the corner of the quaint room and slid it around his muscular frame. It was a fifteen-minute walk from his rented accommodation to the large retail park. He needed to pick up his ingredients from three separate stores so as not to arouse suspicion. He didn't particularly think that the young employees who worked in the supermarkets would know what they were for, but it was better to be safe than sorry.

The last thing he wanted was for someone to question him, realising who he was and that the contents of his trolley were clearly to make an explosive.

Sam slid his keys and wallet into his jacket pockets and stepped outside, appreciating the calming breeze on another clear afternoon. He adjusted his baseball cap, kept his head low, and walked briskly towards the retail park, knowing he was working to a tight schedule and that his only shot at Kovac was merely a few hours away.

―――――

Townsend felt sick to his stomach.

With Kovac on high alert, and the plans irrevocably changed by the re-emergence of Sam Pope, it meant that everything he'd been working towards for the past few years hung precariously from the thinnest of threads.

When Sanders had approached him two years ago, offering him a coffee and a way out of the Bell View Gang, Townsend had thought he was going home. Instead, he was offered the opportunity to help bring down one of the most dangerous criminals in the country.

Slaven Kovac had been on the radar of every law enforcement agency in the country and with the void left behind by Harry Chapman and Sam Pope's death, they expected him to make a serious play for the throne. High-ranking officials scoured every police department, looking for someone who was ready-made to infiltrate the gang and try to help them bring him down.

Jack Townsend was that man.

For two years, Kovac had called him Danny, and the more Townsend had committed to the role, the further from the line of truth he veered. Deep down, he knew he was still a good cop.

A loving husband.

A doting father.

But the further down the rabbit hole he ventured, the darker his path had become. There was a moment, about eight months before, when he begged Sanders to pull him out. The plans were made, and a convincing death was ready to be staged.

But then Kovac opened his door a little further for *Danny* and Townsend discovered the truth.

Kovac was being funded.

He wasn't the head of the snake.

While Townsend had collated enough evidence to bring down Kovac and his crew, the reality was they were replaceable. The powers that be needed the one controlling the purse strings and despite every part of him yearning to return home, Townsend knew he needed to see it through to the end.

He'd watched as Kovac and his crew tortured drug rivals. Townsend himself had brutally assaulted whomever Kovac had turned him onto.

Throughout it all, Townsend had shelved any guilt or remorse in a quiet corner of his mind, knowing that somewhere down the road, he would need to square it with himself. Every drink became one step closer to alcoholism, and he worried what kind of man he would be if he finally returned home.

Now, sat in the back of Kovac's Range Rover, he felt his stomach flip with every jolt of the vehicle. He took a deep breath and stared at the window, trying his best to focus on the streets of Suffolk as they whipped by.

'Something bothering you, Danny?'

Kovac's commanding voice filled the car, and Townsend looked up, trying to compose himself. Kovac, sat in the passenger seat, was glaring into the rear-view mirror, his stern eyes locked onto Townsend.

'Just a bit of car sickness.'

'Pussy,' Luka snarled, his hands firmly planted on the steering wheel.

'Rich coming from the guy we just found bound and gagged like a fucking gimp.'

The car swerved as Luka snapped his head round, glaring at Townsend with the usual animosity. The two had never seen eye to eye, with Luka publicly questioning Kovac's judgement in bringing in an outsider. Any tension was always quashed by Kovac himself, insisting that his decisions should never be questioned and if the two of them couldn't co-exist within his unit, then he would personally kill them both before easily replacing them.

There were a lot of hungry dogs willing to take the meat he dangled from his hand.

'Enough,' Kovac snapped. 'Eyes on the road.'

'*Kurvin sin,*' Luka muttered. Townsend didn't understand the words, but he ventured it wasn't a compliment.

Kovac's eyes were still locked on him in the mirror.

'You never get car sick before,' Kovac claimed, his tone verging on accusing.

'He is scared.' Luka chuckled. 'Scared of Sam Pope.'

Townsend rolled his eyes, trying his best to play the role

he'd become accustomed to. Luka may have been Kovac's guard dog, but the man was smart enough to keep Luka on a short leash. Townsend, however, was seen as the more sensible of the crew. Originally, he'd helped build bridges with local dealers, who seemed less resistant when dealing with a fellow Englishman. Once they'd agreed to peddle Kovac's drugs, that was when they were handed over to Luka who would rule over them with an iron fist and a vile temper.

But in the last few months, Kovac had kept Townsend close to his side, entrusting him with some of the more important details of the operation.

All of which he'd filtered back to Sanders.

Enough to bury the man.

But Kovac was no longer the target.

'Do not worry about Sam Pope,' Kovac said calmly, his gaze returning to the road ahead. 'We will kill him if he gets involved.'

Townsend knew it wasn't an empty threat. In his time within Kovac's crew, he'd witnessed the man murder three people. It was evidence they would use when the empire fell, and the man would be locked away in the darkest hole for the rest of his life.

But Kovac was good.

Informed.

Townsend was certain there was a rat on the other side of the fence, and he'd pleaded with Sanders to sniff them out. There had been too many times that the information he'd fed back had eventually proved useless.

As if Kovac knew they were coming.

On six separate occasions, Kovac had deviated the plan less than an hour before, which meant he knew the police would be waiting.

Which meant he was being fed information.

Townsend woke up every morning certain that it would be the day Kovac was told who *Danny Miller* really was.

Sanders and his team had done an amazing job in crafting his backstory, and his time undercover in the Bell View Gang only added legitimacy to it.

But the day would come soon enough, that Townsend would be sat down in front of Kovac and be told his real name.

And that would be the end of it.

Townsend turned his gaze to the window again, anxious at not being able to get a word to Sanders about the location of the drop or the changes to plan.

The Ukrainian wouldn't be in attendance.

Sam Pope would most likely be.

Sanders would have his team in place, waiting patiently for the location that would never come.

It was building towards a messy crescendo.

With a horrid, panicked ache sat in his stomach, Townsend thought of his girls, and wondered how long it would be until he got back to them. The world was a vile and grim place, and he was tired of living among the worst of it.

He just wanted to go home.

CHAPTER TEN

As the final few crates were expertly carried from the cargo ship, the Port of Felixstowe was bristling with activity. The evening had a gentle breeze, meaning the mood among the workforce was bordering on jovial. Although the work was hard and physically demanding, carrying out their jobs in the freezing cold or pouring rain often made it unbearable. The small mercy of a pleasant evening went a long way in making the job more enjoyable.

As the crane operator placed the final crate in its designated place, the supervisor began his rounds, ensuring all crates were accounted for and could be traced back to the ID number. Unbeknownst to him, the paperwork had already been forged, with the right people in the right places having been paid to ensure the seamless arrival of Kovac's container.

Nobody within the workforce had any idea that the crate, which contained two hundred and fifty boxed and sealed computers, was actually stuffed with packets of high-quality cocaine and disassembled gun parts. The products were signed off, and the clearance was given for the delivery to be transitioned onto the truck. The driver, who had been paid handsomely to not ask any questions, oversaw the transition of goods, even sharing a cigarette and a few laughs with the staff who were working tirelessly to clear the crate and tick it off their list.

A few conversations were thrown around, mostly pertaining to the old football rivalry between Norwich City and Ipswich Town, with supporters of either local team jokingly mocking the other.

By the time the truck was stocked and locked, it was a little after eleven, and under the floodlights of the Port, the driver roared the truck to life and carefully made his way to the entrance, offering mock salutes to anyone he passed on the way out.

Innocent people, making an honest living, all of whom had no idea they were integral to the steady flow of weapons and drugs onto the streets of East Anglia.

The driver turned out of the Port and rumbled up the A14, the headlights illuminating sign postings for the Orford Ness Nature Reserve some twenty-five miles north along the beautiful coastline. Passing through the quiet town of Felixstowe, the A14 was relatively quiet at such a late time, and soon enough, the driver transitioned onto the A12, bypassing Ipswich and following the straight road through a number of small, quiet villages and onwards towards the larger towns such as Lowestoft and Norwich. Being a local man, the driver was familiar with all the towns, but he was under strict instructions to bring the truck to Kirby Cane Quarry, which was situated just outside of Gillingham. It was a journey of over fifty miles, but with minimal traffic, it was twenty past midnight when he approached the entrance to the vast quarry.

An Eastern European man stood watch at the door, his muscular frame wrapped in a leather jacket and when the driver told him he was from the Port of Felixstowe, the man grunted and raised the barrier for him to enter. There was a sense of secrecy hanging over the evening, and the driver reminded himself of the handsome pay packet he'd been promised. Half up front.

Half upon delivery.

On the far side of the quarry, he could see the bright floodlights indicating activity, and with his lights on full beam, he carefully followed the gravelly path that looped around the quarry. With extra attention, he guided the massive vehicle around the spiral ramp way that brought him deeper into the darkness; the gravel flicking up and clattering the side of his truck as its tyres crunched over them.

It took ten minutes to reach the bottom, but as the ramp way levelled out, he continued full steam ahead towards the now clear delivery station ahead. There were a number of other trucks, and a group of men wandering about. In the distance, beyond the portable cabin office, he could see a variety of other construction vehicles that were clearly out of action.

As he arrived, another tough-looking man guided him into the remaining bay, demanding he reverse into the space between two other lorries. The driver did as instructed. Pleased with his smooth parking ability and hoping that those watching were just as impressed.

He killed the engine and began to descend from the vehicle, completely unaware of the part he'd played in this operation.

'Wait.'

A thick, European accent hung from the command and the driver looked up to be greeted by a gruff-looking man.

'Come on, mate. I need a piss.'

'Arms up.'

'Fuck off.' The driver chuckled but stopped instantly. The other man didn't look too pleased. 'Fine. Make it quick before I piss myself.'

The driver lifted his arms and allowed himself to be frisked. After a quick pat down, the large man nodded to the back of the truck.

'Open it.'

'Seriously, mate. Let me take a quick slash and I'll…'

'Now.' The man pulled a Glock 17 from his jacket and pointed it squarely at his forehead. The effect was immediate. The driver crumbled, lifting his shaking hands in the air and ejecting a hot stream of urine down his leg.

'Oh God. Please.'

'Open.'

As the man stumbled around to the back of the truck, he noticed several more men, all clad in black leather jackets, all looking like they wouldn't bat an eyelid if he was killed in front of them. Behind them, five black Range Rovers were parked, with another one already reversing slowly towards them. With his hands shaking, he began to fumble with the lock. He dropped his key and as he bent down to pick it up, he felt the cold steel of the gun press against his skull.

'Quickly.'

The driver lifted the keys with a shaking hand, and from behind, he heard an angered voice.

'Fucking hell, Luka. Give him a break.'

The voice was clearly Scouse and judging from the venomous insult thrown back at him, it was obvious the two didn't get along. It wasn't until he'd unfastened the mighty bolt lock across the back of the lorry that the driver realised he'd been holding his breath and he exhaled gratefully as he did.

'Move.'

The man shoved the driver to the side and hopped onto the small platform at the base of the door and in one, impressive heave, he hauled the metal shutter door upwards, revealing the stacks of tightly packed boxes. The man cast his eye over them and nodded, before turning to the rest of his crew and yelling an instruction in a language the man didn't recognise nor understand. Instantly, three other men swarmed the truck, with two of them hopping into the back of it and beginning the long, arduous process of moving all the heavy boxes.

Luka, who had intimidated the driver for nothing more than his own amusement, turned to the petrified driver and smirked.

'Do you still need toilet?'

The man looked shamefully at the ground, drawing a chuckle from Luka.

Another man stepped towards them, shaking his head. When he spoke, the driver recognised the Scouse voice again.

'Stop fucking about,' the Scouser snapped, drawing a scowl from the driver's antagoniser. For the next forty-five minutes, the driver watched in horror as the crew removed the boxes, revealing bags of drugs and sporadic gun parts. Horrified in the part he'd played, he understood what he was being shown.

The reason he wouldn't be able to leave.

He counted fifteen different weapons being assembled and placed into the back of the first Range Rover. Most of them were assault rifles and handguns.

A crate of what looked like grenades was also shifted from the truck into the backseat of the luxury vehicle.

High-calibre weapons.

Class A drugs.

He'd just dropped off the most dangerous delivery he could imagine and judging from the smirk on the armed man's face beside him, it was most appreciated. The man barked something in his native tongue, and one of his men slammed the car shut. There were still hundreds of boxes in the truck and the driver could only speculate how much it was worth.

How much damage it could do.

With a grunt, the armed man shoved the driver towards the Scouse man who had spoken up before. He regarded the driver with a regretful smile.

'Come with me. We'll get you paid and get you out of here.'

'I just want to go home.' The driver protested. 'Seriously, you can keep the other half.'

The man sighed and offered the driver an apologetic shrug.

'That's not how this works, fella.' He beckoned the driver to follow him. 'Boss needs to speak to ya.'

As the man marched towards the cabin, his boots crunched over the gravel. The driver flashed a glance at Luka, who stared a hole straight through him. The driver swallowed his nerves and quickly scurried after the seemingly more friendly man as the crew continued their swift operation of emptying the truck.

With regretful steps, the driver followed, wondering what the hell he'd got himself into and with every step he took, resigned himself to the fact that he was unlikely to ever find out.

Or make it home.

———

As his team went to work unloading his contraband from the back of the truck, Kovac sat back in his chair and took a long, satisfying puff on his cigar. While a number of his crew wasted their money and lungs on cheap cigarettes, his tastes required something more enjoyable. Reserving his expensive Cuban cigars for nights such as this one, he let the thick smoke filter from his mouth and cloud the small cabin. Usually, it would have been used for the foreman of the quarry, a makeshift office to either hold meetings or get through the mountains of paperwork, and Kovac was respectful enough to not touch the neat piles of paper on the desk.

He didn't, however, care about the sickly stench of tobacco he would leave behind.

The foreman had been paid handsomely to allow the transfer to happen and Kovac knew his reputation meant there wouldn't be any word of contention to his smoking. With the threat of Sam Pope crashing the party, Kovac had brought in six more men with the sole purpose of exterminating the man on sight. The usual process was one man from each of his main districts would attend to help with the unloading and construction of the weapons. Similar to Luka, these men had served with Kovac back in Croatia and were as loyal as they were deadly. They would then return and dispatch the contraband to their armies of dealers.

But tonight, each one of them brought along one of their most trusted men to tackle the possible Pope problem, which meant it weakened Kovac's stranglehold for one night.

But if he was the one to finally put Sam Pope in the ground, Kovac was certain it was worth it.

Despite the extra muscle, Luka had seemed nervous, no doubt embarrassed by the earlier interaction with Sam.

More surprisingly, Danny had seemed on edge, as if something hadn't sat right with him ever since Kovac had made it clear that his boss wouldn't be attending. The threat of Sam Pope showing up hadn't bothered the young man, but Kovac was a little perplexed by Danny's reaction to that decision.

Kovac trusted Danny and had even reached out to his informant within the police to dig into his past.

Danny was clean. Just a tough kid from a rough neighbourhood in Liverpool who had excelled through the gang life and made his way into Kovac's crew through sheer loyalty and dedication.

Danny's unease made Kovac feel similar, and as he took another puff on his cigar, a knuckle rapped against the door to the cabin.

'Come in.'

The door flew open, and Danny stepped in, ushering in a terrified looking man who had a resigned look on his chubby face. Kovac greeted him with a warm smile, his handsome face framed by his thick hair. The man must have been near the same age as him, but Kovac looked a decade younger.

'The driver, boss.' Danny made the lazy introduction.

'Ah, the delivery man. Thank you.' Kovac stood, clasping his hands together. 'I trust you had no problems?'

'No, sir.' The man's voice was trembling.

'And my crew. They polite?' The man hesitated, telling Kovac all he needed to know. Kovac rolled his eyes. 'I can only apologise. What happen?'

Kovac pointed to the man's groin, which was heavily stained with urine. Humiliated, the driver shuffled on the spot. Danny sighed.

'Luka stuck a gun in his face. You need to tell him to rein it in.'

'Do not tell me what to do, Danny,' Kovac snapped, his eyes wide with instant fury. 'Do you understand me?'

Danny held his hands up.

'Sorry, boss.'

Angered at his veil slipping for a millisecond, Kovac clasped his hands together again and offered the driver a warm smile.

'Let's sort you out, shall we?' He reached down into the

desk and slid open the drawer. 'What was the arrangement again? Remind me.'

The man flashed a nervous glance to the stoic Danny, and then back to Kovac.

'Half to take the job. Half on delivery. B-b-but I am happy to just go home.'

'Don't be silly. A man should be rewarded for the work he does. It is strong principle of mine and one that make me a very rich man. Where would I be if I gave people my service for free?' Kovac reached into the drawer. The driver gasped as Kovac retrieved a handgun. 'But I am also very careful man, and I am afraid people who see too much are not allowed to walk away.'

'Please, I swear, I don't even know your name and I'll…'

The driver trailed off as Kovac lifted a finger to his lips. The fear in the room was as thick as the cigar smoke that clung to the walls.

'Do not beg. Begging is weak trait.' Kovac took a final puff on his cigar and then stubbed it out on the wooden desk, burning a grey mark into the surface. 'The alternative is I remove your eyes and your tongue to ensure your silence, and that is no honourable way for a man to live. This will be easier.'

Kovac lifted the gun, and the man screamed in terror as a gunshot echoed.

But from outside.

As all three men turned to the window in shock, a mighty explosion roared through the quarry, shaking the ground and rocking the cabin. Eighty or so feet from the cabin, a piece of heavy machinery was ablaze, with large chunks of metal scattered around as flaming debris. Already, Kovac could see Luka and a few of his men rushing towards the wreckage, guns at the ready, with Luka angrily screaming at them to spread out. Kovac turned to

Danny, who had already retrieved his own handgun from his jeans, and then to the driver, who was pale with fear.

Danny nodded at his boss.

Sam Pope.

Kovac angrily turned to the desk and lifted the walkie talkie and slammed his thumb down. His furious voice would cackle across all his men, with the message brutally clear in its simplicity.

'Find him and kill him.'

As Kovac threw the device back on the desk, he took a deep breath, assuring himself he had the situation under control.

Before he could return to the business of the driver, another gunshot rang out, and threw another section of the quarry into a blazing inferno.

CHAPTER ELEVEN

Sam had been against the clock from the moment he'd left his accommodation. He'd acquired the necessary ingredients, ensuring he picked up what he could from the supermarket before getting the major components of his homemade explosives from one of the large chain hardware stores.

Once he'd taken everything back to his rented apartment, he laid his purchases out on the table. As he placed the paint thinner onto the table, he chuckled, remembering the conversation he had with Etheridge a few days before they eventually went their separate ways over two years ago.

Paul Etheridge had served alongside Sam as part of the British Armed Forces, his genius intellect making him a valuable member of the team as opposed to a deadly soldier. While Sam had built his reputation up from behind the scope of his rifle, Etheridge had channelled his intelligence into becoming an explosives expert. After springing Sam from a police transfer to another prison, Etheridge had taken Sam to an abandoned apartment he owned, giving them a safe place to lie low as he organised their escape from the public eye.

Sam was headed to America to make things right with Alex Stone, and Etheridge, now wanted for his part in Sam's escape, was going completely off the grid. Considering the man practically built the Grid himself, it wouldn't be too hard for him to disappear.

Sam missed Etheridge dearly.

Along the dark path he'd walked, Sam had met a few people he considered friends. People who had gone beyond the call to do the right thing and Etheridge was top of the list. The man had walked away from his cosy life as a millionaire to join Sam's cause, finding true purpose in helping Sam discover the truth of Project Hailstorm and bringing down the Kovalenko empire.

Etheridge had paid a heavy price for it.

He'd sold his company.

His trophy wife had left him.

A bullet to his kneecap would leave him disabled for the rest of his life.

But Etheridge deemed it all worth it. And on that evening, hunkered down in the safe house, while sharing a few bottles of beer, Etheridge had given Sam a brief lesson in how to build a crude, home-made explosive. It was one of Sam's gifts that he could commit things to memory, his eye for detail allowing him to build out his plan of execution or escape in an instant.

In his room, he sat back in his chair and expelled a deep breath. In the two hours since his shopping trip, he'd made four bombs, each potent enough to level his apartment and blow him halfway to hell.

They weren't built to end lives.

They were built to distract.

Sam carefully loaded them into the sports bag, wrapping them in towels he'd found in the cupboard, leaving a note and a few hundred pounds to the owner to replace them.

In his other sports bag, Sam loaded his SA80 Assault Rifle, along with the remaining bullet magazines. The two recently cleaned Glocks were placed in as well, and the zip pulled tight. Outside, he saw the taxi pull up, and he took a deep breath before venturing out of the apartment, the guns draped over his shoulder and the bombs carefully in the grip of his right hand. The taxi driver offered to take the bags, but Sam was insistent on sitting with them in the back seat of the car. When questioned on their drive to the quarry, Sam fed the driver a few vague lies about delivering samples.

It sufficed.

With the majority of the crew already finished for the evening, Sam had the driver pull over half a kilometre from the quarry entrance. With a sceptical raise of his eyebrow, the driver obliged, and Sam soon found himself walking along the perimeter fence of the quarry, his guns strapped to his back and a bag of bombs secured tightly in his grip. The tall mesh fences ran the entire boundary of the massive quarry, with a number of health and safety and warning signs affixed every twenty yards.

Sam marched around the west side of the fence, following the information that Luka had given him under the duress of Sam holding a gun to his sister's head.

The truck yard was on the west side of the quarry, which was behind the white cabin. After fifteen minutes of walking, the trucks come into view, along with the cabin and numerous pieces of digging equipment, all disengaged and shut down for the day.

For a place so large, it was eerily quiet, and with the sun beginning to descend ever so slightly, Sam moved quickly. From his back pocket, he pulled the wire clippers he'd purchased that afternoon and he snipped a hole through the fence and squirmed through. As he ran down the dusty incline, his mind raced back to his days in the army, the numerous missions he'd been on.

From Iraq to the Amazon.

Arriving back to base with a full squadron or being the only survivor.

Through the downpour of rain or gunfire.

As his boots kicked through the dust, Sam felt for the briefest second, like he was back in the camos. But life had moved on considerably since then, with his reason for always fighting long since gone.

Now he fought back, to help those that couldn't fight for themselves. The good people who had to stand by while the rich and corrupt stayed healthy and the law did little to change that.

Men like Frank Jackson, Andrei Kovalenko, Harry Chapman, and Daniel Bowker.

Men like General Ervin Wallace.

Men like Slaven Kovac.

If Sam didn't fight back, all of them would still be alive, feeding off the fear of the country and getting wealthier and more powerful than they could even imagine.

So Sam fought.

And as he slid down the final, steep incline to the flattened earth beneath, he felt a renewed sense of purpose. This wasn't just about getting some extra guns and maybe knocking a few bad guys off the streets.

This was a declaration of war.

A declaration of war not just on Kovac and the vast empire he had. But a war on every person who thought they were above the law.

Beyond justice.

Who saw this country as their kingdom.

Too many good people had died for Sam to still be

standing, and as he surveyed the empty quarry, admiring the sun setting over the far hill, he knew he had to keep fighting.

For their memory.

And the memories that people had yet to make.

Sam eased the sports bag from his back, laid it to rest on the ground, before surveying the scene. As Luka had promised, there were a number of trucks parked beyond the cabin, and Sam took off in a brisk jog, passing the cabin itself and approaching the parked vehicles. With caution, he unzipped the sports bag and carefully removed one of the home-made explosives. Gently, he placed it on the bumper of the truck, tucking it in tightly enough to the headlight so as not to be obvious, but with nothing obstructing it.

Sam needed a clear view.

Ten minutes later, he found himself strolling back to his guns, an empty sports bag in his hand and beads of sweat sliding down his spine.

The quarry had been strategically rigged with explosives. Now all Sam had to do was find his spot.

And wait.

It was an ability that came easily to Sam, one he'd honed over years of sitting behind the scope of his rifle. Tucked away at the top of the ridge that overlooked the main work area, Sam had sat patiently as the evening got considerably darker, and not once did he flinch. As an elite sniper, being locked into one position, without so much as a muscle twitch, was second nature to him. Eventually, the magnificent burst of six pairs of headlights became visible on the horizon, and sure enough, the cavalcade of 4x4s made their way down the gravel heavy ramp. Carefully, the drivers pulled the cars to a stop in a row and the doors opened. Sam counted thirteen men in total, all of them dressed in black. Beside him, Sam had the SA80 Assault

Rifle primed and ready, along with the two Glocks he would keep as a last-ditch resort. He reached into the sports bag and pulled out the cheap pair of binoculars he'd bought on his shopping trip and lifted them to his eyes.

Thankfully, the headlights of the vehicles illuminated the clearing enough for him to confirm that every one of the arrivals looked like they meant business, and he instantly recognised Luka. There was another man close to him who didn't have the same hardened expression as the rest of the crew.

An outsider, perhaps?

A translator?

Then he saw the man that was unmistakably Slaven Kovac.

Well groomed, handsome, and with a rock-solid jaw, the man looked as dangerous as the reputation that preceded him. Barking out a few orders, Kovac made his way towards the cabin, while a number of the men began to scan the perimeter, no doubt trying to find Sam himself. They were all armed, expertly holding their handguns with murderous and well-trained hands.

They wouldn't find him, though.

Sam had taken up a spot above the clearing, over-looking a steep ridge that gave him plenty of cover. He'd pressed himself up against a powerful excavator, which meant his entire body was shielded from their view. With the height, distance, and machinery between himself and Kovac's crew, Sam knew they wouldn't find him.

He was hidden.

For now.

After another half hour of watching the crew slowly circle the quarry and work their way through a number of cigarettes, Sam's attention was drawn to a bright light in the distance. Two headlights sliced through the darkness, accompanied by a thunderous hum of an engine. The articulated lorry wobbled across the quarry floor, before carefully turning onto the ramp way and slowly descending into the pit. Just as Luka had relayed to Sam, the driver parked it where designated and killed the engine. Through his binoculars, Sam watched as an unassuming man exited the vehicle, only to be welcomed with a gun to the face. Clearly terrified, the man struggled to open the back of the truck, falling foul of Luka who seemed to be enjoying himself. The outsider took umbrage at Luka's behaviour, and after a few curt words, the metal shutter flew open. Sam couldn't see what was inside, but as five of the men quickly got to work, he was sure the delivery was as Luka had admitted.

Guns and drugs.

The motherload.

The crew got to work quickly, pulling open boxes and removing bag after bag of cocaine. Then came the gun parts. Sam watched as the heavily trained men assembled the weapons efficiently, before they were loaded into the back of one of the Range Rovers that had been brought to the rear of the truck. They were a fluid machine, with the weapons and drugs being quickly removed, sorted and stored away.

There would be over two hundred boxes on the truck, which necessitated the six cars.

That was a lot of drugs.

And a dangerous number of weapons.

The outsider marched the driver to the office, disappearing inside and no doubt giving Kovac the pleasure of intimidating the poor man who was probably just trying to make a little extra cash on the side.

They wouldn't let him live.

Kovac would be too careful.

'Stick to the plan,' Sam said to himself through gritted teeth, trying to ignore the horrible fate of the driver. The car hadn't been loaded yet, although he'd counted twenty assembled weapons being placed in the back, along with a box of grenades.

Sam was here for an arsenal.

There were too many of Kovac's men here for him to bring the man down tonight, but with those weapons, he could burn everything Kovac had built to the ground.

He just needed to stick to the plan.

Five minutes had passed, and neither Kovac, the outsider, nor the driver had emerged.

More importantly, there had been no gunshot or flash.

Sam thought of his son. Jamie had made him promise not to kill people, and it was a broken promise that Sam regretted with every breath he took.

Sam had to kill people.

But he didn't need to let innocent people die.

'Fuck it,' Sam uttered, and he stepped out from the machine, drawing the SA80 up to his eyeline and lodging the stock into his muscular shoulder. Without a scope, Sam was reliant on the lights of the cars below and his own unrivalled ability behind the trigger.

He aimed for the explosive on the truck on the far side of the quarry.

There was no going back now.

Sam pulled the trigger and announced his arrival as the truck exploded into a ball of fire and shards of metal, sending the whole evening into mayhem.

He had to move.

And quick.

CHAPTER TWELVE

As the first truck exploded in an incredible ball of flames, shaking the gravel beneath, Sam watched as a number of the armed men rushed towards the chaos. The blast had sent one of the men hurtling to the ground and a few of the men rush to his aid.

He wasn't moving.

Sam pushed himself forward, keeping himself low and the rifle expertly held in front of him. There had been no movement from the cabin, which meant he was too late or Kovac was as unflappable as he assumed. As he scrambled across the crumbling ridge that framed the entire quarry, he dropped down to one knee and drew the rifle up again.

On the right-hand side of the quarry, he'd placed another home-made explosive on the front of a rusty, well-worn wheel loader.

It had seen better days.

As Sam pulled the trigger, he consigned those days to the history books.

The bullet ripped through the explosive, causing another mighty eruption, and the machine rose from the ground as the front compartment was blown to smithereens. Among the smoke and wreckage, one of the tyres bounced through the wreckage.

A risible panic had taken a hold of the armed crew, and Luka began barking orders, demanding they fan out and try to find Sam. Some of the men rushed towards the second wreckage, and Sam's focus landed on the Range Rover by the truck.

It had been left unattended.

As he began to take a few careful steps down the steep incline, the door to the cabin burst open. Sam stopped, adjusting his weight to keep himself steady and through the door burst Kovac, looking irate at the situation unfolding before him. Behind him followed the outsider, along with the driver whose appearance drew a sigh of relief from Sam.

And also a pained conflict.

He couldn't leave the driver behind.

The man was clearly terrified and there was no way he would survive the evening. It was likely that the only reason he hadn't been killed yet was Sam's explosive interruption.

A gunshot rang out.

Two feet to Sam's left, a bullet hammered into the stone embankment, sending rocks into the air. Below, Sam heard the shooter calling for support having located Sam.

The man drew up his handgun again.

Sam drew his rifle quicker.

He pulled the sight at the end of the rifle in line with his eye, locked it on the man, and without hesitation, Sam pulled the trigger.

The flash from the rifle would give away his position, but Sam knew, as he absorbed the kickback in his shoulder, that the man below was dead. The bullet caught him clean in the chest, ripping through his lungs, and sending him spiralling to the hard, dark rocks beneath him.

A few more voices rose from the quarry, their owners

pointing towards Sam as they rushed forward, having discovered his location.

A few gunshots rang out.

The bullets hit the stones surrounding Sam, one of them coming dangerously close to his left leg.

Sam pulled the trigger again, the bullet hitting the onrushing henchman between the eyes and sending his head snapping back and a burst of blood and brain onto the rocks. He spun to the left, dropped to one knee, and sent another bullet careening through the headlight lit quarry into the chest of another.

Three dead.

But there were more following, and he looked at Kovac, who stood stoically, staring at Sam's position.

Almost daring Sam to shoot.

With his cover blown, and another eight men rushing towards him, including a vengeful Luka, Sam dropped to one knee and swung the rifle to face Kovac. Behind the fearless leader, a number of his crew were racing towards him, having to pass the cabin as they made their way from the previous explosion.

Sam drew the gun to his shoulder, put his eye to the sight, and took a deep breath.

He needed to make this shot.

His life depended on it.

Another bullet clattered into the embankment beside him, and with the majority of the onrushing, murderous crew rounding the cabin, Sam squeezed the trigger.

Judging from Kovac's reaction, the man had realised that Sam wasn't aiming for the kill.

The bullet shot through the dark, beyond Kovac, and just as the remainder of his crew hurtled past the cabin, the bullet embedded itself below the metal steps that led to the cabin door.

Into the explosive Sam had placed there a few hours earlier.

Kovac yelled in his native tongue, but the ear-shattering explosion drowned him out as the cabin burst into a ball of flames, the impact and fire sending Kovac, the outsider, the driver, and the rest of the crew hurtling to the ground.

Sam had no time to assess the damage.

Judging by their proximity, he estimated that at least half the crew wouldn't be getting back up. Those that did, he would deal with if necessary.

But as he slid down the rest of the embankment, his feet sporadically hitting the ground to keep his balance, he had two targets.

The driver and the Range Rover.

As he neared the bottom of the ridge, another bullet whistled past him, ricocheting off the stones behind. Instinctively, Sam dived forward, clearing the final few feet of the incline, and he hit the flat gravel of the quarry floor. As his shoulder collided with the stone, Sam rolled through, propelling himself back onto one knee and he whipped the rifle up and directed it at the henchman who had already returned to his feet.

Sam sent a flurry of bullets in the man's direction, and three of them riddled his soot covered body and sent him flopping motionless to the floor.

The quarry had begun to fill with thick, black smoke from the explosions, both helping and harming Sam. It provided him with a little more cover, but it also meant his own line of sight was compromised. Keeping low, he hooked the strap of his SA80 over his shoulder and slid it round to his back before retrieving one of the Glock 17s from the back of his jeans.

Stumbling erratically through the smoke, another

henchman came into view, his face smeared with blood and his left leg horribly charred. Sam dropped him with a precise shot to the chest before he was drawn to the sound of footsteps crunching across the gravel. He spun, trying his best to peer through the smoke, and was met with a confusing sight.

The outsider was helping the driver across the quarry, heading towards the Range Rover.

Keeping his gun drawn, Sam gave chase as the quarry continued to fall beneath the fiery chaos he'd unleashed.

———

'What the fuck is going on?'

Kovac angrily yelled into the radio, his fingers clasping it tightly. The usual veneer of calm had slipped slightly, revealing the terrifying commander that Townsend had heard so much about. Beyond the penchant for expensive suits and his usual unflappable calm, Kovac was as dangerous as they came. When Sanders briefed him two years ago, informing Townsend just how dangerous Kovac was, Townsend was sceptical.

He'd been around street criminals his entire life, from his rough upbringing to his time walking the beat.

They were tough.

But not unstoppable.

Kovac was a different beast entirely. The man commanded more fear and respect with the slightest raise of an eyebrow than any street thug Townsend had come across. The man was cold, calculating, and ambitious. The most dangerous aspect was the man's intelligence. There were no ridiculous displays of bravado or attempts to impress with his vast wealth. The man was a ruthlessly efficient businessman, who had steadily guided the rebuild of an empire and made it flourish.

But watching that calmness ebb away as the second

explosion rocked the quarry, Townsend caught a glimpse at the horror behind the mask.

The Man of Stone.

'It's Pope,' Townsend stated.

'Then let's go kill him,' Kovac replied coldly, ushering the two men to the door with his handgun. 'But first, Danny, put this cockroach in the ground before he gets in the way.'

'Oh God…' The driver began to panic again, and Townsend stepped forward.

'With all due respect, sir, he isn't the concern.'

Kovac stopped reaching for the door handle and turned to Townsend, his eyes wide in anger. The venomous gaze sent a shiver down Townsend's spine.

'Just kill him.' Kovac looked the driver up and down with a look of disdain on his face. 'Make it quick.'

At that moment, a flurry of gunshots echoed throughout the quarry, drawing their attention. A few screams of horror followed, meaning two things.

Sam Pope was there.

And some of Kovac's men were dead.

The ice-cold look fell across Kovac's face again and he threw open the door, allowing the chaos that Sam had orchestrated to reveal itself. Two large fires were dancing up towards the sky, with thick, black smoke billowing upwards and no doubt sending a worrying message to any of the local towns. It meant that authorities would be called, and they were now against the clock to not only eradicate Sam Pope, but to also leave with their delivery intact. Kovac turned to the doorway.

'Get him in the truck and get him the fuck out of here.'

Kovac barked the order at a concerned Townsend. With an obliging nod, Townsend ushered the driver away from the oncoming group of men, who were all rushing towards them with their guns raised. Kovac followed their gaze to the embankment, his eyes falling on the expert movements of Sam Pope.

He felt his knuckles whiten with fury.

With his gun in his hand, Kovac steadied himself, ready to embarrass his crew with one pinpoint shot that would send Pope to the afterlife. But Pope dropped to one knee, hoisting the rifle up expertly, and Kovac felt himself in the crosshair. But he wasn't the target.

If he was, he would have been dead already.

Behind him, he saw his crew, led by the irate Luka, charging past the cabin. Beyond them, Townsend was guiding the terrified driver away from them, heading back towards the delivery truck in a desperate attempt to salvage the drop off.

Kovac's eyes widened with realisation, and he opened his mouth.

'Get away from the—' His desperate order was cut off as Pope's rifle clattered behind him, sending a bullet whipping past him and embedding itself in the explosive set against the cabin.

The flash of orange exploded before him, followed by a roar like thunder, and he was sent hurtling to the ground as if hit by an invisible truck. He felt the searing heat against his skin, and as Kovac collided with the gravel, everything went black.

———

Luckily for Townsend, they'd covered sufficient distance when the gunshot rang out. The blast of the explosion sent both himself and the driver tumbling forward, a wave of heat brushing past them like a gale-force wind. Gingerly, Townsend pushed himself to his knees, checking the palms of his hands that had been shredded by the hard impact on the gravel below. Beside him, the driver wobbled as he stumbled to his feet, the man holding his bleeding elbow in severe discomfort.

The driver said something, but it came through like an echo, and Townsend tried his hardest to shake the high-pitch squeal that was still dominating his hearing. He'd seen it in movies countless times, but never imagined that a loud explosion really could send his ear drum off on a different frequency. As he got to his feet, Townsend's hearing began to unmuffle.

'What the fuck was that?' the driver asked, clearly panicked. Townsend shook his head before surveying the scene. Kovac was down, the blast knocking him far enough away for Townsend to know that he wasn't dead. A few of the crew were not so lucky.

The thick smoke spread across the quarry like an unstoppable wave and among it, he heard another burst of fire and the sound of a dead body crashing to the stones below.

Sam Pope was finishing the job.

With the smoke providing enough cover, Townsend turned back to the driver and pointed.

'Move. Now.'

As the quarry burnt around them, the two men shuffled as quickly and as uncomfortably as they could towards the Range Rover, which had been abandoned among the carnage with the door still open and the key hanging in the ignition. Townsend knew that stealing the car and prioritising the safety of the driver meant that there would be no coming back. Kovac wasn't known for his forgiveness and there was no chance Sanders would send him back once he'd got out.

They would have a portion of the drugs and the guns, a live witness, and enough evidence at the quarry to convict every single one of them. Although it was unlikely, their best chance of breaking a man like Kovac was to potentially offer him a deal to give up his benefactor.

It was a long shot.

But Townsend was ready to go home.

Bursting through the worst of the smoke, Townsend rushed to the car, opening the back door and demanding the driver get in among the shipment. It would be safer for him to lie low in the back, and with the man eager to leave the most horrifying night of his life behind him, the driver obliged immediately.

Somewhere in the distance, the faint sound of sirens wailing.

Townsend closed the door, turned to the driver's door, and felt a fist collide with his jaw, rocking him into the side of the Range Rover and crashing to the ground. He spat a mouthful of blood onto the stones and looked up, only to be met by the murderous eyes of Luka.

'Where are you going you piece of shit?' Luka spat, his face covered in painful looking burns and his other hand gleefully gripping his Glock.

'Get the fuck out of my way,' Townsend said wearily, as he got to his feet. 'Boss wants this out of here.'

Luka straightened his arm, the pistol aimed squarely at Townsend's head. His suspicion of Townsend had always been clear, and now, having caught him trying to sneak the driver to safety, Townsend knew he had limited options.

And all of those inevitably led to his death.

'It will be a pleasure to kill you.' Luka smirked, his teeth stained with blood and ash. Townsend saw a flash of his family in his mind's eye, realising that his final moments would be spent thinking about them. A sickening thud interrupted his final goodbye, and Townsend opened his eyes to see an unconscious Luka collide with the Range Rover, before tumbling motionless to the ground below.

Shocked, Townsend turned to the man who had just driven the grip of his gun into Luka's temple.

Stepping out of the smoke was Sam Pope.

'On your knees,' Sam demanded, pointing the weapon at Townsend, who raised his hands immediately in surrender.

'Look, my name is Jack Townsend and I'm an undercover police officer.'

Sam didn't look convinced, then looked beyond Townsend as a few more of the crew were beginning to stumble to their feet, all of them cursing in their native tongue.

'Who's in the back?' Sam asked, his gun still trained on Townsend.

'A driver. He's innocent, and I'm trying to get him out of here.'

A few excited cries echoed behind them, followed by a crack of gunfire. A bullet blew out the left taillight. With his gun still trained on Townsend, Sam rushed to the passenger door and motioned for Townsend to take the wheel.

'Get in,' Sam yelled as another bullet whizzed past, just missing them. 'You can explain on the way.'

'I'm driving?' Townsend questioned, dropping into the car and pulling away before he'd even closed the door. Sam slid the clip from the Glock, letting it clatter to the floor, before slamming in a full one.

'Yup.' Sam held up his gun. 'I think I'm going to be a little busy.'

As Townsend raced towards the ramp way, the headlights of three of the Range Rovers illuminated the smoke behind them, ready to give chase and to stop them from leaving the quarry.

By any means necessary.

CHAPTER THIRTEEN

As Townsend took the bend onto the ramp, the spinning tyre of the Range Rover threw a trail of gravel up into the air. The engine roared as he slammed his foot down, the weight of the car only adding to the incline. Townsend felt his heart racing, the adrenaline coursing through his body pulsed like a second heartbeat, and he shot a glance to Sam next to him. The man had been announced dead a few years before, but here he was, in the flesh and proving first hand just how deadly he was. In the back of Townsend's mind, he worried whether Sam believed him or not, and whether once they'd got away from their pursuers, would he fall the same way as so many other criminals?

'Floor it,' Sam demanded, and Townsend pressed his foot down as far as he could, and the car burst forward into the thick, black smoke that was pumping from the quarry below. In the back of the car, the innocent driver tried to hold himself steady among the weapons and the drugs, their placement making it impossible for him to secure his seat belt. The man was clearly terrified, and Townsend knew it was his guilt for all the other drivers that had caused him to potentially blow his cover with Luka.

The other drivers, all of whom had been shot in the head and buried somewhere within the quarry. Townsend had never had to pull the trigger himself, but he'd held the shovel, and he hoped that by saving this driver, he could at least quash some of that guilt.

Just another thing to add to the list of why he craved redemption and a way back home.

As they approached the top of the ramp, Townsend pulled the wheel into a full lock, the Range Rover skidding across the stones and, as it threatened to veer off course, Townsend used his upper body to eventually pull the car under his control.

The chasing lights quickly emerged through the smoke, with the remnants of Kovac's crew in hot pursuit and fortunately for them, not weighed down by an arsenal of high calibre guns. With his headlights on full beam, Townsend navigated his way through the quarry, weaving in and out of machinery and water barrels, and turning just at the last moment to avoid a severe dip into a water trail. As he did, a gunshot echoed behind them and blew out one of the back windows.

'Stay down,' Townsend yelled, with the driver yelping in fear as he tried to make himself as low as possible.

Calmly, Sam pressed the button on the door and his window began to slide down. As it did, the onrushing air filtered into the car, welcoming in a cool breeze and the unmistakable smell of burning. Sam unfastened his seat belt and turned on his seat.

'Turn left now,' he ordered, and Townsend obliged, pulling the wheel with all his might and causing the 4x4 to sharply spin to the side. As it did, Sam locked his arm in place, with both his hands held expertly around the Glock and he squeezed the trigger.

The gunshot was deafening, catching both Townsend and the innocent passenger by surprise.

But there was no surprise with the outcome.

The bullet launched from the gun and burrowed through the windscreen of the nearest car, ripping through the driver's skull and sending him and his passengers hurtling down the incline and into the water trail. With the dead driver's foot still on the accelerator, the speed caused the vehicle to flip, and it rolled a few times before crashing into a crumpled heap at the bottom.

Sam rocked back into his seat.

'That was awesome,' Townsend cackled.

'Eyes on the road.'

Townsend readjusted his gaze ahead of him, and as he rounded another piece of machinery, they saw the next incline that would take them back towards the exit. Beside them, one of the chasing cars drew close, the driver twisting the steering wheel, so their cars collided. Rattled, Townsend steered back into him, and with both cars neck and neck, Townsend flashed a glance at the murderous driver beside him.

'Sit back,' Sam demanded, and as Townsend did, Sam straightened his arm, the Glock locked squarely on the other driver, and he executed him at top speed. Townsend barked in pain as the gunshot pushed his ear drums to their limit and as he tried to concentrate through the agony, he barely noticed the other car collide viciously with an excavator and explode in a fiery demise.

One car left.

Then they were on the home straight.

Four bullets rattled the side of their vehicle, and Sam looked over his shoulder at the final car that was chasing them. With the lights on full beam, he couldn't make out how many of the crew were in pursuit, or if Luka was among them. Chances were, Luka and Kovac had made their exit pretty sharpish, and with the sirens now painfully close, it was time they did the same. Another round of bullets cackled into the night, with one of the bullets blowing out Sam's wing mirror.

'Aim for the fence,' Sam demanded, pointing with his gun at the chain-link fence a few hundred metres away.

'What?'

'The police will be at the gate by now.'

'I told you, I'm with the police.'

'But I'm not.'

Townsend nodded his agreement and slammed his foot down once more, the Range Rover battling against the weight of three men and an arsenal to drive on towards the metal fence ahead. Behind them, the glow of the head-lights grew as the car gained on them, and then it veered to the side, hoping to pull up beside them. Townsend turned the car towards them, trying to push them off course, but the driver did likewise, the two cars colliding with each other at high speed.

Gravel shot up from the ground.

The horrible sound of metal screeching echoed.

Somehow, both managed to avoid the final piece of machinery before they hit the final stretch of stone before the fence.

The car pulled up beside them, and Townsend saw the passenger lift the double-barrel shotgun to the window.

'Brake now.'

Sam's command triggered an immediate response from Townsend, who slammed his foot down on the brake pedal so hard, he feared his foot would penetrate the bottom of the car itself. The bullet-riddled Range Rover screeched to an almost immediate stop, sending both men shunting forward and Sam used his forearm to absorb the collision with the dashboard. Behind them, the driver clattered into the backs of their seats, doing his best to limit the impact among the clattering of metal.

Caught by surprise, the other car bolted past, with the shotgun blast blowing out one of Townsend's headlights and ripping through some of the licence plate. In desperation, the driver turned the car to full lock, the tyres arching precariously as the mighty vehicle violently jerked to the side.

With a dangerous fluidity, Sam stepped out of the car and instantly raised the Glock, with both hands clasping it and one eye closed. He pulled the trigger, unloading the rest of the clip with devastating precision, sending one of the bullets through the open window and into the throat of the gun-toting passenger.

The rest of the bullets hammered the arch of the wheel, before two of them ripped through the tyre and the suspension. The tyre exploded, causing the already turning Range Rover to flip, and at such a high speed, sent it rolling through the air and onto the hard stones below. In their haste to kill Sam and Townsend, the henchmen hadn't bothered with their seat belts, and their bodies were left to be torn to shreds by the spinning cocoon of broken metal, glass, and gravel.

The car rolled into the fence, completely dismantling it and ripping it from the ground, clearing a pathway for Townsend. As the car rolled to a fatal stop, Townsend realised his mouth was open in awe, and he shot a glance to Sam, who stood, as calm as if he was queuing for a coffee.

Behind him, the quarry was burning to the ground, with a trail of destruction and death following them.

It was in that moment that Townsend realised that despite working for Kovac for over two years, he'd never felt truly afraid at what another human was capable of. Sam Pope wasn't a dangerous criminal, running guns and drugs into the country with the ultimate goal of seizing power.

He was trained.

Capable.

And fighting for something he believed in.

At that moment, with flames flickering in the distance and the smouldering embers floating among the smoke, Townsend saw exactly how deadly Sam Pope was.

Sam stepped back into the car, slamming the door shut, and then nodded to Townsend.

'Let's go.'

Townsend felt his hands shake as he pulled the car into first gear, the wheels of the vehicle crunching over the gravel as they headed towards the shattered fence. On the other side of the quarry, the emergency services began to filter in through the gate, no doubt horrified at the ravenous flames and thick black smoke that had engulfed the entire area. Once they'd got through the initial shock and ventured further into the carnage and burning embers, they would find a trail of bodies that would lead them to one of several conclusions.

One, that Kovac had entered into a gang war with an unknown adversary.

Or two, the rumours of Sam Pope being alive and well had some truth to them.

As Townsend guided the car past the wreckage and into the cold, dark freedom of the night, he could see from the purpose emanating from Sam Pope that he was willing to feed those rumours even more.

———

Luka stared at his charred knuckles; the skin tinged with soreness from the heat of the explosions. He ignored the pain, especially the searing agony that was pumping from the fierce blow to the back of his head, and he gripped the steering wheel tighter.

Amid the carnage that had ensued once Townsend had made off with the weapons, a furious Kovac had awoken him from his enforced slumber with a brisk slap to the face. Like Luka, Kovac's face had born some of the brunt of the explosion and embedded in his now charred face were two eyes that glared with murderous rage.

'Get up!' Kovac had screamed, his voice barely audible over the sound of the other cars roaring into life and the high-pitch squeal that had taken up residence within his ear drum. Luka had woozily risen, his skull still shaking from the clubbing blow Sam had delivered, and he stumbled to his feet. With the majority of the fleet of Range Rovers in hot pursuit of Sam, Kovac shoved his right-hand man towards one of the other parked vehicles.

'Let's go.'

Kovac threw open the passenger door and dropped into the seat, waiting for Luka to shake the cobwebs and start the car. Knowing the interruption from Sam would have drawn the authorities, there was no chance of Kovac having them called off. While his powers of persuasion could ensure a smooth deal went ahead, he knew there was no way his contact could stem the tidal wave of emergency calls based on the noise and the fire.

It meant they had to leave immediately, forfeiting the safety and freedom of his men and more importantly, the treasure trove of weapons and drugs in the back of the lorry. Kovac, overcome with rage, slammed his soot covered fist against the dashboard, as Luka pulled the car into gear and drove towards the back exit of the quarry, hopeful that Sam's merry chase would hold up any potential police interest.

Within five minutes, the flames and smoke of the wreckage had disappeared from their rear-view mirror, and Luka stared at his charred knuckles, feeling them tighten with anger around the cool leather of the steering wheel.

'Danny abandoned us,' Luka finally said, his bulging eyes staring daggers at the dark country road ahead.

'Nonsense.' Kovac batted away the idea with his hand, a cigarette resting loosely between the fingers. He took a long drag and then blew the smoke out of the window. 'He make off with the guns.'

'I'm telling you, that boy is no good.' Luka shook his head. 'I say it since day one—'

'I do not pay you to speak to me like this.' Kovac interrupted, his voice raised with agitation. 'I pulled you from war, Luka, to make you a rich man. You do as I say, you don't tell me what to do. You understand?'

Luka grunted and kept his eyes on the road. Kovac kept his glare on Luka for a few more moments, just long enough to re-establish the balance of power. With a grimace, he took another puff on his cigarette before he flicked it out of the window.

'What do we do now?' Luka finally broke the silence.

'We find Danny and we take the guns he managed to keep and then we go to war.' Kovac slipped another cigarette out of his blazer and lit it. 'We underestimated Sam Pope. He killed many of our men and he has cost us a lot of money. For that, he will pay a heavy price.'

'You will kill him?' Luka asked excitedly.

'No. But I make him beg me to.'

The threat hung heavy in the air, thicker than the black smoke that had engulfed them earlier. As they travelled onwards, Luka took the turn towards the motorway, following the earlier instruction to take them to Kovac's remote abode. Despite his business being central to the urban lifestyle, Kovac operated out of a picturesque mansion deep in the middle of the countryside. It offered optimal privacy, as well as the opportunity to bask in the fortune he'd made.

It was off the grid.

And it was kept that way by paying the right people in the right places.

'How do we find Danny?' Luka said through gritted teeth, clearly disappointed his attempt to execute him in the middle of the battlefield had failed.

'He will come to us,' Kovac said, as he unlocked his phone, and the screen illuminated his face. He began to thumb his way across the touch screen to his contacts. 'He is loyal.'

'Like a dog.'

'We are all dogs,' Kovac said dryly. 'However, soon, I will be the one without a master.'

'And how do we find Sam Pope?'

'Simple.' Kovac grinned and exhaled another cloud of cancerous smoke. 'We call the police.'

Luka shook his head with a wry grin on his face, as Kovac lifted the phone to his ear. He knew the terror that his name caused when it hit the receiver's screen, and within three rings, the call connected. In the background, he could hear the chaos of the quarry as the emergency services tried their best to contain the carnage.

Panicked, the voice finally spoke.

'This isn't a good time.'

'I want Sam Pope. Find him for me.'

Kovac hung up the call instantly and dropped the phone onto his lap. As the darkness of the countryside enveloped the car, he sat back in his seat and enjoyed the rest of his cigarette, and fantasising about the moment that he crushed Sam Pope's skull under his oppressive boot.

Sam Pope had declared war.

And Kovac was a war lord.

CHAPTER FOURTEEN

'Christ on a fuckin' bike.'

Inspector Sanders ran his hand across his bearded chin and sighed. As he stepped across the gravel, he was taken aback at the mayhem that was unfolding before him. Kirby Cane Quarry was as much a crime scene as it was a war zone, and as the fine officers of the Suffolk Police worked alongside the fire department and paramedics, Sanders could only imagine what the hell happened.

He'd been stopped at the entrance by the officer working the cordon and he stepped out of his car and decided to venture in on foot. The gate on the far side had been completely obliterated by the turned over Range Rover that sat a few metres from the gap, with paramedics fighting helplessly to save the life of one of the men they'd hauled from the wreckage.

Beside them, a dead body had already been recovered.

With every crunch of his shoe on the gravel, Sanders felt the weight of his guilt increase.

Townsend hadn't been able to give him the location, which meant he didn't have a team mobilised, ready to bring down Kovac and his boss. That had been the plan, and twenty-four hours earlier, Townsend had been adamant that it would be over.

Sanders would have what he wanted.

And Townsend could go back home.

Sanders had even organised for Mandy and Eve to travel across the country from Merseyside, hoping to surprise Townsend with a quicker return to his family. Despite his better instincts, he knew that the secret rendezvous with his family was all that was keeping Townsend sane.

Was all that was keeping him a copper.

Continuing on, Sanders passed another overturned vehicle, this one at the bottom of a water trench. As the body of the car was still smouldering, fire fighters were working to douse the flames.

The occupants were dead.

None of them Townsend.

A few officers hurried past, working tirelessly under the lights of the vehicles, doing their best to try to secure a crime scene that would be like no other they'd ever encountered. Rumours had already begun to swirl around the quarry, as a few of Slaven Kovac's men had been identified by some of the officers who had dealt with them before. The rumours were of an escalating drug war that threatened to turn East Anglia into a war zone.

The other was even scarier.

Sam Pope.

Sanders had read about the rumours from a few weeks ago, where a security enforcement operation, on the payroll of a wealthy pharmaceutical CEO, had been slain by the resurrected Sam Pope. Having been declared dead a few years ago, Sanders was well aware that his death, along with that of the legendary Harry Chapman, had led to the rise of a new wave of criminals.

Criminals like Slaven Kovac.

For two years, Sanders had been worrying day and night about Jack Townsend, knowing he'd sent him into the belly of the beast and fearing that every day would be the day he received a call to say they'd pulled Townsend's body out of the Waveny. That any day, he would have to go see Mandy and Eve, watching as Townsend's wife crumpled under the acknowledgement of what his home visit meant.

They were so close.

Townsend was adamant that Kovac's superior was ready to reveal themselves and when they had whoever held the purse strings, they could bring everything down. Townsend had made it clear that despite how dangerous Kovac was, he was just a weed.

If they pulled him out, another one would just grow in his place.

The last thing Sanders or Townsend needed was the most notorious vigilante the country had ever known to not only be alive but hunting in their kingdom. Pope was as dangerous as the criminals he went to war with, and if he had targeted Kovac, it meant there would be a reaction.

The walls would go up.

The shutters would go down.

Kovac's boss was unlikely to step willingly into Sam's crosshair.

'You all right, Reece?'

A voice pulled Sanders's focus away from the wreckage of the car. Sergeant James Tyler stood, hands on his hips, looking over the crest of the quarry to the smouldering vehicles on the main surface. He beckoned Sanders over, offering him a cigarette, which Sanders politely declined.

'Suit yourself.' Tyler shrugged, lighting one up and sighing as he exhaled. 'What a fucking mess, eh?'

'You're telling me.'

'Your boy here?' Tyler asked, raising a hopeful

eyebrow. It was a stab in the dark, and Sanders rolled his eyes.

'You know I can't tell you.'

'Just out on a stroll then?' Tyler smirked. 'Don't worry. If he is here, we'll find him. You'll just need to point him out to us.'

'I hope not. For his wife's sake.'

'Too right. What you thinking? The boys are almost cumming in their pants at the idea of Sam Pope being alive and well.' Tyler shook his head and took another puff. 'What do you reckon?'

'I think, if he is, then it's the worst possible outcome.'

'Last thing we need is a person taking the law into their own hands. Especially one like him. You read the reports? The man's a lunatic.'

Tyler took a final puff on the cigarette and then crunched onto the gravel below. Over the edge of where they stood, the fire services were working tirelessly to control the numerous pieces of equipment that were ablaze, bombarding the flaming wreckage with a barrage of water.

'That's the scary thing. I don't believe Sam Pope is a lunatic. I think he knew exactly what he was doing.'

'Knew?' Tyler raised his eyebrow.

'Until we get confirmation that he's alive, then it's just speculation. In the meantime, I'd start thinking about who might have the fucking bollocks to take on Kovac head on.'

'Good point.'

At that moment, Sanders felt his phone rumble inside his blazer, and he dipped his hand into the pocket and pulled it out. He was praying for Townsend's coded name to be plastered across the screen.

It wasn't, and his heart dropped.

It was the boss.

Agitated, Sanders held the phone up to Tyler, who

nodded and waved him on. As he descended the ramp way towards the fiery wreckage below, Sanders took a breath and finally answered.

'This isn't a good time.'

His boss responded curtly and hung up, and Sanders slid the phone back into his pocket. With each step, he felt his stomach flip. The panic and guilt of finding Townsend's charred corpse was as terrifying as being reprimanded by his boss later.

This has been going on for two years.

Two years.

And all that Sanders had to show for it was guilt.

Traipsing through the carnage, Sanders prayed to a god he'd never believed in, that Jack Townsend was elsewhere.

―――――

As Townsend pulled the car into the car park of the hospital, he was still unsure if Sam Pope believed him. After they'd put a safe distance between themselves and the carnage of the quarry, the rest of their journey was travelled in silence, with Sam only given the blunt direction of heading back to Lowestoft.

With a gun in the hand of the most dangerous vigilante in UK history, and his unbelievable confession of being an undercover police officer, Townsend found the tension nigh on unbearable. At one point, the driver in the back just begged to be let out anywhere, but Sam cut him off and told him they were taking him to a hospital. Even if he had escaped the explosion unscathed, there was still the very real possibility of shock setting in. Sam's compassion surprised Townsend.

You didn't expect a man who had killed dozens of

people to care about the wellbeing of someone caught in the midst of a drug and arms deal.

It was a measure of the man Sam was that he still saw innocence as exactly that, and the reports of his unwavering commitment to justice had been almost too far-fetched. As a young, idealistic officer, Townsend had immediately tagged Sam as a dangerous criminal when the first reports came in. Despite bringing down a known crime syndicate, and a wanted mobster in Frank Jackson, he'd done so by breaking the law.

It didn't make him a hero. Not in Townsend's eyes.

But as he spiralled further into his life as an undercover cop and got a true taste of just how ruthless the world can be, those stories didn't seem so bad when he got wind of them.

Taking down a sex trafficking empire and saving a teenage girl.

Exposing a high-ranking terrorist within the UK government.

Killing Harry Chapman, the man who had controlled so much of the UK underworld and had caused so much pain and devastation to so many.

The man may have broken the law, but the further Townsend had sunk into his double life, the more he saw someone like Sam as a necessity.

And here he was, flesh and blood beside him, with his eyes fixed on the road ahead and a loaded gun pointed directly at Townsend's stomach.

There was no doubt in Townsend's mind that Sam would pull the trigger. He just hoped he'd give him the chance to explain the lay of the land.

As they pulled into the drop off bay of the James Paget University Hospital, Townsend killed the engine and took a deep breath. Sam turned in his chair and looked at the innocent driver, who was sitting among the batch of stolen weapons and drugs.

'Next time, if someone offers you money to drop an unmarked truck in a quarry in the middle of the night. Don't do it.'

The man nodded, clearly scared. Sam motioned to the door, and the man pushed it open, his hand shaking as the reality and trauma of the evening began to flood through him. As he stepped out of the car, he turned back.

'Thank you.' He shot glances at both Sam and then Townsend. 'You both saved my life.'

'What's your name?' Sam asked.

'Duncan.'

'Well, take care of yourself, Duncan.' Sam turned back in his chair, breaking their eye contact. 'I hope for your sake, I never see you again.'

Townsend gave the man a fake salute with two fingers and Duncan slammed the door shut and stumbled towards the automatic doors that led to the A&E. It was a warm night, and a few people were standing to the side of the entrance, smoking and willing the time away.

'What do you think he'll say?' Townsend asked.

'Hopefully the truth.' Sam turned to Townsend and readjusted the weapon, making a show of it still being aimed at Townsend's stomach. 'Now drive.'

With a nervous exhale, Townsend put the car into first gear and pulled away, heading out of the hospital car park and back towards Lowestoft town centre. Sam said nothing, apart from the odd direction, and as they drove past the large retail park that housed a few supermarkets and carpet stores, Sam demanded Townsend pull the car in to the deserted car park. Reducing his speed, Townsend navigated his way through the darkness, and Sam demanded he cut the headlights. With his vision impaired, Townsend carefully continued into the darkness, heading away from the bright lights of the streets and more terrifyingly, humanity itself.

Sam was taking him where no one would hear them.

Where no one could find them.

As they rounded the back of one of the large buildings, Sam motioned for Townsend to pull the car down the side of the building, tucking them nicely away in the darkness and completely obscured from any security camera. With his hand shaking, Townsend killed the ignition and took a deep breath.

Sam flung his door open and stepped out. He turned back to his hostage and gestured with the gun.

'Get out.'

Slamming the door shut, Sam strode around the back of the car. A foolish idea raced through Townsend's mind to turn the key and floor it, but having witnessed Sam take out three moving cars in the heat of battle, he knew it would be a fruitless task.

And it would only hasten the inevitable bullet in the back of his skull.

Townsend kept his mind squarely on Mandy and Eve, willing himself to get back to them. The tap of the gun on the window broke his train of thought, and he pushed open the door, raised his hand in surrender, and stepped out. Sam took a few steps back, his arm outstretched, and his fingers wrapped around the gun.

There was nowhere for Townsend to go.

'Talk. Now.'

'What do you want to know?' Townsend asked.

'The truth. Who the hell are you and why I shouldn't put you in the ground with the others?'

Townsend nodded. It wasn't lost on him that a desperate criminal would try anything to survive, even lie about working for the police. But as he looked at Sam, he understood that the strict moral compass of the man probably made him a human lie detector.

If he thought Townsend was lying, then he wouldn't hesitate to pull the trigger.

'My name is Jack Townsend. I'm an undercover police officer for Merseyside Police.'

'You're a long way from home.'

'Yeah, and you're a long way from dead.'

'Touché.' Sam chuckled. 'You have two minutes to convince me not to waste another bullet, which means these are the most important two of your life.'

'You left a hole in this country, Sam,' Townsend said, ignoring the slight crack of fear in his voice. 'You had the whole country shaken when you were active. I was undercover in a gang back in Toxteth, and fuck, even they had a Sam Pope contingency plan.'

'I'm flattered.'

'I say plan… They basically said they had two options. Run the fuck away or shoot as many bullets as possible and hope they put you down. Anyway, like I said, you left a gaping hole in this country when you took down Harry Chapman. Suddenly, a lot of people saw an opportunity. You didn't stop the guns and the drugs from coming in, you just effectively put the business out to tender.'

'One minute…' Sam pretended to look at his watch.

'Then you died. Well, they said you died. Your body had been found in America. That was it. No you. No Chapman. It was a free for all. My superior came to me, telling me of an operation to infiltrate the biggest player who was making a move for the throne. So, I took it, and I've regretted every fucking day since.'

'Kovac.'

'Kovac is the one on the ground, but he isn't the money. He's got plans to take control, but all I know is that he's being funded by a Ukrainian.'

'Who?' Sam demanded, reasserting his grip on his gun.

'We don't know.' Townsend shrugged. 'They were going to be there tonight, however, you decided to beat seven shades of shit out of Luka and Kovac told them to stay away until they dealt with you. I think that's my minute up, right?'

Sam sighed and drew his mouth into a thin line. His strong jaw shook with anger and he lowered the weapon, much to the obvious relief of Townsend.

'Can you arrange another meet?'

Townsend shook his head.

'In two years, Kovac hasn't even mentioned a name. It's been part of his plan. He says it's for their protection, but in reality, he's just spent the last two years making everyone on his payroll loyal to him and him alone.'

'Strength in numbers,' Sam agreed.

'Considerably fewer numbers now.' Townsend held his hands up. 'Why are you back, anyway? I mean, I heard about the stuff in London, but they never said it was definitely you.'

'Because I'm needed. Clearly.' Sam chuckled and shook his head. 'And I needed guns, and my path unfortunately led me to you.'

'So, what now?'

'Now? We regroup and we fight again.'

'We? You mean, you're not going to kill me?'

Sam shook his head. Townsend exhaled with relief and leant forward, his hands clasping his knees.

'But I need to know everything,' Sam demanded. 'Every detail. Where he operates from. Who his men are. How he communicates with the Ukrainian. Everything.'

'I've kept everything. You know, as an insurance policy.' Sam raised his eyebrows. 'I'm certain there's a rat on our team, and if I get thrown under the bus or Kovac comes after my family, then I need something to bargain with.'

Sam smiled.

'You got a family.'

'A little girl.' Townsend couldn't hide the pride on his face. 'She's my world.'

'Where's the information?'

'In a safe house that my handler has arranged so I can see her and my wife. It's on the other side of town.'

'Right, give me the address, and I'll see you tomorrow.'

Townsend obliged, and Sam committed it to memory and headed towards the driver's side of the car.

'Hey, hold up.' Townsend objected.

'You can walk.'

'No, it's not that.' Townsend took a deep breath, clearly building up some courage. 'You need to assault me.'

'What?'

'They know I left in the car with you, right? If I walk back to Kovac looking like you took me for a fucking latte, he'll sniff me out and kill me just as quickly.'

Sam stepped back away from the door and walked towards Townsend with a look of confusion on his face.

'What are you suggesting?'

'I don't know, but mayb…'

Sam drove the handle of his gun into the bridge of Townsend's nose, the harsh steel cracking the cartilage and send a spray of blood shooting down the young man's face. As he yelped in pain and stumbled back, Sam drove a fist into the man's solid body, the impact at least bruising the rib cage and driving the air clean out from him. As Townsend stumbled forward, gasping for air and trying his best to stem the flow of blood from his face, Sam grabbed hold of his collar and the belt of his jeans, and hurled him into the side of the car.

The undercover cop clattered into the solid body of the vehicle, and then hit the concrete below, gasping in pain. Sam hopped back into the vehicle, casting an eye over the weapons he'd procured and then a scowl at the bags of drugs that accompanied them.

When he torched the car later that night, he'd make damn sure that a lot of money burnt inside it. The engine roared to life, and Sam carefully navigated around the prone and beaten body of Townsend before rolling down his window.

'Sorry,' Sam offered. 'I'll see you tomorrow.'

Townsend mustered the energy to raise his hand and give Sam a shaky thumbs up. It was quickly followed by a jovial middle finger, which drew a smirk from Sam, before he drove off into the darkness.

He liked Townsend.

Which meant getting the man back to his family was just another addition to a mission that was escalating rapidly into an all-out war.

CHAPTER FIFTEEN

With the skin on his knuckles slightly charred, Kovac grimaced as he held them against the ice bucket. The cooling sensation was welcome, and he held them for a few moments before reaching in and using the metal tongs to grasp a slippery ice cube and drop it into his drink.

It had been a disappointing night.

The drive from the quarry to his home had been a quiet one, with a furious Luka keeping his eyes locked on the road and his mind set on revenge. Despite his tendencies to fly off the handle, Luka was a dependable soldier.

Loyal as a dog.

As ferocious as one, too.

Having served alongside Kovac in the BSD, Luka was deadly when his mind was right. Years of drugs and drinking had made those moments few and far between. Luka had put that down to part of the job, with the constant access he had to the contraband and no ramifications.

Kovac knew it couldn't continue and had long since come to terms with the facts that when the Kingdom belonged to him, he would likely need to sit Luka out. The man wouldn't take it well, but Kovac hadn't risen to his throne through his sentimentality.

Kovac was cutthroat, and if he needed to slide that blade across Luka's Adam's apple, then he would without hesitation.

But not yet.

Despite Sam Pope's interference, Kovac still had every intention of moving ahead with his coup. Removing Pope from the equation would be a necessary factor in it, but once that annoyance had been snuffed out, Kovac would organise another delivery and invite his benefactor to their operation. She would most likely want to see it in action, lavishing praise upon him for his meticulous operation. He would roll out the charm, knowing that his powerful physique combined with his strong jaw made him an attractive proposition.

On the cusp of seduction, he would reveal that he was taking over the organisation, wiping out the final vestige of her family name before putting a bullet through her skull.

Then it would all be his.

Everything.

Whoever was controlling her finances would be given the option to sit beneath Kovac and funnel the remaining fortune into his operation or be taken apart, limb by limb, for as long as they could stay alive. Every asset and every deed of ownership would be placed in his name.

Kovac would burrow deep into the foundations of their fallen empire, shake whatever was worth something for himself, and then leave the carcass to rot.

They would be a footnote in history, while his name would continue to write more.

But he needed to find and kill Sam Pope before anything else.

If only for his pride.

With an angered grunt, Kovac lifted the thick glass

tumbler to his lips and sipped the now chilled whisky. Despite the cooler temperature, the liquid still burnt the back of his throat with its familiar after taste. As he knocked back the entire drink, he slammed the glass down on the bar and lifted the bottle again.

'You want one?'

Kovac didn't look back to Luka, who was sitting on the leather sofa in the sitting-room of Kovac's lavish mansion.

'Sure.'

As Kovac poured the second drink out, Luka looked around the incredible home. Not wanting to live in the epicentre of his operation, Kovac had procured an expensive house in the middle of the woods on the outskirts of Suffolk, near a small village named Metfield. Kovac's residence was fifteen miles away from the quarry, and a further ten from the centre of Norwich where they had considerable business interests. Along with Lowestoft, they targeted the major towns of East Anglia, with Kovac tucked away far enough to distance himself from it. The house had a half-mile private entrance way, passing through an electronic gate and a long gravel path that was lined with trees. The road eventually gave way to the house, which was stunningly modern for its surroundings. The entire front was on show, with floor to ceiling glass panels showing off the mighty entrance hall, along with one of the many seating areas inside. The hallway offered two staircases, one leading to one of six bedrooms on the upper floor, with the other leading down to the main seating area where Luka was currently sitting.

Behind Luka was the vast kitchen, decked out with every appliance and a square, marble topped island that was illuminated by the hanging lights.

Everything was simplistic, from the white walls to the black trim, and it never surprised Luka that Kovac's home matched his style. The man was always well presented, and his mighty home was no different. Luka looked up to the balcony that overlooked the seating area, the metal rail obstructing his view of the front door. Directly below the balcony was a thick metal door that was always locked. Beyond was another staircase, leading down even further into the earth. It was a place Luka knew well, having dragged multiple people down there for their final moments.

Beneath the pristine home were three soundproof rooms, all of them locked down and under surveillance by Kovac's in-house security.

One of them was the armoury, which housed enough weaponry to start World War Three.

Another, stacks upon stacks of high-grade drugs and vacuum sealed packs of cash. By Kovac's estimation, they had over twenty-two million pounds worth of cash, and double that in narcotics.

The room was a treasure trove, and one Luka had often wondered about testing the security of.

The final room was his favourite.

It was dark, and it was dingy, with a crude dentist's chair bolted to the middle of the floor. A meat hook was also affixed to the ceiling on the far side of the room, along with his work bench full of his tools.

Whenever he took someone in there, they talked.

In fact, they sang.

And once he'd put them through as much pain as their bodies could take, he would slit their throats and let the blood filter through the draining facility that was built into the floor.

As he stared vacantly at the door, Luka envisaged putting Sam Pope in the chair. Even better, he imagined hanging Danny from the meat hook and making him pay for every smart remark he ever made. Luka didn't even realise Kovac stood above him, his arm extended.

'Luka?' Kovac raised his voice. 'Take it.'

Luka snapped back into the room, took the drink and nodded his appreciation. Kovac dropped into the leather armchair opposite, and the two men drank in silence for a few moments, allowing the catastrophic events of the night to play in their minds.

'You think he will find Pope for you?' Luka eventually said, putting the glass on the table. Kovac shot him a furious glare, and Luka quickly procured himself a coaster.

'He better,' Kovac snapped. 'His usefulness is beginning to wane, and soon, I will not need him at all.'

'You want me to make certain?' Luka offered, his charred face cleaner since having a shower.

'Maybe.' Kovac looked at his drink and then necked it in one. 'Let's give him a few hours.'

'Then what?'

'Then you find him, you make his life very uncomfortable, and if he is no more use to us, then you can get rid of him. Nothing more dishonourable than a dirty cop.'

Luka nodded in agreement. Kovac held up his glass, and Luka pushed himself from his seat and retrieved it. As he poured them both another one, Kovac's phone buzzed.

'It's Danny.'

'Traitor,' Luka spat, his fingers dangerously clenching the glass.

'I don't think so.' Kovac turned the phone so Luka could see the screen. Danny had taken a selfie of himself, laying on a hospital bed. His nose was clearly broken, and his eyes were beginning to bruise. It looked like he'd taken a hell of a beating.

'You want me to go get him?'

'No, leave him. Whatever he has to say, he can say in a few hours.' Kovac tossed the phone onto the table and gratefully accepted the drink from Luka. Just as he lifted it, ready to enjoy the burning sensation once more, Luka decided to ruin the moment by planting a seed of doubt in his mind.

'Why did Sam Pope not kill him?'

It was a good question, and one Kovac knew he immediately needed the answer to. Within two minutes, Luka was already headed to the car, more than willing to go and extract the answer.

————

Townsend nodded politely to the nurse who stood by his bed as she put away her blood pressure machine. She was a few years younger than him and despite everything he'd been through, he couldn't help but admire her. He was under no illusion of the pressure and workload everyone in the NHS was under at all times, and as he marvelled at her composure and friendly bedside manner, he felt guilty for questioning how hard he truly had it.

'Can I go now?' he eventually asked, offering her a smile and then wincing immediately. The bandage strapped across his nose was holding the cartilage in place, and the slightest movement of his facial muscles sent a wave of agony hurtling towards his brain.

'You took a pretty big blow to the head.' She smiled warmly. 'And you say you fell down the stairs?'

'Yup.'

'Right,' she replied, clearly aware he was lying. 'How's about we keep you in for a little while longer? Luckily, you don't have any signs of a concussion, but we need to make sure. I could have someone bring you a coffee?'

'I got that covered.'

The voice at the door broke their conversation, and Sanders stepped in, two coffees in his hand. The nurse shot a glance to Townsend, who nodded his approval, and she winked at him and walked out of the room. Sanders watched her go and raised his eyebrows.

'Don't be that guy,' Townsend said with a sigh.

'Hey, I'm not the one who could try to wrangle a sponge bath.' Sanders approached the bed and handed Townsend the coffee. 'How you feeling?'

'Like someone smashed my face in.'

'Really? You can't tell.'

Townsend smiled and immediately regretted it. He took a sip of his coffee and adjusted himself on the bed, sitting up a little further. He'd text Sanders the moment he'd been checked into the hospital, and the relief of seeing his superior officer was quite overwhelming.

'Thanks.'

Sanders pulled up the plastic chair to the bedside, manoeuvring it round the unused apparatus, and took a seat. After a sip of his coffee, he leant in and lowered his voice.

'What the hell happened, lad?'

Taking a deep breath, Townsend relayed the entire series of events to an exasperated Sanders. The story seemed too insane to be believable, from the re-birth of Sam Pope to the way he singlehandedly took out Luka and his crew. Townsend felt himself shaking as he spoke about the fear of being sat in the car with Kovac and the rest of his men, knowing he couldn't get a message to Sanders to warn him of the events to come. Despite Sanders's dismissal of it, Townsend was racked with guilt that not only could they have apprehended Kovac and stopped a lot of people from being killed, they would have been able to stop Sam Pope.

'What's he like?' Sanders asked casually. 'Pope.'

'Intense.' Townsend shook his head. 'But he saved my life. And the driver, too.'

'He saved your life?'

'Well, when I tried to get the driver to safety, I got jumped by Luka. That guy is just begging me to give him an excuse, and he almost had one. Sam stepped in, and that's how we got away.'

'You willingly drove Sam Pope and a carload of guns to safety? Jesus fucking Christ, Jack.'

'He had me at gunpoint. Look, I can handle myself, but you're talking about a man who hunts down criminals for fun.'

'Exactly. He does it for fun, whereas we do it as a duty. There's a big difference.' Sanders rubbed the bridge of his nose in frustration. 'Hang on, why didn't he leave you behind?'

Townsend sheepishly looked at the corrugated cup in his hand.

'I had to tell him—'

'You gave up your cover?'

'He had a gun to my fucking head.' Townsend slammed his fist on the mattress, shaking the entire bed. 'My only concern was getting out, getting back to my girls.'

Sanders stood from his chair and walked up the room, his hands on his hips. It was a hell of a mess, and Townsend knew he had made a potentially case-destroying call. After a few moments, Sanders seemed to recompose, and he returned to the bedside, this time asserting his authority by standing over Townsend.

'This is a big fucking mess.'

'I know.'

'How the hell will you explain it to Kovac?'

'I sent him a message. Showed him I was pretty banged up and told him Sam left me beaten on the side of the road. He told me to meet him tomorrow.'

'And you think that will work?'

'I don't know. I hope so.'

'What about Sam?' Sanders leant on the metal bar that

ran down the side of the bed. The very mention of the man seemed to put him on edge. 'Where did he go?'

Townsend knew he should tell Sanders about the deal he'd made and that they planned to meet later that day at the safe house. But he'd already burnt a lot of trust with his superior, and willingly working with a vigilante would be the final straw.

He would be aiding and abetting one of the most wanted men in recent history. Meaning he would trade his life inside Kovac's operation, to a life behind bars. With the guilt dripping from him in cold beads of sweat, Townsend shrugged.

'I don't know. All I know is, we don't have a lot of time before he goes after Kovac again and ruins everything we've worked for. We need to move on him, Reece.'

'It's Sir,' Sanders snapped, clearly irritated. 'And we don't have nearly enough to get Kovac's boss.'

'Maybe…I've compiled everything. I've got files, phone records, all of it on a USB stick,' Townsend began, drawing a surprised look from Sanders. 'I needed some kind of bargaining chip if things went tits up.'

'Fuck me, Jack. You've been withholding evidence?' Sanders anxiously ran a hand through his thinning hair. 'Where are they? These files?'

At that moment, Luka stepped into the room, blocking the doorway with his monstrous frame. He looked like hell warmed up, and he fixed Townsend with a furious glare. Then his eyes fell on Sanders, regarding him with a mixture of confusion and intimidation. Townsend felt his body tense, certain that the game was up.

Sanders, however, adjusted his tie and turned to Luka.

'Can I help you?'

'I am concerned friend,' Luka said, his voice betraying his words.

'Do you know this man?' Sanders turned to Townsend,

who nodded. 'Okay, well thank you, Mr Miller. Your answers have been useful. If we catch the man who mugged you, we'll be in touch.'

Townsend thanked him, grateful for Sanders's quick thinking. Trying to assert his authority, Sanders turned on his heel and marched towards Luka in the doorway, before silently waiting for the large man to step aside. Eventually, he did, and Sanders left, shooting an anxious glance back in Townsend's direction as Luka settled down on the plastic seat beside the bed, stretching its support to the limit.

'What did he want?'

'I told them I'd been mugged when I came in.' Townsend pointed to his face. 'He's just doing his job, I suppose.'

Luka flashed Townsend a fiendish grin.

'As am I.' Luka lifted the remote control for the television and turned it on, a random show about sports cars filling the screen. 'When can you leave?'

'A few hours...'

'Then we wait.' Luka made a show of placing the remote control carefully on the side table. 'Boss wants to see you. We have some questions that I am very excited to ask.'

Luka stared at the television screen as Townsend tipped his head back, wondering how the hell he would be able to convince Kovac and Luka of his loyalty.

Worst still, he had no idea how he would make his meeting with Sam, which was his best shot of bringing it all to an end.

Townsend thought of his girls and hoped beyond hope that he would see them again.

CHAPTER SIXTEEN

When Sam woke up the next morning, the first thing he smelt was smoke. The heavy, undeniable stench of the burning quarry had etched itself between every fibre of his clothes that hung over the chair by the desk. It clung to his skin, trying to infiltrate every pore, and it was laced into every strand of hair on his head. He checked his watch that was on the side table and realised he'd slept for over six hours, which was close to a record for him.

For the past two years, with his war over and his life hidden away from the world, he'd fought the demons of his past every time he went to sleep. Refusing to drown his sorrows in alcohol, and instead, dedicating his time and pain to improving his fitness, Sam realised he had no barrier against the visions that haunted his dreams.

The rows of dead bodies, all belonging to people who'd been on the other end of his scope.

The open, lifeless eyes of the criminals he'd put in the ground. Frequently, the bleeding body of Frank Jackson would visit him, often appearing beside him as he watched his son play on the climbing frame. As the first major criminal Sam had killed during his crusade, Jackson was his subconscious, bringing him back to the realities of the path he'd trodden. Despite the bullet-riddled body, Jackson would often point out the fallacy of Sam's motives, claiming that he was nothing more than a cold-blooded killer who was merely scratching an itch.

There was no good in what he did.

The only difference between Sam and the criminals he brutally hunted was at least they got paid.

The nightmare would always end the same way.

His best friend, Theo Walker, would crawl through the sandpit of the graveyard, his body obliterated by a grenade, and he would reach for Sam with his charred hand. Sam would reach back, but the guilt of Theo's death would hang too heavy around Sam's neck for him to be able to make it before Theo's time ran out. As Sam turned back, Jackson had bled out, and it would only be then that Sam would notice the mountains of corpses that were now littered across the playground, a monument to the chaos he'd created.

Then he would hear the scream.

Jamie was no longer playing idly on the climbing frame, indulging in his adventurous nature in the relentless summer sun.

He was at the bottom of the climbing frame, motion-less and his body broken, twisted in the unmistakable way he was the night he was killed. It was an image that was tattooed on Sam's brain and at that moment, Sam would snap back to consciousness. For two whole years, with the world thinking he was dead, Sam often wished it to be the case.

The lure of an alcoholic slumber was tempting, knowing that a drunken sleep would at least block out those demons. But it would open the door to so many more, and Sam knew that if he'd turned to the bottle, the night would come when it didn't slam the door shut on everything that had come before. It would only exacerbate it, and instead of swallowing another drink, Sam would likely swallow the end of his Glock.

But since Sam had re-emerged from the shadows to avenge Sean Wiseman and keep Marcus, Lynsey Beckett, and his old friend, Adrian Pearce safe, those nightmares had gone away.

His renewed sense of purpose had overtaken his guilt, and as he sat up in the warm bedroom of the modest rental, he could feel it.

Part of him felt guilty for not allowing his son's death to haunt him on a nightly basis.

But it had been a long time.

While the pain had never once subsided, it didn't dominate him anymore, and having been around death his entire life, Sam knew he was in the final and endless stage of grief.

Acceptance.

There would never come a day where his heart would ever heal. Losing his son was a permanent wound that would never scar, and he didn't want it to either. It was a reminder that the world was a cruel and unfair place, and one where the most innocent of person could meet the most devastating of fates.

Jamie had been just five years old when a drunk driver had swerved into him, killing him in front of his mother. Sam could have, and for every second since, told himself he should have stopped it.

But he'd come to terms with the loss, accepted it as part of his life, and now used it as fuel.

Fuel to get up every morning.

Fuel to put the wrong things right.

Sam stepped out of the bed and headed to the bathroom, which was comprised of a small sink, a toilet, and a shower cubicle, all crammed into a space no bigger than a wardrobe. The two years of rigorous exercise had certainly added a new layer of muscle to his already impressive frame, and Sam found the shower cubicle a pretty tight squeeze. For the next twenty minutes, he vigorously scrubbed his entire body, using an entire bottle of shower gel. As he squeezed the last few drops onto his hand, he could smell the aroma of the gel finally replacing the smoke and he soon stepped out, feeling as refreshed as he could.

He quickly dressed, sliding on a pair of jeans and another well-fitting T-shirt and then he ran his hand through his short, brown hair, which had just started to grow long enough that it spiked upwards. He flattened it and made a mental note to get it clipped short as soon as he could. Despite keeping it short, he'd noticed the greying at the temples growing even more prominent and a timely reminder that despite the physical shape he was in, he was now in his forties.

Time would start catching up with him soon, and there was only so much punishment his body could take. The T-shirt, which clung to his physique, covered a tapestry of scars, from burns to stab wounds to bullet holes, all in the name of fighting for the cause.

One day, he wouldn't be so lucky.

Sam looked down at the table where three assault rifles had been placed, all of them with their ammunition removed and all in pristine condition. Alongside them, he'd taken a few more handguns, along with the batch of grenades that had been loaded into the Range Rover before he'd made his presence at the quarry known. After leaving Townsend in a bloody mess in the car park, Sam had driven the vehicle back to the Airbnb he was staying at, unloaded the weapons he wanted, and then returned to the vehicle, driving a few miles out to a deserted carpark beside an abandoned factory on the outskirts of Lowestoft.

As he drove, he silently lamented the fact that there hadn't been a sniper rifle among his recently procured collection, but he'd still been able to significantly upgrade his armoury. He'd wanted to keep all the guns but transporting an entire shipment of weapons without drawing attention was nigh on impossible.

He left the discarded guns in the back of the car, along with the piles of drugs he had no use for. Once he'd set the car on fire, he jogged away from the wreckage with a sense of satisfaction that Kovac wouldn't be able to pollute the streets with them.

That they wouldn't get cut and shipped out to men like Ryan Marsh to prey on those who were addicted.

Sam turned on the TV for the local news, and sure enough, there was a report on the incident at the quarry, which had been labelled as 'gang warfare'. Either the police had no clue he was in their domain, or they wanted to keep it quiet. It was swiftly linked to the following story, about the abandoned guns and drugs that he'd set ablaze.

The police had sealed off the area and all remnants of the weapons and drugs would be disposed of as appropriate. Sam turned off the television with a grin, wondering if any of the police would offer him a thank you for what he'd done.

One of them had.

Jack Townsend.

Despite his reservations, Sam had given the young man the benefit of the doubt and checked his watch. He had plenty of time until he would head towards the address the man had given him. It could quite easily be a set up, and Sam would make sure he was prepared for any outcome, but there was something about Townsend that spoke to Sam.

The man just wanted to get back to his family.

To his daughter.

When Sam had been in the army, there had been many times where he'd found himself in the same boat. Whether that was under fire from a deadly sniper in the Amazon Rainforest or battling the Taliban in a derelict city in Afghanistan. The thought of seeing Lucy and then, when he arrived, Jamie, was what had driven him forward.

Had brought him home.

Had kept him alive.

Townsend was in deep, and after what happened at the quarry, Sam doubted there would be much chance of a lifeboat. If Kovac was as brutal as Sam had been told, then he wouldn't accept being infiltrated.

The police wouldn't want to compromise any of the work that had been done.

Townsend, in the crudest way possible, was expendable.

But not to his family.

Which meant he wasn't to Sam.

If Townsend had the evidence he claimed, then Sam could take it to Kovac and make him give up his boss in exchange for his own possible freedom. If not, then Sam had other ways of getting what he wanted. He would take down Kovac's entire operation, and to do that, he needed the person who was controlling the money.

That was where the real power was.

Sam checked through the blinds at the weather outside. The warmth of the day before had gone, and a steady downpour of rain had taken its place. Having grown quite fond of the quaint little high street half a mile away, Sam slipped on his bomber jacket, pulled his baseball cap onto his head, and stepped out into the rain with the sole purpose of getting a coffee from the local coffee shop.

The brisk walk, chilled rain, and caffeine shot would be well needed, especially as he had numerous weapons to check and clean before he visited Townsend.

After that, he planned to finish things with Kovac for good.

———

'Where the fuck is it?'

Sanders ran his hand through his thinning hair and blew out his cheeks. He'd essentially ransacked Townsend's flat, with every drawer pulled from its place and every cushion on the floor. Strewn across the tabletop were the contents of several drawers and boxes aggressively dispersed during his frantic search.

He'd found nothing.

Which wasn't good.

Sanders had felt guilty from the first moment Townsend interacted with Kovac's gang, and each day since, as his officer followed the dangerous criminal further into his world. Townsend was a good man, who was driven by doing the right thing, and Sanders knew he would never be able to live with himself if something happened to him.

But it was a necessity.

Sanders was given a near impossible task and turned to one guy he knew had the capability and more importantly, the guts to do what was required. Sure, he may have laid it on a little thick when he proposed the mission to Townsend, but he knew anything other than Townsend's complete agreement would lead to disaster.

It would cost Sanders everything.

But now, with the end so close, the sudden emergence of Sam Pope threatened to hijack what should have been the easy final moments of Sanders's mission and had turned it into chaos. The man had taken down half of Kovac's army, along with obliterating the drop that would take a heavy toll on Kovac's operation.

It meant that they were further from Kovac's benefactor, making the trip to the UK, and bringing the whole thing down.

Sanders was so close.

Townsend revealing that he'd been compiling his own insurance policy against Kovac had also sent the entire plan off course. As a unit, the police operation to bring Kovac and his benefactor down had done everything by the book. While Sanders had been reprimanded several times for the things Townsend had been forced to do, he'd always been able to talk them into acceptance based on the need to maintain the illusion.

The case they'd pulled together was watertight, but if Townsend had gone off the script and gone into business for himself, then it would undermine every time Sanders had gone to bat for him.

Sanders needed the USB stick.

He needed to see the information Townsend had been collating to ensure that it didn't interfere with the bigger picture. Plus, despite proving his ability to handle himself, Townsend was playing with fire.

If Kovac or one of his men found it, then Townsend would be killed, and most likely, anyone who had anything to do with him.

That meant Sanders.

That meant Townsend's family.

As he stood in the centre of the destroyed apartment with his hands firmly on his hips, a jolt of inspiration struck Sanders like a bolt from the stormy skies.

His family.

Sanders shuffled through the paperwork on the table, riffling through numerous bills that were made out to Townsend's alias until he found one of the hidden photos Townsend kept close by.

It was a picture of his wife, her beautiful face curving upwards in her stunning smile. In her arms was Eve, a few years younger than she was now, her blue eyes filled with love for the man behind the camera.

Kovac knew where Townsend lived, but he didn't know about the safe house. Which made it the perfect place to store something he never wanted Kovac to see.

Scampering towards the door, Sanders hauled his jacket from the back of the armchair and ignored the carnage he'd left the flat in as he slammed the door behind him.

If the USB stick was at the safe house, then maybe, just maybe, they all stood a chance of surviving what was to come.

CHAPTER SEVENTEEN

The drive out to Kovac's hideout was as silent as it was tense. Despite Townsend's protest, Luka demanded that he cable tie Townsend's hands behind his back. Luka had been suspicious of Townsend since the day he'd joined Kovac's crew. Due to the aftermath of Sam's assault on the quarry, Luka was looking a little worse for wear, and Townsend would have fancied his chances.

However, Luka had him at gunpoint when he made the demand, and Townsend knew there was no bluff to call.

Sat in the back of the car, with his hands strapped behind his back, Townsend stared out of the window as they turned into the woodland that surrounded Kovac's impressive estate. With the recent sunshine replaced with a downpour, Townsend caught his reflection in the window and realised the bruises on his face looked as bad as they felt.

'Don't worry.' Luka smirked from the driver's seat. 'You were ugly to begin with.'

'That's rich coming from you.'

Luka scoffed and kept his eyes on the country lane that sliced through the trees, his scarred hands tightly gripping the steering wheel. Ignoring Townsend's request to the contrary, Luka lit a cigarette and casually puffed on it as they neared Kovac.

'Can you at least open your window?' Townsend asked, coughing at the second-hand smoke that wafted into the back of the car.

'It's raining,' Luka replied, taking a final puff on the cigarette before turning and blowing it directly at Townsend. 'Besides, this smoke is last thing you should worry about.'

The ominous threat sat with Townsend for the duration of the journey as Luka finished his cigarette and approached the gate to Kovac's private home. The impressive, modern building was shrouded in the privacy of his gated residence, with the surrounding trees hiding it even further from the public eye. Unless you were given directions, it would be near impossible to find.

It was so far off the grid that one of Townsend's jobs when he first joined the crew was to collect and handle any post that was sent to a PO Box in Ipswich.

They were in the middle of nowhere, and Townsend was about to be marched into a crime lord's home, with his hands tied and his loyalty heavily questioned. On the rare occasion that Luka had spoken since he'd taken the seat beside him in the hospital, he'd made it clear what he thought of Townsend. In Luka's eyes, Townsend was a rat, and despite continually insulting the man for his perceived lack of intelligence, Townsend had secretly given the man credit for his instincts. Kovac had been swift to shut down Luka's misgivings from the beginning, confronting his right-hand man on whether he believed he had better instincts than Kovac himself.

Kovac trusted Townsend. To him, 'Danny Miller' was a loyal soldier, and Townsend knew he would be haunted for life for some of the things he'd done to prove that loyalty.

But he was close to the end.

All he had to do was convince Kovac of his loyalty, get the hell out of dodge, and then give Sam Pope what he needed. Then, there was a chance he could go home to his girls and have a serious think about the rest of his life. Despite his marriage to doing the right thing, his vows to his wife had taken a back seat, and it was a situation he wanted to remedy with every waking moment he had left.

The car rumbled to a stop in front of the glass of the house, and Luka stepped out and hauled open the door beside Townsend.

'Out.'

As Townsend shuffled to the open door, Luka reached in with his meaty hand and grabbed his collar and tugged. Townsend crashed to the gravel below, unable to stop the sharp stones from welcoming his face to the ground. He grunted with pain, and as Luka hoisted him to his feet, Townsend could feel the blood trickling from his eyebrow. He shot a glare at Luka, who smarmily grinned.

'Accident.'

Townsend turned to the door and, as he walked towards it, Luka needlessly gave him another shove in the back. A henchman that Townsend didn't recognise opened the door to them, clearly brought in as re-enforcement after Sam had depleted Kovac's numbers. As they walked towards the staircase to lead them down to the grand living room, Townsend could see Kovac by his drinks cabinet, pouring himself a drink. Upon hearing their footsteps echoing down the steps, Kovac stopped briefly, but he didn't turn around. He waited until they stepped off the bottom step and then held up the glass.

'Drink?'

'I can't,' Townsend replied, and Kovac turned. Townsend leant to the side, showing his bound wrists.

'For fuck's sake, Luka. Cut those.'

With a grunt of displeasure, Luka obliged, maintaining eye contact with Townsend who rubbed the soreness from his wrists. Kovac approached and handed Townsend his drink.

'You look like shit,' Kovac said. 'Pope do this to you?'

'I'm lucky he didn't kill me.'

'What about the driver?' Kovac asked, his usually calm demeanour slipping and putting Townsend on edge. 'Where is he?'

'Pope made me drop him at the hosp—'

'Why he do that?' Luka interrupted, drawing a furious scowl from his boss.

'Because the man is a fucking boy scout,' Townsend spat back. 'Learn to read and then pick up a newspaper.'

'Enough,' Kovac snapped. 'Luka, you do not ask questions. I do. Now, Danny, Luka tells me he saw you running to escape with the driver. Now, I disagree because surely, after everything I've done for you, you would not betray me. I have given you a good life, lots of money. I think there is no way that Danny would help Sam Pope escape. No, the Danny I know would kill Sam Pope and bring me his body so I can take a piss on it. So, is Luka lying?'

Townsend felt his body tense. All eyes were on him, and for the first time in a long time, he felt the full force of Kovac's intimidation. Many people had crumpled at the merest glare from the man, but coupled with his calm delivery, the man was terrifying.

Townsend took a breath.

He had only one way to play it.

'No, Luka's right. I did make a run for it with the driver.'

'I told you.' Luka slapped his thigh and then stood up with excitement. 'The man is a fucking rat.'

'Sit down,' Kovac demanded, not taking his eyes from Townsend. 'Your life hinges on your next answer, Danny. Why did you run?'

'Because, despite what fuckwit over there thinks he saw, I was trying to get to the main stash. Only one carload had been removed from the lorry when Sam hit us, which meant five more carloads were still packed neatly in the back of that lorry. Now, my maths has always been pretty good, but I'd say that's a fuck ton of money, so I took the one person who had the fucking keys and tried to get it out of there as quickly as possible. Until Luka stopped me and then Sam Pope got the drop on both of us.'

Kovac was silent. His chiselled jaw jolted from side to side as he contemplated Townsend's answer. He took a sip of his drink and then turned to Luka.

'Did you see him with Sam Pope?'

'I saw him running to the Range Rover and—'

'Did you see him with Sam Pope?' Kovac repeated, his voice raised, and the venom increased.

'The fuck he did,' Townsend said. 'Pope dropped him from behind when he threatened to kill me, then Pope stuck a gun in my face and made me drive him out of there. I'm guessing the police confiscated the lorry? And everything inside?'

Luka stared at the ground, a horrible realisation shaking his entire bulky frame. Kovac shook his head in disgust, and then hurled the glass tumbler across the spacious room until it exploded against the white stone wall. As the shards clattered against the floor, Kovac's phone buzzed in his pocket. He angrily held up a finger, pausing the conversation and lifted the phone to his ear.

'Have you—' Kovac was cut off by the caller. His

angry face suddenly relaxed, as if whatever was being relayed to him had caught him off-guard. 'I see.'

Kovac hung up the call and turned back to them. He nodded to Luka, who stepped towards Townsend. Caught off-guard, Townsend failed to get his hand up in time as Luka drove the grip of his pistol into the side of his skull, the hard metal connecting expertly with his temple.

Townsend felt his legs wobble, and as gravity welcomed him, everything went black.

Stepping towards Townsend's unconscious body, Kovac shook his head in disappointment, and then turned to a smiling Luka.

Kovac's words were laced with hatred.

'Take him deep into the woods and kill him.'

————

Sanders approached the curb outside of the safe house and brought the car to a stop. There was nothing remarkable about the residence, just another house among a row of others in a nondescript residential area just north of Norwich town centre. It was far enough away from Lowestoft that Townsend could escape with his family, but near enough that he could return within enough time as to not raise suspicion.

A tinge of guilt rumbled through Sanders's nervous system as he stepped out of the car, knowing he was responsible for every necessary visit to the house over the past two years. He'd put in motion everything that had caused the Townsends to consider it a home away from home. When he was given the brief regarding Kovac's operation, it was Sanders himself who had dangled the carrot in front of Townsend, leaning heavily on the man's inbuilt nobility to coerce him to take the mission. Try as he might to rationalise it in his mind, with things clearly coming to an end, Sanders fought tooth and nail to reason with himself that it wasn't emotional blackmail.

It had been a selfish move, one he regretted, but one that Sanders knew he had to make.

Now, he was dedicated to getting Townsend out, hoping beyond hope that he would be able to get him back to Mandy and Eve and hopefully close the door on the entire operation.

He just needed those files.

Without them, there was no hope for Townsend, and he himself would find life extremely difficult. He puffed out his cheeks and marched towards the opening in the brick wall that separated the modest patch of grass that resembled a front garden from the pavement. As he stepped across the threshold, he only then realised that the light in the living room was on.

The house was supposed to be empty.

Perturbed, Sanders felt his fist clench with tension, and he brought his wiry frame to the door and thudded against the faded paint of the wood with a balled fist. He felt his heart pick up speed, the relentless anxiety of the entire situation seemingly reaching a crescendo.

Someone was in the house.

Possibly looking for the files?

His mind raced, wondering which of Kovac's men would greet him and how on Earth he'd be able to talk his way out of there. He didn't even have a set of handcuffs on him, so trying to make an arrest would prove difficult.

Kovac's men had little regard for the law, and as the footsteps approached the door, Sanders scanned the drive-way, looking frantically for a loose brick or stone he could potentially use.

The door opened a crack, and instantly, all that fear melted away.

'Reece?'

Mandy stood in the small opening of the doorway, holding the door open just enough to reveal her face.

'Mandy.' Sanders sighed. 'Oh, thank God.'

'What are you doing here?' Her brow furrowed, pulling her pretty face into a frown.

'I could ask you the same question.' Sanders made to step into the house, but Mandy drew the door slightly, catching him off-guard. 'Can I come in?'

'Is Jack with you?' she asked, flashing her eyes back into the room.

'No, he isn't.' Sanders frowned. 'Is he with you?'

'No. I'm worried.'

'We've been over this, Mandy. Jack knows exactly what he's doing, and we are so close to bringing this all to a close. He'll be home before you know it.'

'I hope so.'

'Look, let me come in and we can talk it through.'

'I was just about to have a bath.' Mandy looked back into the house. 'I figured with Eve at her nanna's I could have some peace and quiet, you know? Try to collect myself to be strong for him.'

Sanders clenched his teeth. He had no strong reason to be there, and especially not one that could justify interrupting her evening.

'I didn't know you were coming today. There was no contact with my team.'

'I know, I'm sorry. Last time I spoke to him, I could tell he was struggling. He didn't tell me, but that's our Jack, right?' Mandy forced a smile. 'Anyway, when he answers his phone to me, I'll let you know when he's here. Goodnight, Reece.'

'Oh, Mandy, wait.' Sanders stepped forward. 'Jack told me he left something here, something that could be imperative to the case.'

'Wait here, and I'll go get it. What is it?'

Sanders felt his fists clench in frustration.

'It's just some files on the case he forgot to hand in.'

'Where are they?' Mandy asked, keeping her grip on the door.

'Maybe if I were to come in and look…' Sanders realised his desperation was seeping through and he scolded himself as he made a lame attempt to step forward. Mandy pulled the door closer.

'Sorry, Reece. I'm not comfortable with you rooting through the place when he isn't here.' She offered him a polite smile. 'I'll get him to call you when he's back, or if you speak to him first, bring him home to me. Well, what passes as home these days.'

Sanders motioned to dispute, but then gave up, his hands dropping to his side in defeat.

'Will do. Goodnight, Mandy.'

'Goodnight, Reece.'

As she closed the door, Sanders silently cursed to himself and stomped back down the pathway towards the street, slapping both hands on his head as he realised the situation was truly beginning to slip through his fingers. As he walked out of sight of the peephole of the front door, Mandy pulled the metal cover back across and, with her hands pressed against the door, she blew out a big sigh of relief.

'He's gone.'

'Why couldn't he come in, Mummy?' Eve scrambled across the outdated living room, rushing to her mother's side and wrapping her delicate arms around Mandy's legs.

'Because your daddy isn't home yet.' Mandy gave her daughter a loving smile. 'Why don't you get your pens and we'll do some drawing while we wait?'

'Okay.' Eve giggled before turning back to the other person in the room. 'Do you like drawing?'

Sam stood by the side of the window, obscured from

the outside by the wall of the room, but with enough of an angle to peer through the net curtains. He looked at Eve, basking in her angelic innocence, and smiled.

'I sure do.'

Eve celebrated as she raced towards the stairs, heading upstairs to the makeshift bedroom to procure her art supplies. Sam stepped away from the wall and into the room as Mandy regarded him with a stern glare.

'I don't like lying to Reece. He's been good to us.'

'I know. But he's with the police, and I'm not exactly high on their Christmas card list.'

'Well, I'm putting a lot of faith in my husband's judge of character. And Christ knows he hangs around with some wrong-un's.' Mandy shook her head in annoyance. 'If he gave you this address, then he must trust you.'

'I guess so.' Sam shrugged before he apprehensively sat on the arm of the armchair. Mandy bit her bottom lip anxiously before shooting another glance at the door.

'Reece is a good guy. He could really help us.'

'What I'm planning isn't exactly what Reece, or his team, would call *by the book*.'

Mandy stepped forward, her fingers twitching with nerves.

'What are you planning to do?'

Sam offered her his most comforting smile.

'I'm planning on bringing your husband home. Let's leave it at that.'

Mandy took a few seconds before she finally relented and tried to relax. Upstairs, she could hear her daughter impatiently rummaging through her suitcase. Although she didn't follow it religiously, Mandy did her best to keep up with the news, usually swiping through the BBC app while enjoying her morning coffee. It had been impossible not to read about Sam Pope a few years ago, especially after he'd been caught after the death of a high-ranking government official. But despite the charges he was found guilty of, there had always been the common theme running through them.

The people he killed had been criminals.

She would never condone the things he did, but the man clearly had a moral code somewhere within his muscular, war-torn frame, and despite his crimes, she inexplicably knew she was safe.

As was her daughter.

And by the sounds of things, soon her husband would be too.

After a few moments of contemplation, she clasped her hands together, just as Eve bound down the stairs with her pens in her hand and a beaming smile across her face.

'Right. Tea?'

Sam returned her smile.

'I'd love one.' He then turned to Eve. 'Right, where's the paper?'

———

Sanders had only driven for ten minutes before he pulled the car into a dark alleyway behind a row of old, derelict shops and stumbled out of the car. He rushed to the wall, placed one hand against the graffiti laden bricks and hunched over, emptying his stomach onto the floor below. As he violently vomited, he knew it was driven by guilt.

After a few final dry heaves, Sanders stood up, doing his best to catch his breath before he stumbled back into the car. He dropped into the seat and reached for the bottle of water in the drink's holder. He took a mouthful, swashed it around his mouth, and then spat it out of the door. It didn't completely remove the horrific aftertaste, but it did at least soothe some of the burning.

'Fuck's sake, Jack.'

He slammed his fist angrily against the steering wheel. Everything had been going to plan. Everything he'd worked so hard for over the past two years was now hanging by a dangerously thin thread.

Townsend had evidence outside of the investigation.

Sanders understood why Townsend had gone to such lengths. With Sam Pope's apparent return, Kovac was on edge, and would most likely be looking for leaks. Looking for someone to blame. And if that finger fell on Townsend, and he felt there was no way out, then he at least had a bargaining chip to try to save his life.

Townsend had a lot to fight for, and Sanders knew just how much fight was in the man.

A good man.

A good man who had given him no other choice.

Tears were already streaming down Sanders's face as he thumbed through his phone before pressing the call button. As he lifted the phone to his ear, he caught a look of himself in the rear-view mirror and hated the pathetic man staring back at him.

The phone rang twice before Kovac picked up the phone.

'*Have you—*'

'Danny Miller is an undercover police officer called Jack Townsend. He has information on you outside of my control.'

'*I see.*'

The phone line went dead.

Sanders didn't move a muscle but allowed the phone to slide from his hand and crash somewhere on the floor of his car. He tried his hardest not to draw another breath, but when his body finally made the decision for him, he turned, leant out of the open door, and once again vomited on the ground.

He had just sanctioned the death of Jack Townsend.

CHAPTER EIGHTEEN

Three Years Ago...

'Can I get another?'

Sanders's voice drunkenly slurred as he lifted his empty glass and waved it at the young bartender. The woman offered him a sympathetic smile before flashing a knowing glance to the bouncer who stood a few feet from the bar, his gargantuan arms folded across his barrel-like chest. Sanders was perched on one of the beaten stools that were dotted against the bar of the grimy, back-alley watering hole and as the bartender placed another double whisky, neat, in front of him, he grunted his thanks.

'Let's make that the last one, eh?' she said, looking at him with disapproval.

'Whatever you say, ma'am.'

Sanders refused to even look at her as he lifted the glass to his lips, staring vacantly at the mirror behind the bar and smirking at the pathetic man that returned his gaze. The drinking had definitely worsened, but somehow, he'd been able to hide it well enough at work as not to arouse suspicion. On the days when he was meeting with Townsend, who had just infiltrated the Bell View Gang, he smartened himself up, even going as far as to shave the greying stubble that framed his gaunt, pointy face to at least allude to being a man in control.

To Townsend, Sanders was his only link to the world he had left behind.

To Sanders, Townsend was the only link keeping him in it.

It had been six months since Ange had kicked him out, tired of the increasing booze and the receipts in his pockets. Sanders had always enjoyed a flutter on the weekend football, often throwing a tenner into whatever gambling app offered a few freebies and it raised the stakes for him when following along with the scores. Annually, he would take his family to the betting shop to put down bets on the Grand National, a British institution, and they would all back horses to win the historic race.

But those weekly flutters became daily, and as the stress of tackling organised crime took its toll on Sanders, so did the gambling on his marriage.

That and the drinking.

As he spiralled further and further into addiction, Sanders fell drastically away from the respected police inspector and doting husband he had been.

Ange didn't want him in the house, nor did she want a man with such weakness and reckless tendencies around their two teenage sons.

Sanders didn't even fight it when he was served the papers.

To keep appearances after the divorce, Sanders had committed to a round of golf at the weekend until they cancelled his membership. There was only so long his behaviour would be tolerated, especially as his payments continued to fail. His reputation, which had brought him as much pride as his two sons, was now as distant as they were.

Often, he would lie about having them at the weekends, hoping the idea of his divorce being purely amicable would divert attention from his problems.

But he was alone.

He was on the verge of complete ruin.

And all he wanted was to divulge himself in his vices until someone shut off the lights for him.

As he put down the empty glass, he stood, stumbling against the bar and bursting into a fit of laughter at his own drunken stupor. The few regulars, all nursing their beers in the quiet pockets of the dingy bar, looked on with pity. The barmaid stepped forward.

'You okay, Reece?'

'Just stick it on the tab.' He waved her away, trying his best to stand straight. Once he finally did, he wobbled towards the door, only for the bouncer to step in his way.

'Tab's gotta be settled.' A different voice echoed behind him, and Sanders froze, feeling a tinge of fear tap dance down his spine. Slowly he turned and was greeted by three men, two the same size as the bouncer and the one in the middle, offering him a gold tooth infused grin. 'Hello, guv.'

It belonged to Charlie Baker. A charming, balding Cockney in his late fifties, with a penchant for fine suits and even finer wine.

He also happened to be one of the most feared loan sharks in the country, and if he'd made the trip to Merseyside, then he would have had a damn good reason to.

Sanders felt his knees weaken as he realised he was the reason.

'Look, Charlie—'

'Excuse me.' Charlie cupped his ear. It was a pointless power play, but Charlie's playful side only made him more terrifying.

'Mr Baker…'

'That's better.'

'I am an inspector of the Merseyside Police. You need to be very careful…'

'Oh, I've had enough of this bollocks. Everyone, if you look away now, the next round's on me.'

The patrons all turned back to their lonely beers, as one of Charlie's henchmen drove a rocket of a right hook into Sander's stomach, doubling him over and extracting the air from his lungs.

'Take it outside,' the bar woman yelled, and Charlie motioned for his boys to oblige. Spluttering for air, Sanders felt himself being lifted *from the floor and as he looked back to the bar as he was hauled from the bar, he saw Charlie drop a roll of notes on the bar to ensure every-one's silence.*

Ten minutes later, he found himself lying among several black bags of rubbish in the alleyway, his nose broken, along with a number of ribs. But worse than that, was the outcome of his negotiation.

His gambling had put him over fifteen thousand pounds in Charlie's pocket, and the loan shark had offered to scrub it out completely if Sanders would promise him a favour.

He never said what it was, but in Sanders' desperation, he had agreed. And lying there, among the foul aroma of trash, he wept at not only where his life had ended up, but where it was likely to go.

The only question was when…

One Year Later…

Stepping foot into the Halo Lounge in Norwich town centre caused Sanders' stomach to flip, and that wasn't due to the temptation to have his first drink in a year. Having found himself at his lowest ebb among the trash that harrowing evening a year before, Sanders had been insistent he wouldn't drink again.

And he had been true to his word.

Giving up the booze, along with kicking his gambling addiction had put him somewhat back on a steady pathway, and although those roads would never lead him back to Ange, it had at least built a few bridges with his sons.

But as he walked through the empty bar towards the two men sat at the table in the middle of the room, he realised he was walking into a situation that there was no walking away from.

His stomach flipped because he had locked eyes with Slaven Kovac.

The man needed no introduction, as news was beginning to filter across the country of the power the man was beginning to reportedly yield. No one had been able to get close to Kovac, despite him stepping into the void left behind by the now deceased Harry Chapman, courtesy of the also recently departed Sam Pope. The UK underworld was a free for all, and the classic phrase 'no honour among thieves' had never been so apt.

Accept Kovac was no thief.

He was a smart, calculating soldier who knew what needed to be done and whose palms needed to be greased.

The fact that Deputy Chief Constable Dennis Chase of the Norfolk Constabulary was sitting beside Kovac, a bottle of beer in his hand and a mocking grin across his face, was evident to that. The two men couldn't have been more different, with DCC Chase clearly enjoying the plush salary his senior role afforded him, combined with whatever cut he was getting from Kovac. His uniform was pulled tight against his flabby body, and he greedily guzzled his beverage. Beside him, Kovac was the personification of cool, with his hair slicked back and a smart blazer and polo shirt clinging to a well-toned physique.

A soldier's physique.

Charlie Baker had called on Sanders nearly ten months after he'd beaten him in that alleyway, cashing in his favour with the strangest request.

Drive across the country to Norwich and meet with two people at the Halo Lounge. He gave him the date and time, and as long as Sanders didn't piss the two men off, he and Charlie were even. As Sanders approached the table, he wondered whether Charlie was being paid in cash or in product. Either way, Kovac had more than enough, and as the premier arms dealer in the UK, he also had the arsenal to keep it that way.

'Sit.' Kovac's voice was smooth and authoritative, and he gestured to the seat in front of Sanders, who obliged. 'Drink?'

'No. Thank you,' Sanders stammered.

'Probably for the best, eh?' Chase chuckled. 'Don't be surprised. We didn't pick you at random.'

'Pick me?'

Chase knocked back the last of his beer before continuing, as Kovac burnt a hole through Sanders with his piercing stare.

'Do you know who I am? I'm Dennis Chase, Deputy Chief Constable of this fine county, and this man is Slaven Kovac. Now, I'm not going to sugar coat it, Mr Kovac here pays me a generous amount of money to ensure he is left to his own devices. However, despite my considerable influence, calls are being made for my constab- ulary to do more to try to stop Mr Kovac and shut down his operation—'

'This cannot happen,' Kovac interrupted. 'It would be very painful for a lot of people.'

'Which is where you come in, Reece.' Chase offered a slappable smirk. 'Your history of addiction is well documented no matter how hard you tried to hide it, so unfortunately, you ended up in a bad spot and owed a pretty shifty man a big favour. Well, that shifty man happens to be on Mr Kovac's payroll as he looks to expand his opera- tion and therefore, your favour, has become Mr Kovac's favour.'

'Sorry, I don't follow,' Sanders said, trying to swallow his nerves.

'He means you work for me now,' Kovac stated bluntly.

'Exactly,' Chase continued, signalling to the young man behind the bar for another drink. 'Like I said, the pressure is growing, so I've agreed to a dedicated task force that will focus on nothing more than bringing Mr Kovac to justice. And I want you to lead it. Now, when I say lead it, I'll expect you to do everything possible to make it look like a thorough investigation. Despite your plight, Reece, you do have a solid reputation and certainly have the credentials for this sort of thing. Your work on the Bell View Gang has been impressive my peers at Merseyside tell me.'

'I can't do this…' Sanders croaked; his throat dry from the hope- less situation unfolding before him.

'Well, you don't really have a choice, I'm afraid.' Chase's smug grin reappeared. 'That fifteen grand you owed Baker, you now owe Mr Kovac. And he doesn't accept non-payment. Your transfer has already been approved, and I need you to start putting together your team and start doing your best to stop Mr Kovac. But, in reality, your job is to feed Mr Kovac any pertinent information that will ensure you will only ever get so close. Do you understand?'

Sanders sat, his eyes wide with fear as he stared at the table in disbelief. Kovac, without moving his whole arm, slammed his hand down on the table to snap Sanders back into the room.

'Do you understand?' Kovac echoed, his eyes locked on Sanders, who nodded feebly. DCC Chase stood as the bartender approached and gratefully accepted his beer.

'Good. I'll see you tomorrow morning to discuss the logistics. Now, gents, if you don't mind, I believe there are some ladies in the back room who will do anything for the right price.'

Chase gave Sanders a sickening wink, before meandering across the lounge's dance floor towards the private area out back. Sanders watched him leave, his skin crawling at now being associated with the man. He turned back to Kovac, who hadn't broken his glare once, and he leant forward across the table.

'If you fuck this up, I will personally kill your children in front of you. Do you understand?' Sanders felt the tears forming in his eyes and he nodded. Kovac sat back in his chair. 'Now go. Fat boy will give you the details tomorrow.'

With that, Sanders scrambled from his chair and with his knees weak, stumbled back towards the door of the exclusive bar. Once outside, he found the first public bin he could find, and he vomited violently, not caring for the disgusted civilians who passed by. After years of dedicating himself to upholding the law, his weakness had led him to breaking it. He was now working for one of the most dangerous criminals in the country, with not only his own, but his sons' welfare at stake. There was no way out of it, and Deputy Chief Constable Chase would make sure, if anything did go wrong, he would bury Sanders so deep into the earth, he'd come face to face with the core.

Sanders knew, if he had any hope of surviving, he needed to be proactive. He also needed some leverage, a way of possibly collating his own insurance policy against both Kovac and Chase without them knowing it.

What he needed was someone inside Kovac's crew feeding him information he could use, not only to show willing in the face of helping Kovac elude the authorities, but information he could potentially use to burn his ties with the brutal criminal and hopefully regain a semblance of credibility.

It was with a heavy heart that he knew what he needed to do, and who the only person was for the job. The guilt was already manifesting as he began to formulate a plan to introduce Townsend into Kovac's gang without Kovac knowing.

Townsend was a good man, and Sanders would do whatever he could to keep him alive. But his family was at stake, and to him, keeping them safe and hopefully getting a version of his whole life back meant more to him than Townsend.

Sometimes, you just had to do what you had to do.

Sanders made his way back to his car, ready for the long journey back to Merseyside, and to put 'Danny Miller' into a Norfolk based prison.

CHAPTER NINETEEN

When Townsend began to stir himself back to consciousness, all that greeted him was a blurred grey colour. A low hum emanated from somewhere beneath him, and every so often, he felt his entire body shake. He tried to push himself up, but found his hands clasped behind his back, the plastic of the zip tie so tight, it threatened to break the skin and draw blood.

His head was pounding, the back of his skull throbbing from what must have been a hefty blow. Clarity began to seep into his vision, solidifying the colourful blob before him and he soon realised he was lying on the backseat of a car, which explained the bump that rattled his body and caused his head to slap against the leather seat.

Townsend grit his teeth and groaned.

'Wakey wakey.' Luka's voice joyfully boomed from the front seat. Smiling evilly as he pulled the car to a stop, Luka turned round in his seat and locked eyes on the restrained Townsend. 'I was right the whole time.'

Townsend did his best to respond, but the agony of his rattled skull had taken control and refused him the permission to speak. Squinting through the pain, Townsend looked back to the front seat, where Luka was sitting, casually rolling a cigarette between his murderous fingers. Beyond him, Townsend could see the leaves of a tree, indicating they were out in the surrounding woods somewhere.

Away from civilization.

Away from any chance of being found.

Gritting his teeth, Townsend engaged his core and began to haul himself up without the use of his hands. Just as he was about to find his balance, the back of Luka's hand caught him flush in the face, the connection wreaking havoc with the broken nose Sam had kindly given him. Townsend hit the leather once more, grunting in pain as Luka chuckled. He lowered the window slightly and clicked his lighter and the dank smell of smoke filled the car.

'Sit the fuck down,' Luka said, clearly enjoying himself. 'You are no more than a rat.'

'What the fuck is going on?' Townsend demanded. The last thing he remembered was standing opposite Kovac, protesting his innocence and seemingly doing a good job of it. Everything was going swimmingly, and all he had to do was rendezvous with Sam back at the safe house and everything would be over.

Then Kovac had received a phone call.

Then black.

'It seems that Danny Miller is not your name. You are a police officer.'

'Bullshit,' Townsend snapped, trying his best not to show his fear. 'Whoever told you that's lying.'

'I don't think so.' Luka shook his head. 'I think you are filthy rat. And Kovac, he does not like filthy rats. I am… pest control.'

Luka let out a cruel laugh at his own joke before taking a final puff on his cigarette and flicking it out of the window. Townsend took a few deep breaths, to try to not only control the pain from Luka's strike but also the rising fear within his gut.

He thought about Mandy and Eve and realised it was unlikely he would ever see them again.

If Kovac had discovered that he was an undercover police officer, then he knew first-hand how ruthlessly he would be dealt with. Considering he'd gone from being offered a drink by Kovac to know being bound and beaten by his right-hand man, Townsend understood the gravity of the situation. Luka let out a sigh, stretching his back before turning to Townsend.

'Please, Luka. Let me speak to Kovac.'

'It's too late.' Luka grinned. 'This will be fun.'

Luka pushed open his door, allowing a gust of fresh air to filter into the car, eradicating the stench of smoke and offering Townsend the promise of a cold, wet evening. A few moments later, the door by Townsend's feet opened, and despite his struggles, Luka easily overpowered him, grasping both of Townsend's ankles and hauling him carelessly out of the car. Without his hands to break his fall, Townsend hit the earth hard, his hip absorbing most of the impact. Desperation caused him to try to army crawl away, his body slithering through the mud and broken twigs of the secluded spot, only for his progress to be cut short by a solid boot to the stomach. Gasping for breath, Townsend eventually managed to haul himself up onto his knees as the gentle drizzle splashed against him with its welcome freshness.

Luka stepped around him, standing a few feet in front, and he mockingly squatted down so they were almost at eye level.

'My one question is who you actually are?' Luka smiled. 'What is your real name?'

'Go fuck yourself,' Townsend spat, defiant to the end. He'd known for a long time that he'd been walking a tight rope, and despite Sanders's insistence, there was never a safety net below. If he was going to die, at least he wouldn't beg for his life.

'That is a shame.' Luka patted him on the head. 'When I do find out, I will see if you have family. Then I will pay them many visits. Take my time.'

Townsend grit his teeth, refusing to show any inclination of a family. The last thing he wanted was for Luka to even pick up a hint of his girls. The man was many things, but a liar wasn't one of them. Townsend had no doubt that Luka would be as brutal as he claimed just to send a message out to anyone who ever tried to double cross Kovac.

'Let me speak to Kovac. This has been a misunderstanding.'

From the back of his jeans, Luka brandished a Bowie knife, the immaculate blade sending a chill down Townsend's spine. 'Give me a chance to explain...'

Luka waggled the blade in front of him and began to laugh. As he did, he failed to notice Townsend slide one of his legs forward, allowing him to plant a foot on the ground. There was a slim chance Townsend would make it out of the woods alive, especially with his hands bound behind his back. But if Kovac knew who he truly was, then Luka's threat towards Townsend's family was very real.

He would find them, and Townsend couldn't even fathom the sick pleasure Luka would have in butchering them.

Townsend had to fight.

Until his final breath.

Luka took a step towards him, seemingly unaware of the change in position, and as he nonchalantly lifted Townsend's face upwards by his chin, Townsend sprung upwards with as much force as he could possibly generate. The impact of Luka's solid jaw crunching under the impact of Townsend's skull caused Townsend to stumble, but the large Croatian came off worse. With his jaw snapping shut, Townsend heard the crunching of teeth as he slammed them together, before the rest of the blow's impact shuddered through Luka's skull, knocking him a few steps back and into the open door of his car.

Luka fell to the ground, howling in a furious cocktail of agony and blind rage, and that sound echoed behind Townsend as he raced into the labyrinth of the woods as fast as his feet could carry him.

It took Luka two minutes to finally get to his feet, trying his best to shake the pain of Townsend's sneak attack, and by the time he did, he stared out at the trees with murderous intent.

He reached down and lifted his knife, grasping it tightly until his charred knuckles turned white.

Blood poured down his chin, a constant stream that had already stained the front of his shirt.

Townsend was long gone, lost to the endless woods that would provide him with sanctuary for now. Luka angrily slammed his fist on the bonnet of his car and then dropped back into the driver's seat. His desire to murder the man he knew as Danny had doubled inside but was only outweighed by one thing.

The fear of telling Kovac that he'd failed.

Again.

————

As soon as Sanders returned to his flat, he threw up again. Barely making it to the bathroom in time, he vomited into the sink before collapsing to his knees and weeping over the side of the bath. He felt pathetic, physically and mentally, and the guilt from betraying Townsend was refusing to relent. The situation he'd found himself in was his own doing, and despite doing his best to convince himself his back was against the wall, he'd always had another option.

It was his gambling and reckless living that had put him in the pocket of Kovac, and thus, put his family in danger.

It was his choice to accept Kovac's offer, and it was his own choice, out of self-preservation, to put Townsend in Kovac's crew.

It had been a risky decision; one he'd made to try to cover his own back when the powers that be either fed him to the wolves or threw him behind bars.

But now it had collapsed.

Townsend, a good, honest cop, had most likely been killed, his body unlikely to be found. His daughter will never know what had happened to him.

Then there were the very real and imminent repercussions of his betrayal to Kovac. The man was a violent criminal, a man whose reputation was forged in the wars he'd fought and the people he'd killed. Despite his neglect for the law and the human lives it was built to protect, Kovac still lived by a code.

And that code was built on loyalty.

Loyalty to and from the people he kept close.

After two years of feeding Kovac the information he needed, Sanders had broken it. It was a desperate attempt to salvage whatever chance he had to survive, and by outing Townsend and scuppering the police investigation, he hoped that Kovac would see beyond the betrayal and appreciate the loyalty.

Enough to spare him his life.

Even if it had meant giving up Townsend.

As he stumbled from the bathroom towards the crummy, messy kitchen, Sanders soon realised he wouldn't have to wait long, when a knuckle rapped against his front door. Sanders froze, hoping his silence would fool Kovac into thinking he was elsewhere.

'I watched you come in.' Kovac spoke through the door. 'Open the door.'

Sanders swallowed his fear, and with a sweaty, shaking hand, he twisted the metal lock on the front door.

A boot crashed against the base of the door, flinging it backwards and the sharp edge caught Sanders in the mouth, splitting his lip and sending him spiralling back into the kitchen. As the blood gushed from the wound and the pain shook his skull like a maraca, Sanders had barely gathered his bearings before he was set upon by two of Kovac's soldiers. Decked in black and with shaved heads, the two men roughly grabbed Sanders by an arm each, wrenching it backwards until his tendons begged for mercy and held him against the fridge.

Kovac calmly closed the front door behind them and then stepped into the kitchen with a disappointed look on his face. The burns were still fresh from Sam Pope's exploits at the quarry and the usual calm that sat behind Kovac's eyes had been replaced by murderous rage.

'I liked Danny,' Kovac began, his gloved hands held casually in his lap. 'He was a loyal man. Just to the wrong man it would seem. It is unfortunate that I had to kill him.'

Sanders hadn't seen the point of fighting his restraints, and he felt a tear slide down his cheek.

'Is he dead?' He finally managed.

'Last time I saw him, his unconscious body was being loaded into Luka's car. And you know how much Luka hated him. Is a shame. A real shame.' Kovac shook his head and then turned to Sanders. 'As for you, you have ten seconds to tell me where these files are...'

Ring. Ring.

Kovac's phone buzzed in his pocket. Irritated, he

pulled it from the inside of his blazer, saw the name *Luka* and answered. Immediately, his brow furrowed.

'You useless fuck,' Kovac spat. 'Find him and kill him.'

Kovac hung up the phone and slid it back in his pocket. Sanders felt his own heart beat a little faster, part of him grateful that it appeared Townsend had been every bit the fighter he knew him to be. That gratitude was quickly eradicated by the very real threat that it brought his way.

'It would seem that Danny is a fighter. Unlike you.' Kovac took another step towards him. 'But if he is alive, then I need those files before he gets them, so you have ten seconds to tell me where I find them or else I'll start to skin you alive from the belly up.'

Kovac flicked open his pocketknife, revealing a sharp, serrated blade that shimmered under the bright light of the kitchen.

'I don't know, Slaven. I swear.'

'Lift his shirt.'

Sanders finally began to squirm and fight for his life, as one of the henchmen grabbed at his shirt, roughly pulling it from the waistband of his trouser. As he struggled, Kovac roughly struck him across the face with the back of his hand. As his head snapped back against the fridge door, Kovac pressed his hand to Sanders' forehead, pinning it in place. He then lifted the tip of his knife to his eye, stopping it less than an inch from his retina.

Sanders went still with fear. His stomach flipped.

'Maybe I take an eye, just to make us even.'

'Please. Please don't,' Sanders begged. 'I think I know where they are…at the safe house…but I couldn't get to them because his wife was there…'

Kovac took a step back, his eyebrows raised with surprise. A light bulb had clearly activated in his mind.

'He has a wife?' Kovac asked, his words cruelly

carrying a layer of excitement. He collapsed the knife and took another step closer to Sanders, assuming his dominance over the man. 'You take my boys to her, and you bring her back to me.'

'She has nothing to do with this…' Sanders tried to reason, knowing it was nothing more than his own guilt.

'Maybe not.' Kovac stepped back, heading towards the door. 'But if Danny is the man I think he is, then he will be willing to trade them for her. And if not, then her blood will be on your hands.'

Kovac barked something in Croatian to the two men on either side of Sanders, and they roughly relinquished their grip. For good measure, one of them clubbed Sanders with a rough shot to the kidney, rocking his body and every one of his internal organs. Sanders tried to breathe through the pain, but as they marched him past Kovac and to the door, all he could do was cry.

He wasn't a fighter.

And now, it was a very real possibility that he'd made an orphan out of Eve Townsend.

CHAPTER TWENTY

'Do you have the green?'

Eve's eyes lit up at Sam's question, and she began to rummage through her pencil case, searching for the pen. As she did, Sam looked up at Mandy from his seat at the modest dining table and offered her a warm smile. She reciprocated and took a sip of her tea. It made her yearn for the return of her husband, and the absence of Jack in Eve's life during his undercover operation, had deprived their daughter of more moments like this.

The fact that the UK's most dangerous vigilante was sitting opposite her daughter, wilfully indulging her in a colouring in contest made her question just how their lives had got to such a place.

According to Sanders, Jack was working round the clock to bring down one of the worst criminals the country had seen in years.

To Sam, he was a desperate man whose only route home was with Sam's help.

Despite everything Sanders had done to maintain a connection for Mandy and Jack over the past few years, she couldn't help but trust Sam. The man had nothing to lose, and he'd voluntarily shown up based on her husband's confession.

If Jack did have a way out, and all other doors were closed due to the very real prospect of death, then she knew she needed Sam just as much as Jack did.

All she wanted was her husband home and her daughter to have her father back.

'You don't have to do that, you know?' Mandy shrugged, finishing her tea and placing the mug down on the table beside the sofa. She shuffled uncomfortably on the arm of the chair.

'It's my pleasure,' Sam replied, smiling at Ede. 'Besides, I think this is looking good. What do you think?'

Sam held up the sheet of paper, where he'd almost completed colouring the cartoon image of a Tyrannosaurus Rex. Eve looked up at the sheet and nodded her head.

'It's not as good as mine.'

Sam chuckled at Eve's strong mindedness, and he watched as she carefully coloured between the thick, black lines of the image, her tongue poking out the side of her mouth in concentration. Considering his life for the past three years had been one raged in blood and death, the innocence of a child was a wonderful tonic, despite the circumstances. Mandy lifted herself from the sofa and walked across the room, peering over her daughter's shoulder and raising her eyebrows.

'That is very good. Is that for Daddy?'

'Yup. Red is his favourite colour.'

'Come on, it's late.' Mandy leant down and kissed Eve on the top of her head, her blonde hair giving off the sweet smell of her strawberry scented shampoo. 'Let's put this away.'

'Okay, Mummy,' Eve politely answered, carefully placing the lids back on her pens.

'You go up and brush your teeth and get your jammies on, then I'll be up.' Mandy winked and smiled at her daughter, who dropped down from her chair and headed to the stairs. As she climbed the first few, she poked her head through the wooden slats of the banister.

'Will you read me a story?'

'When you're tucked up—' Mandy began.

'No, not you, Mummy. Sam?'

Taken aback, Sam shot a look at Mandy who nodded her approval.

'You betcha. But you need to have clean teeth before I do.'

Eve let out a cheer as she rushed up the stairs, and as she disappeared from sight, the sound of brushing quickly followed. Sam turned to Mandy and smiled warmly. 'She's a good kid.'

'She's the best.' Mandy felt a weight of sadness fall upon her. 'She misses her dad something rotten.'

'I'm sure he does, too,' Sam said, standing from his seat. 'Not seeing your kid every day is torture. Trust me.'

Guilt hit Mandy in her gut like a sucker punch and she turned to Sam with a regretful grimace on her face. While the news around Sam Pope had disappeared with his own apparent death a few years before, she recalled one of the most heartbreaking pieces that a now deceased journalist, Helal Miah, had written. It was about how Sam's quest for justice had stemmed from the death of his child.

A needless death that went by with minimal punishment.

The thought of losing Eve caused her stomach to knot, and she reached out her hand and rested it on Sam's shoulder.

'I'm so sorry, I didn't mean to…'

Sam patted her hand and forced a brave smile.

'It's okay. It was a long time ago.' Sam took a breath.

'But the pain doesn't go. I live with that loss every day, and every day, the details of Jamie's face get a little less clear. It feels like the edges are starting to smudge. But I've accepted what happened, and because of that, I can keep going. The pain might ease, but the scars they never leave. Now, you might hate your husband for what he's done, but he did it for a good reason. Those are hard to find nowadays. Good things to fight for. But believe me, all he wants is to get home to you and that girl upstairs.'

Mandy dabbed at the corner of her eye, shaking her head with embarrassment.

'Can you help him? Really?'

Sam fixed her with a cold, powerful stare.

'I'm going to try.'

Just then, Eve's head appeared through the panels of the banister at the top of the stairs, pulling her lips back to reveal her clean teeth.

'Story time.' She yelled joyfully and then rushed back towards her room. Sam chuckled, and then reassuringly patted Mandy on the shoulder. Mandy took a breath, recomposed, and then stepped across the room to collect her mug.

'You don't want to keep her waiting.' Mandy warned with a wry smile. 'I'll pop the kettle on.'

Sam gave her a thumbs up before he headed up the stairs, recounting all the bedtime stories he read to his son. Jamie had been an avid reader, and with each step he took, Sam felt more guilt for the fact that he'd stopped dedicating as much time to reading in his son's honour. Growing up with a military father, Sam had always put more emphasis on following in his father's footsteps. General William Pope was a highly respected man, and when Sam's mother left while he was too young to really forge a lasting bond with her, his father had done what he could to raise him.

He instilled a set of values that Sam still held dear.

To do the right thing.

Whatever the cost.

With Jamie, Sam had struggled to do the same. Whether it was due to being away on an ill-fated Project Hailstorm mission, or the fact that his son had such a passion for the written word, Sam found bonding difficult.

But he'd loved him completely.

And in the aftermath of losing Jamie, Sam had promised him that he would read as much as he could.

But somewhere along the way, whether it was taking down General Wallace or fighting biker gangs in South Carolina, Sam had fallen short on that promise.

Just another way in which he'd failed his son.

He stepped into Eve's room, ensuring the door remained open, and he sat down beside her bed as she handed him a copy of *The Gruffalo*. An instant image of Jamie echoed in his mind. Whenever they arrived at the snake, Jamie would comment on how nasty he was.

The things kids hang onto always baffled Sam, and he often marvelled at Jamie's memory when it came to his books.

Mandy wandered towards the bottom of the stairs, and just as she was about to ascend them, there was another knock at the door.

Sam heard it, and instinctively his hand went to his gun, which he realised was in the inside pocket of his jacket that was hanging on the back of one of the dining room chairs downstairs.

He stood, putting his finger to his lips, and Eve adorably played along. Edging to the door, Sam peered over the top of the banister to get a look at the door.

Mandy opened it slightly, welcoming in a chilly gust of rain.

'Reece,' Mandy exclaimed. 'What are you doing back here?'

'Is Jack here?' Sanders' voice was heavy with defeat.

'No, I told you…what the hell happened to your face?'

Mandy swung the door open wider to get a look at the vicious, bloody split that had sliced Sanders' lip and as she did, she noticed the two muscular men stood behind him. The rain clattered off their leather jackets, and as she saw the cold, uncaring gaze in their eyes, she instantly tried to slam the door. One of them put his foot in the way, and the door slammed helplessly against it.

With one powerful shove, the man hurled the door open, sending Mandy spiralling back towards the sofa. As Sanders and the two men entered, she sat up in a blind rage.

'What the fuck, Reece?'

'I'm sorry, Mandy.' Sanders couldn't even maintain eye contact. 'But you're going to have to come with me.'

'The fuck I am.'

'Is Jack here?' Sanders pleaded. 'It's imperative that you tell the truth.'

Mandy shot a quick glance up to the top of the stairs, and she caught a quick glimpse of Sam, who shook his head. She turned back to the two men who were rifling through every possession in the room, and Sanders who stared solemnly at the ground.

'No. I told you. It's just me.'

Another burly man appeared in the doorway. Sanders sighed as the driver clicked his fingers, beckoning him to make it quick.

'Mandy. Please don't make this difficult. These men just need to talk to Jack.'

'Well, I'm not Jack, am I?'

'No.' Sanders felt a small bubble of rage at the entire situation. Mandy treating him with such disrespect felt like yet another straw being added to his already weighted spine. 'But he will talk to us if we have you. Take her.'

The driver lunged into the room, and with his powerful advantage, he soon had his arms wrapped around Mandy and hauled her from the front room and out into the rain. Sanders watched on helplessly, before turning to the two men who were still searching the room.

'Kovac said not to kill him if he turns up.' Sanders offered, in hope more than anything.

'We will do our best,' one of them responded in his sinister accent. Sanders shook his head and followed Mandy and her captor out of the safe house, slamming the door behind them. As the two men rifled through the remaining parts of the living room, Sam looked down at Eve, who he'd held tightly against his chest.

As soon as the men burst into the living room, Sam had turned to Eve and held his finger to his lips once more. Again, she followed, and he knelt beside her bed.

'We need to stay very quiet, okay?'

Eve nodded, keeping her finger to her lips, as Sam scooped her from the bed and tiptoed across the small room to the wardrobe. Carefully, he nudged the already open door with his elbow, and he stepped in. Among the few clothes that were hanging, Sam had enough space to kneel on one knee, and he held Eve close to his chest. Despite the sudden upheaval, her heartbeat was calm, a sure sign that she felt safe.

Sam pulled the wardrobe door closed, and for the first time in over fifteen years, he thought back to that horrifying afternoon in Chakari in the Kabul Province of Afghanistan. Nursed back to health after being blown from a cliff face by a local doctor named Farhad Nabizada, Sam had taken refuge in the man's home while the Taliban searched for him. Eventually, they were led to Farhad's door, and the doctor insisted Sam hide in a secret partition in the wall along with Farhad's young son, Masood.

For his bravery, Farhad was shot at point blank range.

Sam's presence had killed a good man and orphaned his two sons, one of whom had already been swayed by the terrorist's propaganda.

Now, trapped in another confined space, grasping tightly to another good man's child, Sam hoped that fate would offer a different outcome.

For the next two hours, he knelt, thankful for the years spent in position as a sniper that meant his body didn't falter.

Eve had fallen asleep against him.

Downstairs, the two men sat speaking to each other in Croatian and waiting for the likely arrival of Townsend.

Behind them on the dining room chair, Sam's jacket hung carelessly.

Sam hoped beyond hope that they didn't see the gun in the pocket, because if they did, he was outnumbered and most likely, out gunned.

All he could do was wait.

And do whatever necessary to keep a sleeping child safe.

———

The eighty-minute drive from the safe house to Kovac's hideout was a tense and silent journey. Mandy had enough sense not to put up a fight, knowing full well that the driver clearly held little regard for her wellbeing. Whoever Jack had pissed off, they were clearly powerful, and knowing she was nothing more than a bargaining chip made sure she kept her mouth shut.

The one time she did speak was to tell Sanders to go fuck himself when he'd attempted to apologise. As the driver navigated through the woodland paths, peering through the wet windscreen and the frantic wipers, she found her eyes bulging at the sheer size of Kovac's lavish, secluded home. The modern building was stowed away in the wilderness, hidden from the world, and Mandy knew, as she stepped out of the car, that the man was certainly worth a lot of money.

Jack had kept the details of Kovac to a minimum during their secret meetings, adamant that the less she knew, the safer she was.

But a man who was the target of an undercover operation, who had senior police officers on the payroll and lived in a home that the Hollywood elite would envy, didn't get rich by stealing cars.

Whoever Kovac truly was, she knew he was dangerous.

As all of them stepped away from the car, the front door to the house opened, and a large, terrifying man stepped out to greet them. He had fresh burns on his face, along with recent swelling around his mouth. Judging from the way he glared at her, Mandy assumed her husband was responsible for some it.

She smiled.

Jack was a pain in the arse when he wanted to be.

Behind the hulking behemoth, a well-groomed man emerged. His handsome face was well chiselled and framed by a good head of hair. He had the physique and stature of an experienced soldier, and he greeted Mandy with an almost apologetic tone.

'You must be Mrs Townsend,' Kovac said calmly. 'I can only apologise that we are meeting under such circumstances.'

'Where is my husband?' Mandy snapped, ignoring the rain and the helpless situation she was in.

'Good question,' Kovac snapped, scowling at Luka. 'My associate here lost him in the woods. Now, your husband has some information I need. As he didn't want to hand that information to me—'

'You took me.' Mandy shook her head and turned to Sanders. 'You pathetic man. You're supposed to be his friend.'

Sanders couldn't even look at her and he stared towards to gravel. Kovac nodded.

'You are right. He is pathetic man who has dug a hole that he may never get out of. And he will pay the price for what he has done.'

'My Jack is a good man—'

'Maybe so. But I am not.' Kovac motioned for them to step inside. Leading the way, he brought them all down the stairs and into the open-plan lounge area and across the room to the next staircase. 'But I am a fair man. If your husband does as he is asked, you will live.'

'And Jack?' Mandy asked. The silence told her what she'd feared the most, and her eyes watered.

'Luka will escort you to your room, and you have my word. He will not touch a hair on your head.' Kovac bore a hole through Luka with his piercing eyes. 'If he does, he will watch me do the same to his sister.'

Luka shuffled angrily in place, and then roughly took Mandy by the elbow, leading her towards the next staircase that led down to his torture room.

'Wait.' Kovac held up a hand. He beckoned Sanders to them and then pointed at his legs. 'Open your legs.'

'Excuse me?' Sanders stammered.

'Spread your feet. Wide.' Confused, Sanders did as he was told, and slid his feet outwards, straightening his legs as much as his limbs would allow. Kovac turned to Mandy. 'For his betrayal, feel free to kick him.'

Sanders gasped in horror, and turned, foolishly, to Mandy, searching for sympathy. Mandy stomped forward, and with all her might, drove her trainer straight into

Sanders' crotch. The man howled in agony, collapsing to the tiled floor with both hands clasping his crushed genitals. Kovac nodded approvingly, and Mandy was swiftly hauled down the staircase by an impatient Luka. As he wept on the floor, Sanders tried to catch his breath.

Kovac squatted down beside him, the serrated blade casually held in his hand. He twirled it slightly, mocking Sanders and asserting his dominance.

'Now I know you have a set of balls. I know what I will cut off first if I don't get my files. Understand?'

Sanders nodded frantically, tears streaming down his cheeks. Kovac stood, shaking his head in disgust as he stepped away from the crumpled heap of a once respected police officer. Downstairs, Mandy was no doubt terrified as the beastly Luka locked her away.

Somewhere, in the dark and the rain, Townsend would soon discover that his wife was in very real danger.

With all those thoughts rushing through his guilt-ridden mind, Sanders came to the conclusion that if anything, Mandy should have kicked him harder.

CHAPTER TWENTY-ONE

By the time Townsend had stumbled onto the street and saw the safe house, he was dead on his feet. After somehow surviving Luka's attempted execution, he'd run aimlessly into the woods, allowing the trees and the rainfall to engulf him and keep him hidden. Knowing Luka would be thirsty for revenge, he never stopped running, ignoring the twigs and branches that lashed at his skin as he raced past.

After a solid five minutes of running, he stopped, scanning the woods for any sense of direction, before he lost his footing and rolled down a muddy incline, landing less than a foot away from a sharp rock. Blowing out his cheeks in relief, Townsend shuffled across to the pointed stone, lined up the centre of the cable tie, and began rubbing it against the sharpened edge. As he felt the cable tie begin to give way, he ignored the pain of the rock against his skin and when he finally broke the tie and freed his hands from behind his back, he ignored the blood he'd drawn from his wrists.

The next hour he spent traversing the woods, weary of the impending sunset and he picked up the pace to try to hit a road before he was plunged into darkness. Any fears of being lost or attacked went out of the window.

He needed to get back to the safe house.

The game was up. Kovac knew he was an undercover cop, which meant he would soon be looking for revenge.

Given the nature of the situation, Townsend doubted that Sam Pope would hang around if he didn't show. The man had already hindered Kovac's delivery and acquired his arsenal of guns.

Townsend didn't have Sam pegged as the sentimental type, so if he had any chance of making it out of the situation alive and getting home to his girls, he had to make that meeting.

With his phone out of battery having spent the previous night and day in hospital, Townsend tried to tap into his pigeon's instinct, and he shocked himself when, as the sun began to fade from the sky, he found his way to a country road. Although there were no cars, the signage stated that the town of Metfield was only a few miles away. Townsend broke into a jog, ignoring the hunger in his stomach and the aches in his legs until he saw the street lights. As the orange glow welcomed him into the town, he found the nearest bus stop and checked the timetable. He waited thirty-three minutes for the next bus that went to Norwich town centre, and from there, he changed to another route that would take him within the vicinity of the safe house. Just north of Norwich town centre, Townsend eventually jumped off the bus by Waterloo Park and then walked a few streets further until he eventually stumbled onto the street.

He doubted Sam would still be waiting.

The man didn't owe him anything. When Townsend didn't show, it would arouse suspicion, and for a man in Sam's position, that would be more than enough reason to vanish.

All he hoped was that he would be able to lie low in the safe house, retrieve the files and hopefully make contact with Sanders to get away and to somewhere safe.

To get back to his girls.

Shuffling down the street, he felt the soles of his feet screaming under the intense pain of the blisters he'd accumulated, and his head was pounding. The blow he'd taken to the back of the skull had shaken his brain, and he was pretty certain he was experiencing a concussion. Coupled with his hunger and exhaustion, Townsend needed to collapse on the sofa, knock back a few painkillers and pray that there was something edible in the house.

With his mind focusing on just keeping him standing, he failed to notice the black car parked out the front of the safe house, and as he approached the front door, only then did he realise the lights were on. He stopped, doubting that Sam would draw attention to his occupancy, and as he rooted around in his pocket for his keys, he let out a sigh of relief that Sanders had no doubt realised what had happened and had been waiting for him to return.

Feebly, he turned the key in the door and fell into it, stumbling into the room. He caught himself before he fell, just in time for the two large men to rise from their seats, their eyes sparkling like a pack of wolves who had just come across an injured deer.

'What the fuck?' Townsend muttered.

'Welcome home.' The nearest man chuckled in his thick accent, before he lunged at Townsend, grabbing him by the scruff of his dirty jacket and hurling him across the small front room. Townsend hit his shins against the coffee table and stumbled, only to be caught by the next man, who welcomed him with a rocking uppercut to his stomach. As the front door slammed shut, Townsend collapsed to his knees, gasping for breath.

The two men circled him, cracking their knuckles in an obvious display of intimidation.

'Kovac say you are police officer.' The first man snarled. 'I hate police officers.'

He followed that remark up with a sickening kick to Townsend's side, exacerbating his struggle for air. Refusing to lie down, Townsend began to drag himself across the cheap carpet, knowing it was a pointless attempt at escape. After moving no more than a few inches, the other man placed his heavy, army-grade leather boot on the centre of his spine.

'Kovac wants you alive,' the man said coldly. 'But he did not say he needs you healthy.'

'Fuck you,' Townsend yelled, his face pressed against the floor.

'You do have balls. Unlike Sanders.'

'Sanders?' Townsend felt a rush of anger flow through his body, causing his fists to clench. The realisation of his handler's betrayal pulsed through him like a sonar, and as he tried to struggle up, the henchman drove his boot down onto his back, pinning him against the floor once more.

'He led us here. Unfortunately, you not here. But your very pretty wife....'

As Townsend's eyes bulged with blind fury, a sickening thud echoed behind him, and the man who had greeted him at the door fell to the floor beside him, crashing through the glass table, his eyes wide, as the fresh dent in the side of his skull pumped blood down his twitching face.

———

As soon as Townsend burst through the door, Eve stirred. Disorientated, she quickly began to panic, forgetting that she was clinging to a stranger in a dark cupboard. Immediately, she began to panic.

'Shhhh,' Sam encouraged, stroking her hair. 'Eve, you're okay. We just need to stay quiet, okay?'

'Daddy?' Eve squeaked, before Sam pulled her in close.

'Eve. We need to be quiet, okay?'

As the little girl threatened to break, downstairs the unmistakable sound of Kovac's heavies assaulting her father echoed up to them. Sam grit his teeth, not wanting to let go of Eve.

He'd failed to protect a child once.

The permanent image of his own son's lifeless body still burnt on the back of his retinas.

He couldn't fail again.

Downstairs, the sound of a sickening kick rocked Townsend, who grunted in agony, as the two men mockingly goaded him. Having already taken Townsend's wife, Sam knew that they would keep him alive just long enough to get what they wanted. But there was no telling just how close to death they were willing to beat him.

The man was fighting for his family.

To get back to them.

Having been double-crossed by his senior officer, Townsend had been living a lie. Sacrificing everything dear to him for what he believed was the greater good, when in truth, he was nothing more than a useful tool in someone else's quest to get rich.

Sam could relate. General Wallace had used Project Hailstorm as his own personal hit squad, coercing Sam into multiple missions based on the fabrication of peace and freedom.

Townsend deserved better.

He deserved a chance.

A chance to fight back.

Sam pulled the sniffling Eve away from his body and gently looked into her eyes.

'I need you to be a big girl, okay?' Eve nodded in

response. 'Good girl. So, I need you to close your eyes and cover your ears. Can you do that for me?'

Eve nodded and then proceeded to prove it, over emphasising how tightly she could close her eyes, drawing a genuine smile from Sam. Despite everything going on, the innocence of a child had the ability to cut through any situation like a knife through butter.

'Like that?' Eve whispered.

'Exactly like that.' Sam gave her the thumbs up. 'I'll be back in two minutes, okay? You need to sit still, and remember, cover your ears as tightly as you can.'

Again, Eve pressed her hands to her ears and scrunched her face up, following Sam's instructions to the letter. Delicately, Sam pushed open the wardrobe door and stepped out, shooting one final glance back at Eve who hadn't moved.

She was a good kid.

He understood why Townsend was willing to fight for her.

Sam etched out of the room until he could peer down over the banister, where the two large men had their backs to him, both of them standing over the prone body of Townsend. The young officer was soaked through, his trousers covered in mud. He looked like he'd been through the ringer and considering Kovac had sent his men to collect Townsend's wife, Sam assumed Townsend had already dodged death that day. One of the men had his heavy, black boot pressed on the centre of Townsend's spine, pinning him to the ground, as the other chuckled beside him.

'You do have balls. Unlike Sanders.' The man spat.

'Sanders?' Townsend barked with anger, realising the gravity of the situation and how it had come to pass. Consumed with rage, he tried to struggle, only for the other man to drive his boot down in the centre of his spine.

They were going to maim him. Sam knew that Townsend wouldn't give up, which meant they would need to do more to subdue him.

With their attention focused on the man before them, the two men failed to realise as Sam crept down the stairs, thankful that each step offered next to no creaking. As he got to the bottom, he reached for the thick marble ashtray that was stationed on the cabinet at the bottom of the stairs. It was heavy and lifting it one handed without making a sound took every fibre of Sam's considerable strength, his muscular forearm straining as he lifted it into his grip.

A few feet away, Townsend struggled under the weight of his captor, the realisation of Sander's betrayal and the helpless situation he was in.

The other man chuckled again, ready to pour petrol on the raging fire that was Townsend's turmoil.

'He led us here. Unfortunately, you not here. But your very pretty wife….'

THUD.

The impact shook Sam's arm, and he knew as soon as he swung the ashtray, he would kill the man. The sharp edge of the marble hexagon drove into the man's skull, cracking the bone on impact and sending a torrent of blood spraying from the sickening wound. The man flopped forward, decimating the glass coffee table as he collapsed, the last remnants of his consciousness twitching through his body as his life pumped from the dent in his skull.

The other man took his foot off Townsend and turned, a murderous glint in his eye, and he lunged at Sam. The weight of the ashtray combined with the velocity of the swing had shaken Sam off balance, and the man took advantage, driving his shoulder into Sam's gut, charging a few steps before slamming Sam through the wooden slats of the banister. Sam crashed against the stairs, the edge of one of the steps catching him under the ribs and winding him. The hulking man reached through the remains of the banister and hauled Sam back through by the scruff of his T-shirt, but Sam drove his head forward, connecting with the other man's nose.

The man stumbled back, blinking away the pain, and then swung a right hook, which Sam dodged. Sam rocked the man's sturdy body with a few hard body shots before the man swung wildly with the left. Sam absorbed most of the blow into his body before he locked his arm around the man's arm and pulled it straight. Then, he drove his right knee up as hard as he could, connecting with the man's elbow and snapping it upwards.

The snap of the bone was almost as stomach churning as the sight of the bone piercing the skin and panicked, the man tried to struggle free. In the midst of the man's panic, Sam drove his other knee into the back of the man's leg, dropping him onto his own knees. In one fluid motion, Sam pressed his hand against the man's forehead and then slammed his knee as hard as he could into the back of the man's skull.

The man flopped forward, into the pool of blood that had begun to form courtesy of his dead partner. Sam stared at the carnage he'd caused, registering two more deaths in his karma that he was certain would one day come back around looking for him.

But for now, he'd done the right thing.

He may have killed two men, but he'd saved Townsend, who had begun to get to his feet with a palpable fear in his eyes. Having witnessed Sam expertly kill two men with his bare hands, he suddenly felt very aware of his own limitations and the very real and very dangerous world he was locked in.

'You okay?' Sam asked, raising his eyebrow.

'Yeah…uhh…thank you.' Sam raised a hand as if to say 'don't mention it'. Townsend looked at the two dead men and shook his head. 'They mentioned my wife….'

'She was here when I got here.'

'Fuck.' Townsend slapped both hands to his head and ran his fingers aggressively through his short hair.

'Mandy's a tough woman. She gave them some shit before they took her.'

'Why didn't you save her?' Townsend turned to Sam with anger.

'Because she wanted me to keep your daughter safe.'

'Eve?' Townsend stumbled slightly at the mention of his beloved child. The thought of her being anywhere near any of this made him feel sick. 'Where is she?'

'She's safe and sound. She's upstairs in her wardrobe, waiting for you.' Sam nodded to the now decimated stairs. 'Go to her. I'll sort this mess out.'

Townsend shot forward like an Olympic sprinter, and bound up the stairs two at a time, ignoring the shards of wood that now littered the staircase. He pushed through her door and bound to the wardrobe, pulling both doors open, and then he dropped to his knees.

There, sat obediently, with her eyes closed and her hands to her ears, was Eve.

His beautiful little Eve.

Slowly, she cracked one of her eyelids open, and a massive smile took over her face as she jumped forward, wrapping her arms around her father's neck and burying her head into his chest. Townsend held her as tightly as he could.

Suddenly, all the pain that was coursing through his

body subsided. The fear of his wife's abduction momentarily left him.

The seething rage for Sander's betrayal.

All gone. For a few seconds.

And in those few seconds, Townsend held Eve as tightly as he ever could, and he wept.

CHAPTER TWENTY-TWO

As the night rumbled on, Sanders danced dangerously on the precipice of a panic attack. Sat in Kovac's spacious mansion, he was surrounded by ex-military men, all of whom would tear him to shreds at Kovac's command. While they maintained an experienced calm, Sanders was sticky with sweat. Somewhere in the catacombs beneath the living space, Mandy Townsend was being held against her will, knowing that her and her husband's chances of survival were minimal.

Kovac was a ruthless man, and despite the measured calm he often exuded, Sanders was under no illusion that he would want to tie up every loose end as quickly and efficiently as possible. With his guilt intermittently creeping through in the form of a tear, Sanders knew that having brought an undercover police officer into Kovac's crew, he'd effectively signed his own death warrant.

Given the fact that he was likely to have made an orphan out of the adorable Eve, he understood that it would be richly deserved. His only hope was that it was as painless as possible.

'This is waste of time,' Luka barked from the back of

the room, where he was seated at the vast, oak dining table. He slammed his fist against the wood, shaking the drink in front of him.

'Patience.' Kovac raised his hand. Asserting his authority, Kovac stood from the chair opposite Sanders and strode casually into the middle of the room, his glass of whisky in his hand. 'They will call as soon as Danny shows his face.'

Right on cue, the vibrations of a phone echoed around the room like a hornet, and instinctively, Kovac reached for his phone that was on the coffee table before him. As he lifted the phone, his eyes squinted with confusion.

His phone wasn't ringing.

He shot a glance to Luka, who having checked his own, shook his head. All eyes then turned to Sanders, who lifted his phone with a concerned look.

'It's him,' he said meekly.

'Answer. On speaker,' Kovac demanded, and stood before him, his arms folded. Luka also rose from his seat as Sanders answered the call.

'Jack…' He began, trying to maintain a friendly tone.

'You piece of shit,' Townsend spat. 'My wife, Reece? My fucking wife?'

'Look, Jack. We need to sort this out and—'

'No, you need to realise that you've made a big fucking mistake, Reece. Not only have you put my wife in danger, but you've been a fucking rat this whole time? I'm going to make sure I burn you to the fucking ground.'

'Where are my men?' Kovac cut in, his dominant voice wrestling control of the conversation.

'They've been handled,' Townsend retorted. 'They were trespassing.'

Kovac raised an eyebrow at both Luka and Sanders, clearly worried that maybe they'd underestimated him.

'I see you are very angry, Danny.'

'My name isn't Danny. It's Jack,' Townsend snapped. 'And seen as how that gutless coward has led you to my wife, I guess we can do away with any formalities, right?'

'I always did like you.' Kovac chuckled. Almost impressed.

'What do you want?'

'I want all the information you foolishly kept. Information on me, the operation, my benefactor. Every single shred.' Kovac leant forward, his mouth a few inches from the phone. 'I want everything, otherwise you lose everything.'

'And my wife? I want proof she is okay.'

'She's okay, Jack…' Sanders began, before a clubbing right hand from Luka rocked his jaw. Sanders fell onto his side, his hands clutching his split lip and Luka scowled at him.

'I swear, if you so much as lay a finger on her—'

'That is very much up to you, Jack,' Kovac cut in. 'You have until 8 p.m. tomorrow to bring me my files. You know where I live. You bring them to me, and you come alone. Once we've checked them, then we let your wife go. I can guarantee you now, she will be safe, and I will forget her name forever. You, on the other hand, we may have to have a discussion about whether you survive.'

'I have your word that she will be safe?' Townsend's voice cracked slightly. The realisation that his wife was being held captive by such dangerous men suddenly became very real.

'You have my word. You, having been by my side for so long, should know that is iron clad.' Kovac lifted the phone and took it off speaker. 'If you're not here by eight, I will lock Luka in that room with your wife and will only open the door when she is dead, regardless of how long it takes. Is that understood?'

Kovac expected the silence that followed, knowing that

the threat of unleashing the animalistic Luka on the wife of a man he hated would conjure the most horrendous nightmares. After a few moments, he heard Townsend recompose himself.

'I'll see you tomorrow.'

—————

Townsend hung up the phone and dropped it on the sofa beside him. He could feel his fist clench with fury and a nauseous tremble in the bottom of his stomach. Kovac had essentially confirmed he would be killed when he showed up, but there was no other choice. Mandy was trapped within Kovac's command, and Townsend had seen the very room Kovac had threatened to lock her in with Luka.

The fortified room was impenetrable without the key, meaning the only way for Townsend to ensure she was safe was to get her out himself. Which meant he had no other option but to acquiesce to Kovac's demand.

Shaking through a mixture of hatred and fear, Townsend lost any track of time until Sam's voice welcomed him back to the room.

'You okay?' Townsend shook his head before shooting a glance up the stairs. 'She hasn't made a peep.'

'No, I'm not fucking okay.'

'Hey, calm down.' Sam held his hands up as he stood across the room. 'I'm just asking—'

'They have my wife. They have her locked in a fucking vault beneath the house and if I don't go there by eight o'clock tomorrow night, then that sick bastard is going to have her killed in ways I can't even think about.'

'Okay.' Sam could see his practicality was infuriating Townsend. 'Then you need to find those files.'

'Don't you get it, Sam?' Townsend gestured wildly with his hands; fully aware he was verging on hysteria. 'I won't walk out of there. Neither will Mandy. Kovac doesn't leave a breadcrumb trail. He's too fucking smart for that. Either way, Mandy is going to be killed, and the man has enough firepower to put even you in the ground.'

Sam sighed. He stepped forward towards Townsend, who apprehensively raised his hands. Sam didn't stop and as he approached Townsend, he outstretched his arms and wrapped them around him. Townsend tried to fight it off, but as soon as Sam embraced him, he relented and, for the next thirty seconds, he allowed himself to finally confront the terrifying reality he was in.

His life was in imminent danger.

Mandy's too, and she was trapped with a very real monster.

Eve might be left alone and orphaned.

For those thirty seconds, wrapped in the embrace of the UK's most dangerous man, Townsend felt enough safety to unload a flurry of tears. Sam held him tight, understanding the need for him to get it out of his system, and once the tears relented to a few sniffles, Sam stepped back slightly, his hands clasped to the back of Townsend's neck.

'We will get her back.' His words were cold enough to send a shiver down Townsend's back.

'The man has an army.' Townsend shook his head. 'I can't ask you to do this for me.'

'Tough.' Sam smiled. 'That's not your choice.'

Townsend took a few steps back and again, turned a parental gaze up the stairs. A clarity evidently fell over him and he took another deep breath before turning back to Sam with his hands on his hips.

'Okay. But I need to know why. This isn't your fight, Sam. So why fight it?'

Sam extended his hand for Townsend to shake.

'Because I can.' Townsend shook it. 'And it's the right thing to do.'

'Thank you.' Townsend fought, unsuccessfully, against his voice breaking.

'Besides, throughout that entire phone call, they didn't mention my name. Which means they have no clue that I'm here and that I'll be coming with you.' Sam could see the hope appear in Townsend's eyes, so he nodded to encourage it. 'Which means I'm going to hit them as hard as I can.'

Townsend's newfound optimism quickly changed to concern as he was drawn once again to the bedroom door of his daughter's room.

'What about Eve? I can't leave her...'

'I know someone who can help.' Sam stated with authority. 'Now go to her, get some rest. We have an early start tomorrow.'

———

The following morning had seen the previous evening's downpour replaced with a fresh sunrise, the beams of the sun twinkling off the moisture that coated every part of the town. As she drove through the quiet streets heading towards her practice, Amy Devereux pressed the button on her door, allowing the window to slide down a few inches to let the brisk morning air swirl through her car. The seven o'clock drive to her office on the outskirts of Lowestoft was often one of her most cherished parts of the day.

The streets were clear of any rush hour or school run traffic, and the fresh spring morning eradicated any memories of the gloomy winter months before.

The only thing she was disappointed about was abandoning her usual stop for a morning coffee.

But only two more months and she could indulge her past vice. And given that she would have welcomed her baby into the world, she was pretty sure that caffeine would become a very necessary ally.

As she stopped at a red light, she took a moment to glance into the rear-view mirror.

Her short, blonde hair had been straightened, her pregnancy giving her bob a thicker, fuller look, and it was one of the things she was appreciative of. Luckily, her tiny frame had been able to handle the bump and despite her increasing appetite, she carried all the baby weight in her bump. Her husband, Andy, often commented that unless she turned to the side, you couldn't tell she was pregnant.

Driving on, she smiled warmly as she felt their little boy wiggle, another sign that he was happy and healthy and hopefully, excited to come and meet them soon.

After what had happened in London over three years before, she'd been nervous about moving so far away and starting afresh. Having been targeted by a corrupt police force and a dangerous criminal, it had taken the intervention of Sam Pope to keep her and her husband safe, but it had come at a price.

Andy had been left partially disabled by the bullet that had been blasted through his leg.

Sam Pope had lost his best friend, Theo Walker, who had sacrificed himself to save her and her husband from a vicious onslaught.

The world was a messed-up place, and her husband, who had struggled to overcome the trauma, often wondered if bringing a child into such a world was a good idea.

Amy was certain of it.

Children offered hope. They gave people a chance to be better than they were, and to mould a generation that can put right what previous ones put wrong.

Andy would make a tremendous father; Amy was sure of it. He worried about his lack of manliness at times, but his loving and caring nature always made him twice the man he thought he was. Ever since they discovered they were pregnant, he'd gone above and beyond to keep her comfortable through what had been an enjoyable pregnancy. And now, entering her final month of work, she was confident that her practice could survive her absence and potentially, her part time return. After a few years working for the Metropolitan Police as an occupational therapist, Amy had decided to take the risk of opening her own 'Trauma Recovery Centre', which had been a passion of hers for as long as she could remember. Having seen what the loss of Jamie had done to Sam Pope, and the wild path he'd forged since she'd last seen him, she wanted to focus her expertise on helping those who had experienced life altering hardships. While a few of her newer therapists offered a broader range of therapy, Amy worked with those who had been to the brink of hell and made it through.

Loss.

Rape.

Assault.

The damaging trials that real human beings were put through, by a world that never prepared them through their upbringing. When she'd approached the local education board to raise mental health awareness as a genuine part of the curriculum, she was met with a surprising silence and a door slammed in her face. But she continued on, and although helping people through such horrors only intensified Andy's views on the world, Amy still clung to the notion that their son would offer them a new perspective.

For her, he already had.

She pulled into the usually empty car park outside the plush glass offices. Usually, the car park was empty at this time, besides the odd cleaning van, but today, there was a car already parked a few spaces from the front door. A permanent mental scar from her ordeal in London instantly put her on hiatus, and as she pulled into her parking spot on the opposite side of the car park, her eyes were glued to the rear-view mirror.

The doors to the car opened, and a man stepped out, his arms stretching the sleeves of his T-shirt and the stubble clinging to his jaw.

Her mouth dropped, and she stepped out of the car instantly, not even realising what she was doing until she was stepping towards the man, who sheepishly approached. Behind him, another man had stepped out of the passenger side of the car and was helping an adorable young girl from the backseat, her eyes wide with excitement as she clung to her treasured bear.

Stopping about ten feet from him, Amy shook her head in disbelief.

'Sam?'

'Hello, Amy.' He shrugged, almost embarrassed. He pointed to her stomach. 'Congratulations.'

'Thanks.' She regarded Sam with shock, before her gaze was directed behind him towards Townsend and Eve. 'This is a surprise.'

'I know.' Sam looked back at his travel companions and then back at Amy with hope. 'I need a favour.'

CHAPTER TWENTY-THREE

Despite her best intention, Mandy hadn't been able to sleep. It wasn't just the very real threat to her life that had kept her awake the entire night, but the thought of Jack and Eve. She had no idea where her husband was. Based on what she'd heard from Kovac and Luka, he'd managed to evade their first attempt on his life, making her the ultimate bargaining chip. She knew her husband well enough to know he was a survivor.

If there was even an ounce of strength left in his body, he would fight.

It was one of his most beautiful qualities, and she was hoping that there was at least that left for him to give.

Her mind was also stuck with Eve, her beautiful daughter, and how she'd left her fate in the hands of one of the most dangerous men the country had ever known. Yet she knew she was safe. Having spent time with Sam the evening before, she could see that beyond the rough exterior and the dangerous aura that he was someone she could trust. Everyone he'd killed had been a criminal, profiting from being just beyond the full reach of the law. But the two men that Sanders had left in her house were clearly dangerous, and she found her eyes watering at the thought of them finding her baby.

Eve meant more to her than anything in the world. It was a joke she and Jack often made, both of them agreeing that if push came to shove, they would choose Eve over the other. The thought of her being subjected to or brought into a dangerous world full of drugs, guns, and murder terrified her, and she found little comfort on the concrete floor. She took a few moments to compose herself, and as she did, she heard the echo of footsteps approaching the steel door to her cell. A rattling of keys followed, and as the heavy lock clanged loudly, she drew her knees to her chest and wrapped her arms around them.

Her eyes had adjusted to the dark over the duration of her imprisonment, and the sudden invasion of light into the room caused her to arch her head away, the brightness stinging her eyes.

She couldn't see who entered the room, but she knew she wasn't alone.

'Good morning.'

Kovac's voice was full of warmth, and he stopped a few steps away from her. As she struggled to blink through the searing pain of the light, her other senses kicked in and she could smell the fresh coffee that had followed him into the room. The welcoming aroma combined with the smell of bacon, and she forced herself to peer through the light and lock eyes on Kovac.

He looked less terrifying today. Clearly, whatever her husband had done had set the man off on a dangerous spiral which had seemingly been corrected by a good night's sleep and a shower. His wet hair had been combed neatly backwards, dropping in wet strands to the back of his neck. His strong, chiselled jaw had been freshly shaved and the clean, white T-shirt popped in the room. It clung to a body that was clearly meticulously looked after.

The man looked like a soldier.

Albeit one who had long since strayed from the idea of protecting the innocent.

In his hand, Kovac held a tray, and he quietly groaned as he bent down and placed it in front of her. Instantly, Mandy reached for the piping hot mug of coffee, and for a split second, she contemplated throwing the contents in Kovac's direction.

He seemed to read her mind.

'I wouldn't try anything stupid.' He spoke eloquently, with a strong command of the English language. 'I have kept up my end of the bargain. So let us be friendly, at least.'

'Fuck you.' Mandy scoffed, sipping the coffee and looking towards the sandwich.

'You should eat,' Kovac said, before lowering himself onto the edge of the steel chair in the centre of the room, bathing the room behind him in a thick shadow. Mandy had noticed it was bolted to the floor when she'd been shoved in the room by Luka, who had since removed all of his treasured tools of torture. Kovac looked at her and sighed. 'Your husband has caused a fair bit of trouble.'

'Jack is just doing his job,' Mandy retorted, picking up the sandwich and shovelling half of it into her ravenous mouth.

'Jack? I know him as Danny.' Kovac leant forward, his fingers interlocked. 'Do you know how many people he has hurt for me? How many bones he has broken? Does he tell you this?'

'It worked, didn't it? I mean, you believed him.'

'I did, yes. Because he looked like he enjoyed it. The fact he is a policeman surprises me greatly. Because the man is a criminal, and no badge can hide him from the things he has done.' Kovac shrugged. 'I am man enough to accept my actions. Yet he pretends to be a good man when he is no better.'

Mandy finished her sandwich and did her best to ignore Kovac's words. Yet, he'd tugged at a dangerous thread that existed in her mind. In the few years her husband had been undercover, Mandy had noticed him changing. By spending so much time in the gutter, less and less of him had been coming home. It had worried her, especially with an impressionable child relying on them both.

But now, locked in an underground cell, under the capture of a dangerous and violent criminal, she was desperate for any part of her husband to be there with her. She finished the sandwich and tried to put on a brave front.

'So what's the plan? Are you going to keep me down here like a fucking pet?'

'Not at all.' Kovac stood. 'Your husband has until eight o'clock this evening to bring himself and what I want to my door. If he is the man you say he is, then he will do it and you will be free to go.'

'And that's it? You'll let us leave.'

'As I said. *You* will be free to go. "Jack" has a few things he has to atone for.'

'Well, if I know my Jack, he'll be here. And considering he's already got away from you once, I wouldn't be so confident.'

'He is just one man.' Kovac smirked. 'And this time, I will do what is necessary myself.'

At that moment, a little hope flickered in Mandy's stomach. At no point had anyone mentioned Sam Pope. If they knew that her husband was with him, the entire house would be on high alert. But there hadn't been so much of a mention. They'd spoken to Jack since she was captured, which meant Jack was still alive. Kovac hadn't said anything about their daughter either, which meant his goons hadn't found her.

Or worse for them, they'd found Sam.

For the first time since Sanders had cowardly led her from the house with his head bowed in shame, she felt a slither of a chance that they might make it out alive.

It was unlikely.

But she needed to cling to something.

She took a final swig of her coffee and placed the mug back on the tray alongside the empty plate. Kovac nodded and lifted it before he headed towards the door.

'If your husband doesn't have the spine to show up this evening, I am sorry for what must happen,' Kovac said, with the threat of sincerity loitering with his words. 'But he has left me no other choice.'

'There is always a choice,' Mandy replied. 'But you made yours a long time ago. It's why my husband wanted to bring you down.'

'Very well. If we don't see him, then I'll lock this door one more time, only with Luka on the inside with you. And I will let him kill you in *any* way he likes. Do you understand?'

The chilling threat sent a surge of terror through Mandy's body, and despite the recent food, she felt incredibly weak. The hope of Sam Pope and her husband aligning for a brave rescue had been quickly diminished by the very real promise of her future.

'Do you understand?' Kovac repeated, his words stern and commanding a response. Mandy nodded. 'Good, now get up and follow me.'

'Where are we going?' Mandy asked anxiously, using the concrete wall to help herself to her feet. Kovac offered her a smile.

'I figured you might like to use bathroom.'

The sudden show of manners caught Mandy off-guard, but she gratefully followed Kovac as he stepped out into the corridor beneath the house. As she did, she prayed that Jack was coming for her, as if not, then she had less than half a day to live.

───────

Amy exhaled a sigh of relief as the elevator doors opened and they were greeted by no one. Although she was always the first one in, there had been the odd occasion when her receptionist, Deesha, had decided to come in early to catch-up on some of the copious admin her work created. Thankfully, this hadn't been one of those days, and she ambled as fast as her pregnancy would allow her towards the floor to ceiling glass doors that led to her side of the office. Townsend followed her; his hands clasped around his daughter who took in her surroundings with wonderment. He doubted she'd ever been in a large office block before, and even he was impressed by the clearly expensive carpets and high-quality furniture. Sam stepped out of the elevator last, shooting quick glances towards the stairwell, knowing that his training would never let him lower his guard.

It was how he was. Years of training embedded in his brainstem meaning he absorbed the details of everywhere he was, ensuring he could mentally work out an escape route if needed. After years of being an elite marksman, he'd avoided perilous situations of heavy fire thanks to that very ability.

Using her fob, Amy opened the glass door and pushed it open, leading the three of them past the embossed signage on the wall that read *'Devereux Recovery Clinic'* and out of sight of the public to a plush reception area. The curved oak reception desk was unmanned, and all the comfortable, stylish seats were empty. A black glass table was the centre piece of the room, with magazines and pamphlets neatly stacked for the perusal of waiting clients.

'This way,' Amy said, unlocking the door to her office and stepping in. The sunshine eagerly filled the room through the glass wall, and Eve dropped down from her dad's arms and rushed towards it, admiring the wonderful view that it offered. Townsend and Amy shared a smile and Sam closed the door, peaking through one last time for reassurance before it shut.

'Right, can I offer you both a drink?' Amy said, shuffling to the fancy coffee machine at the back of the office. Although she'd cut coffee out of her daily routine for the past seven months, her clients often were grateful for one.

'That would be great.' Sam smiled, and Townsend nodded in agreement. As she fumbled with the capsules and the milk, Townsend knelt beside his daughter, his arm lovingly pressed to her back as she pointed out to the world before them. Sam watched on, enjoying the clear bond the two of them had and re-emphasising why he needed to be there.

Why he needed to get involved.

Quietly, he joined Amy at the back of the office as the coffee machine kicked into action.

'It's good to see you,' she finally said. 'How's the reading going?'

'Off on and on. Mainly off nowadays.'

'You should stick at it. It's good for you.' Amy's smile turned to a forlorn grimace. 'I thought you were dead.'

'I was meant to be,' Sam confirmed.

'So, what happened?' Amy fiddled with another capsule. 'I mean, I followed in the press. They said you did some awful things. But then there were others who painted you out as a hero.'

'Which one do you believe?'

'I think it's somewhere in the middle,' Amy said clinically, stirring the first coffee before handing it to Sam. 'I mean, we spent months talking and I never once deduced that you would become a murderous vigilante. But then again, you saved mine and my husband's life, so I don't think that's a fair assumption, either. How do you see yourself?'

'Amy, I didn't come here for therapy—'

'No, you came here for help. And before I do that for you, I want to try this for you. How do you see yourself? If you had the chance to walk away from it, have the world think you're dead, but then you came back. I'm interested. How do you see yourself?'

Sam took a sip of his coffee and then looked towards Townsend. More specifically, towards Eve, whose smile was brighter than the sun that bathed the room as she looked at her dad with nothing but complete adoration.

There was a very good chance that when they left, she would never see him again, and that thought was all the reason Sam needed. He took another sip of his coffee, and then turned to Amy, who was waiting impatiently.

'A necessity.'

'Then I'm very sorry, but I don't think I can help you.'

'I'm not asking you to help me, Amy. I'm asking you to help them. That man is an undercover police officer whose boss got into bed with one of the most dangerous criminals in the country and then sold him out. Now, that criminal has his wife and I'm pretty sure will kill both of them, leaving that little girl without a family.' Sam lowered his voice. 'You, of all people, should know how dangerous a corrupt police officer can be.'

Amy grit her teeth before responding and then walked across the room to Townsend and handed him the coffee.

He gratefully accepted, and then looked on with worry as she marched back to Sam.

'What do you want from me?' Amy asked, her arms crossed above her prominent bump.

'I need you to keep her safe.' Amy began to protest, but Sam held up his hand. 'We have no one else. We can't go to the police, because they don't know she's here. Please, Amy. You're the only person I can trust with this. Whatever problem you have with what I'm going to do, don't take it out on her.'

Amy sighed.

'What are you going to do?'

Sam's jaw clenched.

'What I do.'

'Okay. Fine.' Amy waved her hands. 'But I'm doing it for her. She doesn't deserve to be caught up in your world.'

'Thank you,' Sam said softly, finishing his coffee and placing the mug back on the cabinet. 'You'll make an excellent mum, you know that?'

'Just try to keep her parents alive, okay?' Amy felt a smirk appear at the corner of her mouth. 'And maybe yourself if you have the time.'

Sam smiled and rested a hand on her shoulder. He'd walked a long and arduous path since he'd last seen her, but she'd been the catalyst for it all. Amy was a good woman, trying her best to help people, and the world decided to put her in its cross hairs. By saving her, he ultimately saved himself, as he realised that despite how much the world pushed and pushed, most people never pushed back.

That's what he was for.

To fight for those who couldn't.

To put the wrong things right.

Townsend had been betrayed by the one person he could trust, and now he could lose everything.

Eve could lose everyone.

Sam nodded his goodbye to Amy and then strode across the office, tapping Townsend on the shoulder and motioning to the door. Townsend's eyes watered, and with shaking hands, he put down his half-finished coffee and drew his daughter in close.

'I need you to be a good girl, okay?' Townsend struggled to keep his voice steady. 'My friend Amy is going to look after you today.'

'You can help by being my assistant?' Amy chimed in with a smile. 'Does that sound fun?'

'Yeah!' Eve exclaimed. She turned to her dad. 'Where are you going?'

'To go get your mummy. Then I'll be back.' He wrapped his arms around her. 'I love you, pickle.'

'I love you, too, Daddy,' Eve said, breaking all the hearts in the room. She let go of her dad and walked to Sam, beckoning him down with a finger. Sam knelt, and to his shock, she wrapped her arms around him too. Sam patted her on the back, then stepped away and headed to the door. Townsend ruffled Eve's hair and then turned to Amy, who had clearly been moved by Eve's display of affection.

'Thank you.' Townsend shrugged. 'I know this is strange but—'

'Sam explained.' Amy smiled reassuringly. 'It's fine. We'll have fun.'

'We'll be back. I promise.'

'I know.' Amy nodded in Sam's direction. 'Just listen to him, okay? He saved my life once. He might be a criminal, but there is a very clear difference between a bad man and a broken one.'

'He's not a bad man,' Townsend agreed.

'No. But he is looking to fix something that can never

216

be fixed. Some people just can't be put back together. Not fully.'

Townsend saw the sadness in Amy's eyes, and he gently reached out and rubbed her arm. Then, he turned on his heel, waved to his daughter, and dashed off after Sam, hoping his daughter didn't see the tears that were rolling down his cheeks.

CHAPTER TWENTY-FOUR

The rest of the day felt like one long migraine.

Townsend found it impossible to concentrate on anything at hand, his mind locked on the oblivious look on his daughter's face as he left her in the care of a complete stranger. From the few minutes he spent with her, Amy seemed like a responsible and caring woman, well suited to the profession she'd clearly excelled at. But as a parent, there was nothing worse than not knowing if your child was okay, and despite his long absence, Townsend had always known that Eve had Mandy by her side.

Not today.

Now, she was happily playing assistant to a woman she'd never met, fully expecting her mummy and daddy to come for her at any minute and take her home. The reality was much darker and there was a very real possibility that he'd laid eyes on his daughter for the last time.

Coupled with the pain of leaving his daughter, Townsend was fraught with worry for his wife. While Kovac often adhered to a certain code of ethics, which confused Townsend greatly considering the man's brutal empire, the man was a ruthless killer at heart.

He hadn't forged the nickname of The Man of Stone without bloodshed.

Worse was the prospect of Luka. Unhinged and untrusting, Luka had revelled in the idea of being able to kill Townsend, thrilled at the revelation that he was a rat. Their rivalry had been instant, from the moment Townsend was initiated into the group, and despite his best efforts, Townsend had never been able to convince Luka of his loyalty. Kovac had seen him as a useful soldier, whereas Luka saw him as an outsider.

And maybe even as a potential threat.

But what Luka now had was an opportunity to hit Townsend where it hurt. The man was a brutal and vile war criminal, with a shady past as being involved in more than one baseless atrocity under Kovac's regime. Now, operating as a high-functioning crime organisation, Kovac had managed to rein Luka in, but there was only so much give on the chain. And with Townsend on a timer, he had no idea what state his wife would be in by the time he got to her.

If he got to her.

Sam had taken them both to get a coffee and discuss strategy after leaving Amy's, but none of it registered with Townsend. His mind was elsewhere, struggling under the combined weight of fear and guilt.

Sam could see it, so put the discussion on hold, before taking Townsend back to the safe house. As they entered, Townsend remembered the two dead bodies that Sam had stacked in the back of the kitchen, the destruction of the living room all the evidence he needed to remember.

It brought home how real the situation was.

People had already been killed.

More were likely to follow.

And both Kovac and Luka would have him right at the top of the list.

The man who followed him into the safe house was his only shot at survival. Kovac would undoubtedly have back-up, but hopefully not enough to counter the fight that Sam would bring to their door. Townsend took a second to size Sam up, as the former soldier quietly tried to pile up the broken table into a somewhat neat pile.

For someone without any skin in the game, he was willing to put his life on the line for a family he'd just met and save a woman who he didn't love. Townsend had read the stories of Sam Pope from a few years ago, although they were always skewed by whatever political view the media outlet stood for. Either painted as a danger to the public and the fabric of our justice system, or a hero for the people, there was always one part of the story that Townsend found staggering.

That Sam Pope had never hurt an innocent person.

People had died along the way, but the only ones to have met that fate by Sam's hand were those he'd deemed necessary.

And Sam had deemed Kovac and his crew as necessary.

He'd got the guns he'd wanted and burnt an almost unrecoverable hole in Kovac's business, but now Sam was fighting for Townsend.

For Mandy.

For Eve.

Fighting so that Townsend could have the life that was cruelly taken from Sam.

Sam turned around and met Townsend's gaze and nodded.

'Right. Where are the files?'

Townsend bound up the stairs, and Sam heard the shuffling of furniture before the wrenching of floorboards. Moments later, Townsend returned with a USB stick in his hand.

'All of this for something so small.' Townsend shook his head.

'I've seen good people killed for one of these,' Sam said solemnly. 'The most powerful weapon in the world isn't a gun. It's information.'

'So, what's the plan?' Townsend asked, for once looking as vulnerable as the situation called for. Sam marched back to the car, indicating for Townsend to follow, and moments later, they were driving back towards Lowestoft. They drove past the pub where Ryan Marsh was accosted by Sam, triggering this entire series of events. Soon enough, they were outside a quaint little holiday home on one of the main roads leading down towards the quay.

Sam let himself in, indicating Townsend to follow, and then shut the door.

'Nice place,' Townsend said, his hands in his pockets.

'It's done its job,' Sam said, stomping across to the bedroom and hauling out the sports bag from under the bed. Judging by the tensing of his muscular arm, it was heavy. 'Stick the kettle on.'

Townsend obliged, scampering into the slither of a kitchen and getting to work in hunting down the required crockery. Two minutes later, he stepped back out with two cups of piping hot tea.

'Fucking hell.'

Townsend's exclamation drew a wry smile from Sam. On the table and sofa, laid out precisely, was Sam's recently acquired arsenal. Three SA80 Assault Rifles, all cleaned and ready for action, along with four Glock 17s. Multiple clips of ammunition were laid out, along with a few grenades. It was only a crumb from Kovac's table, but in Sam Pope's hands, Townsend was certain the man could bring down an entire empire with it.

Judging by the look on Sam's face, he was planning to.

Sam checked the cheap watch on his wrist, clicking the button on the top of the face and summoning a beep from it.

'We have five hours until your time is up.' Sam gratefully took his mug and sat on the chair beside the table. 'So you need to tell me everything I need to know.'

'With all these weapons, I think you have all you need.' Townsend shook his head in disbelief. 'You'll need them.'

'Kovac has guards?'

'There's usually one. The house is so secluded that it wouldn't draw attention. But yeah, he usually has one guy on the door, come rain or shine.'

'Armed.'

'Always. All of them are. Fuck, even I had a piece from time to time.'

'You ever fire it?' Townsend shook his head, and Sam sipped his tea. 'Keep it that way. Give me the layout of the place.'

'It's big. The front door leads into a balcony that overlooks the main living area. So once you're in…you're in.'

'And where would he keep Mandy?'

'Underground. He has a fortified basement made up of three rooms. An arsenal, a safe, and Luka's playroom.'

'Playroom?'

'It's where he takes people when he needs them to talk or disappear. The guy's a psycho.'

'And that's where they'll be keeping her?' Sam asked, absorbing every word.

'I'd say so.' Townsend took a sip of his drink. 'Kovac wouldn't want this mess to infiltrate his personal space. Besides, the second I show up, I'll imagine that's where they'll take me.'

'Good.'

'Good?' Townsend snapped. 'Do you have any idea what Luka is capable of?'

'It doesn't matter. I need you and Mandy out of the way when the time comes.' Sam stood and began to load the weapons. He slid the ammunition into a couple of the Glock 17s and placed them back on the table. 'Your only focus is to get to your wife, you hear me? Don't try playing the hero.'

As Sam began to load up his SA80 Assault Rifle, Townsend lifted one of the handguns, staring at it as he turned it in his grip.

'Sanders is mine,' Townsend said coldly.

'What are you planning to do, huh? Kill him?' Sam's frustration was clear, and drew a scowl from Townsend.

'He put my family at risk. He sold me out to save his skin.'

'Trust me, Jack, you pull that trigger on him and it will change you. Forever.' Sam reached forward and put his hand over the gun, intimating he wanted Townsend to hand it over. 'It will change you from a good man to a desperate one.'

Townsend stared at the weapon for a few more moments and then sighed, before allowing Sam to claim it from him. Sam nodded his approval and placed the gun in the sports bag along with the SA80, another Glock 17, and a grenade.

'So, I'm just going to walk in unarmed?'

'Exactly.' Sam pulled the zip on the bag.

'And you?'

Once the bag was closed, Sam hoisted it over his shoulder, and turned and looked at Townsend, his expression calm. It dawned on Townsend that this was Sam's world, and that gearing up to take on a dangerous criminal was as normal as going to the football. For a split second, despite depending on the man to help him get his life back, Townsend saw something in Sam that chilled him to the bone.

Sam was at ease.

Emotionless, Sam answered the question.

'I'm going to bring it down around them.'

As the sun slowly faded behind the trees and cast the mansion in an ominous shadow, Kovac agitatedly glared at his watch. It was a little after seven, and he felt a wave of fury rush through his body. Townsend was cutting it close, leaving himself less than an hour before Kovac's deadline. A man of his word, Kovac didn't want to give Luka the satisfaction of a strong-willed woman, but there would be no going back. If the big hand of his watch made it round once more, then Townsend's wife would be in for an extremely uncomfortable death.

Luka could sense it, too. As he paced the room, Kovac could almost hear the cogs in Luka's head turning, conjuring up a myriad of painful and evasive ways in which he would torture the poor woman. Judging by the twinkle in Luka's eye, he was willing for Townsend to be a coward.

To run.

To leave him to it.

But something told Kovac that wouldn't be the case. Considering Townsend had already fought off Luka and taken out two of his men, Kovac didn't have him down as a coward. Townsend was a fighter. It was an admirable quality, one that Kovac would respect, but it would make no difference. The man was an undercover cop and had seen too much. He knew too many of the intricate details of Kovac's operation and more importantly, had apparently kept extensive files on all of it.

Although Kovac was close to being in a position to

overthrow his benefactor and ascend to the throne, he wasn't quite there.

It wasn't his kingdom yet.

With an angered grunt, he turned back to the room, marching across the open room and past the seating area to pour himself another drink. On the sofa sat Sanders, pathetically limp, accepting the painful fate that awaited him. On the other sofa was one of the re-enforcements, part of the elite squadron Luka had called at Kovac's behest. Eight of Kovac's finest men had been pulled from their usual locations, told to halt their drug and gun dealings for the foreseeable while Kovac handled his business. Every single one of them had served either under Kovac or beside Luka, and all of them were large, muscular men with a ferocious blood lust and little regard for human life.

They weren't soldiers.

They were killers.

Cold. Ruthless. Needed.

Two of them were positioned outside the house, walking the perimeter of the grounds that were blocked off to the world by the high, white brick wall. Including the man who was staring a hole through Sanders, another six were present, all of them patiently waiting their orders. Sanders looked at a few of them who were casually sitting at the dining table, shuffling a deck of cards, before turning back to Kovac, who was sipping his drink, his back to the room.

'Is all this necessary?' Sanders asked, his voice trembling.

'Yes. It is.' Kovac turned with a disgusted snarl. 'Because you made it so.'

'Jack won't be any trouble.' Sanders pleaded. 'He'll just come for his wife. You don't need all these men here.'

Kovac slammed his glass down on the wide oak table

between the sofas, stepped forward, and slapped Sanders across the face with the back of his hand. The impact reopened the cut across the man's lip.

'You fool. These men are not for Jack.' Kovac grabbed Sanders by the face and held it steady. 'When this situation is handled, you will bring me to Sam Pope.'

'I-I-I don't know where he is?' Sanders begged.

'Then you will do whatever to find him. Call whoever. Someone knows something.' Kovac pushed Sanders back onto the sofa. 'Once Jack is here and his wife is home, then we'll be going hunting for that piece of shit. And I'll bring back my guns and I will also bring back his head.'

Kovac snatched up his glass and finished the last of his drink. Sanders blew out his cheeks in desperation. The task of hunting down Sam Pope was nigh on impossible, and he knew that if he couldn't deliver, then Kovac would make sure his death was as drawn out and as painful as possible. Sanders had betrayed him, tried to put himself in a position of power, and it had backfired spectacularly. Now, a good man was possibly on his way to his death, his wife unlikely to live, and when it soon became apparent that he couldn't deliver, Sanders would get what was coming to him.

Part of him wanted to stand up, smash a glass, and charge at Kovac with a broken shard, willing the trained marksmen to unload their weapons and end it all quickly.

But Sanders knew he didn't have the stomach for it.

He was a coward and would cling to whatever possibility of survival he had.

He wouldn't fight for his life. He'd just hope he could wriggle free with it.

A radio cackled.

'Car approaching gate.'

Kovac responded, ordering them to open it. A few

moments later, much to the evident disappointment of Luka, the radio confirmed what Kovac already knew.

Jack Townsend was a fighter.

And he'd come for his wife, and for his own execution.

CHAPTER TWENTY-FIVE

As the metal gate folded open, Townsend realised he was holding his breath. The sun had set on the day, welcoming in the dullness of the evening, the surrounding trees only casting more shadows across Kovac's impenetrable fortress. The lights in the vast forecourt were already on, spraying beams of light up against the glass and white stone of the house, illuminating it in the ever-increasing darkness.

Two men were standing near the front door of the house, both of them holding heavy artillery, and a clear sign that Kovac had beefed up his security.

As Townsend rolled the car through the gates and towards them, a few speckles of rain began to dot his windscreen, and as when he pulled it to a complete stop, a spring shower was well underway. Stepping out of the car, Townsend held his hands in surrender.

One of the guards had his assault rifle trained on Townsend, offering little doubt that he would happily pull the trigger.

'Easy, fellas,' Townsend said, as the other guard roughly grabbed him by the back of his jacket collar and shoved him towards the door. With the rifle still aimed straight at him, Townsend headed to the door, not reacting after another needless shove in the back. As he approached the glass, he saw another new recruit climbing the final few steps before marching to the front door to let him in. As he stepped in, he realised how much the temperature had dropped outside; Kovac's home offering a warm, welcoming hug.

And another gun shoved in his face.

'Move,' the man said coldly, his hands gripping the Glock 17 a few inches from Townsend's skull.

'Just take me to my fucking wife.'

The man motioned to the stairs before saying something in Croatian to the guard who had undoubtedly drawn the short straw and headed back out into the rain. Townsend made his way down the wide staircase, his wet footsteps squelching as he did, and the room opened up to him. The first thing he saw was Luka, stood by the doorway to the dreaded staircase across the room, his arms folded, and his eyes locked on Townsend. A sickening smirk spread across his charred face, indicating to Townsend that he planned on having an eventful evening.

They all should have been.

Five other men were in the room, three of them sitting at the main table by the back of the room, their view of the grounds undone by the darkness that had quickly ascended upon the house. Another henchman sat idly in the seating area, casually laid back on a sofa with one foot resting on his knee.

Opposite him was Sanders.

Townsend felt his fists clench with rage as his former boss couldn't even muster the courage to look at him.

To witness what he'd set into motion.

There was no pity from Townsend for the situation Sanders had found himself in. Whatever path he'd taken that had led him to Kovac's pocket, it was of his own doing. To try to pull himself out, he had put not only Townsend, but his family in danger. And for that, Townsend prayed that he would get at least a few moments alone with the man before Kovac did what he needed to do.

Kovac stepped away from the bar area and walked towards the staircase, maintaining the air of calm and control that Townsend had seen a million times.

'Jack,' Kovac said with a smile. 'It feels strange to call you that.'

Townsend stepped off the final step and showed little fear in approaching Kovac, causing a slight stir from the table behind him. The henchman in the seating area also shot his hand to his gun.

Kovac waved them down.

'Where the fuck is my wife?'

'She is fine.' Kovac spoke with assurance. 'We take good care of her. Like I said, she is not part of this.'

'Then why is she here?'

'Because I needed you here.' Kovac sighed. 'This is a big mess. I truly liked you, even if I not know your real name. Unlike some police, you have guts. You have the fight in you. It's why I believed you were one of us. Why you should have been one of us. But instead, you not only lie to me and my crew, but you keep records of it all. Evidence. You know how I feel about loyalty, Jack?'

'I was just doing my goddamn job.'

Kovac swung his hand and caught Townsend with the back of it. Unlike Sanders, Townsend didn't even flinch. His face snapped to one side, but he took the blow with minimal fuss. It drew a wry smile from Kovac and an eye roll from a slightly envious Luka.

'You just prove my point.' Kovac turned to Sanders. 'You. Do you have anything to say to this man?'

All eyes fell on Sanders, who begged for the floor to

open up a gateway to hell for him to roll in to. Instead, he looked at the henchman sitting opposite who indicated to his gun, making it clear that Sanders needed to respond. With a pathetic groan, Sanders got to his feet and trudged towards the man he'd betrayed, his head down. As he began to speak, he looked at Townsend with tears in his eyes.

'Jack, I'm so sorr—'

Townsend rocked Sanders with a thunderous right hook, sending him spiralling to the sofa, with blood gushing from his now broken nose. Instantly, the henchmen left their seats, their hands hovering by their weapons. Townsend raised his hands in surrender, and Kovac nodded in approval.

'I guess that was fair.' Kovac's grin quickly faded. 'Now, give me my files.'

'I want assurances,' Townsend said with as much conviction as he can muster. 'I want proof my wife is okay, and I want her out of her before I hand them over.'

'You do not trust me?' Kovac sounded offended.

'Not when it comes to my wife. I don't fucking trust anyone in this room.'

'Unfortunately, you will need to take me at my word—'

'Then I ain't giving you shit….' From Townsend's left, a hammer-like fist drove into his cheek, rocking his entire jawbone, and sent him hurtling to the floor. Luka shook the impact from his knuckles and then followed it up with a nasty kick to Townsend's already fragile ribs. Kovac watched on, emotionless.

Made of stone.

'The files, Jack.'

As Luka held Townsend down, one of the other henchmen rooted through his pockets before pulling a USB stick from the inside of his jacket pocket. The man handed it to Kovac, who briskly turned and strode to his

231

laptop. A few minutes later, he nodded to Luka, who hauled a woozy Townsend to his feet.

'You have held up your end of the bargain,' Kovac stated coldly. 'Now I will hold up mine. Luka, take him to his wife.'

'With pleasure.' Luka grinned as he pulled Townsend's hands behind his back, and for the second time in two days, he bound them with cable ties. As Townsend was led from the room, he locked eyes on Sanders once more, the man refusing to look at him. They both knew that Kovac had no intention of anyone but Luka coming back upstairs, and Sanders refused to even acknowledge him. As Luka and Townsend disappeared into the underground stairwell, Sanders let out a deep sigh of regret.

Kovac didn't take long to pile on the agony.

'The blood of that family is on your hands.'

Feeling helpless, Sanders wondered how terrified Townsend must have been. Little did he, nor Kovac, nor anyone else in that house know, that up until a half mile from Kovac's premises, he wasn't the only man in the car.

———

'Keep fucking walking.'

Luka tried, but failed, to hide the excitement in his voice as he followed Townsend down the concrete steps to the corridor that ran underneath Kovac's home. With Townsend's hands bound behind his back and walking closer and closer to his death, Luka felt a sense of vindication with every passing moment. Ever since the moment Kovac had welcomed 'Danny' into their operation, Luka had been sceptical. There had been wild theories that he was envious of the newcomer, especially as Kovac trusted him with responsibilities that had usually been held for him. But Luka knew where his loyalties lay.

He'd been alongside Kovac in the BSD, following every command and spilling blood for the man. Never had Luka questioned his position within Kovac's operation nor his mind. His loyalty was something Luka had prided himself on, and for every person he'd strapped to the chair and taken apart, he knew he would do it again at the first request. Kovac had financed and engineered Luka and his sister's arrival in the United Kingdom, setting them up with prosperous jobs that would lead them to a better life. After mercilessly carrying out orders for eight years in the BSD, Luka was thrilled to enjoy the finer things in life that Kovac had offered.

He owed Kovac more than his loyalty. For that, he owed Kovac his life.

Which is why, as he watched Townsend reach the bottom of the staircase, he knew that he'd always been right to trust his gut. That he'd been proved correct in his assessment that he wasn't to be trusted.

It was never a case of jealousy. Just protection.

Protection for everything he'd helped Kovac build and the bizarre blindside his boss seemed to have when it came to this man.

This arrogant, foolish man who thought he could take them down from the inside.

Four steps from the bottom of the staircase, Luka lunged his foot forward, the sole of his boot shunting viciously into the base of Townsend's spine, sending him hurtling forward. With his hands strapped behind him, Townsend tried his best to take the brunt of the fall on his side, hitting the edge of the steps before sprawling forward onto the unforgiving concrete below.

Blood seeped from a few scrapes on his arms, and he was certain he had bruised, possibly even fractured a bone in his forearm. But to Luka's frustration, he gave him no indication of the pain. Instead, Townsend engaged his core, pushed himself to his knees, and stared back at Luka who had followed him down to the final step.

'Just take me to my wife, you prick.'

Enraged, Luka swung another boot towards Townsend, burying it firmly in his stomach. Without his hands to protect him, Townsend absorbed the blow, the impact causing him to heave for air as it was driven from his body. After a few panicked gasps, he composed and then spat a dollop of blood on the floor before them.

'Let me take you to her.'

Luka chuckled, hoisting Townsend up roughly by his jacket and shoving him past the armoury and the safe until they arrived at Luka's favourite door of the house.

Townsend knew what went on in this room, and as Luka opened the door, he squinted, fearing he would see a blood bath.

All he saw was Mandy.

Strapped into the chair, but without so much as a mark on her.

'Jack!' she exclaimed with delight.

'Babe…' Townsend burst forward, oblivious to the foot that Luka slipped between his own feet. Beaten by his own momentum, Townsend toppled into the room, hitting the floor hard and rattling his brain inside his skull. Mandy gasped in horror, and Luka chuckled as he stepped into the room and then ominously pushed the door closed.

'Jack…are you okay?' Mandy struggled against her restraints to no avail. Townsend stirred slightly, groaning in pain as Luka sized him up. 'Leave him alone.'

Despite Mandy's pleas, Luka charged forward and drilled another sickening boot into Townsend's ribs, lifting him off the floor and sending him clattering into the metal table of utensils. During the day, after Mandy had been treated to a basic lunch, Luka had decided to return to the room. As much as it pained him to resist, he refused to hurt the woman, but he forcibly put her in the chair. He'd then wheeled in his table of torturous tools and had left Mandy in the dark to stew over her potential future.

Now, with his wife watching on helplessly, Luka was basking in the idea of beating Townsend to death.

Coughing out another dribble of blood, Townsend refused to stay down, pushing himself to his knees once more and turning to face Luka.

'You have the files. You have me,' he said through sharp breaths. 'Let her go.'

'I'm not leaving you,' Mandy remonstrated.

'Just go.'

'I will let her go.' Luka launched forward, hoisted Townsend up by his shoulder and then drove his skull viciously into Townsend's face. The sound was sickening, and to follow it up, Luka then hurled Townsend towards the wall, knowing the man had nothing to break the impact. He tried to turn his body, but he collided with the unforgiving brick cheek and shoulder first. Luka chuckled as Townsend slid down the wall, trying his best to catch his breath.

'Please stop,' Mandy begged, and Luka leapt towards her, grabbing a handful of her hair and pulling her head back. With his face a mere inch from hers, he smiled at the fear in her eyes.

'Your husband is a rat.' Luka spat, before turning back to Townsend, who valiantly tried to pull himself to his feet. 'Once I kill you, Danny. Then your wife...maybe I show her what a real man is.'

Despite knowing he was being beaten to death, Townsend foolishly lunged towards Luka, trying to use his bodyweight to cause any sort of blow. Luka moved before drilling him with a nasty right hook that sent Townsend sprawling in front of his wife, blood dripping from his lip and his eyebrow. He looked up at her, offering her a hopeful smile that she couldn't see through the tears.

Luka, basking in his dominance, began to shuffle through the items on his table, deciding which one to use on Townsend. Behind him, he could hear the pained groans of Townsend, along with the terrified weeping of his wife.

It was music to his ears.

Music that was abruptly halted by a thunderous explosion that caused the entire room to shake, sending Luka and Townsend to the floor as the power went out and the room was plunged into darkness.

CHAPTER TWENTY-SIX

'This will do.'

Sam held up his hand, and Townsend pulled the car to a stop.

'Really? There's still like a half mile till we get there?'

'I can make that on foot,' Sam said, throwing the car door open. He was wearing a black T-shirt, black trousers, and black boots. Smeared across his face in thick, threatening stripes was dark shoe polish. Townsend had mockingly called him Action Man when he'd done it, but Sam had quickly cut him down with a remark about saving his life.

It was true.

Sam was Townsend's only hope of walking out alive.

As Sam reached into the back of the car and hauled out his sports bag, Townsend leant across the chair to speak to him.

'I'll drive slow to give you enough time to get into position.'

Sam pulled out one of the Glock 17 handguns and slid it into the back of his jeans and nodded. The rain had already begun to cause his T-shirt to cling to his impressive frame, and the sleeves looked fit to burst as he swung the bag full of weapons over his shoulder.

'You just do as we discussed. Get downstairs, get to your wife, and stay down.' Sam reached in and extended his hand. 'I'll do my best to get you out.'

Townsend took Sam's hand and shook it.

'Thank you, Sam. For everything.'

'Don't thank me yet.' Sam joked and Townsend smiled. It eased the tension, but the young man frowned as he stared out through the wet windscreen. Sam dipped his head into the car. 'Just keep your daughter in your mind.'

'I always do.'

'Well then, fight for her. We all have to fight for something, otherwise we die for nothing.' Sam slapped the roof of the car to emphasise his point. 'So fight for her.'

Townsend nodded, his faith seemingly restored, and as he took a deep breath, he slid the car into first and pulled away, leaving Sam stood among the trees. As the rain increased its downpour, Sam turned and rushed into the trees, following the similar direction to the road, but veering off slightly. With the extra weight on his back, he pushed through his energy reserves, grateful for the extra time he'd put into the gym ever since he'd returned from America. Although he'd never had any intention of returning to the life he had, it had kept him away from the bottle and the inevitable spiral into self-hatred that would only end one way.

There was a lot of blood on his hands, and a number of faces of those he'd killed locked in his memory. The last thing he needed was to drunkenly follow them down the pathway that would inevitably lead to his son.

Just as he'd told Townsend, Sam knew he had to find something to fight for. Over a decade ago, under heavy fire in the Amazon rain forest, his commanding officer, Vargas, moments before he sacrificed himself for Sam's escape, asked Sam what he'd fought for.

It was his son.

It had always been his son.

And even though Jamie had been dead for years, Sam still knew that in his own way, he was honouring his memory every time he put a bad guy down. The justice system had failed Jamie, allowing a drunk driver to end a five-year-old's life but to be released less than two years later.

The further Sam peeled back the layers of the system put in place to protect the people, the more he saw how it stepped on them. How it allowed those in power to get greedy, and those who broke it to profit. The same thing had happened to Townsend.

A good man, trying to uphold the same law that had stabbed him in the back. That could cost him his family.

Someone had to fight for him.

Fight to put that wrong right.

As Sam raced through the woods, he soon saw the high, white brick wall that undoubtedly hid Kovac's home. Having reached the perimeter, Sam carefully scaled the wall, digging his rough, dangerous fingers into the ridges of the brickwork and managing to haul himself up a few feet. With his other hand, he clasped the top of the wall, and impressed himself with his ability to pull himself and a bag of weapons up with minimal fuss. As he peered over the top, he could see that he was still heavily shielded by the woodlands, but through the gaps in the trees, he could see the bright lights of the house, and the spacious fore-court where Townsend had just arrived.

Two men had come to greet him, one even going as far as aiming an assault rifle directly at the unarmed man.

Seeing the man at gunpoint put in the perspective just how out of his depth Townsend was, and Sam knew he needed to act fast. He dropped down from the wall as silently as he could and unzipped his bag. Expertly, he slung the SA80 Assault Rifle over his shoulder; the strap sticking to his wet shirt. He took the two grenades from the bag and hooked them onto his belt loop before removing the final Glock 17.

Armed and loaded, Sam briskly ran through the woods, circling the house until he could see head-on through the door from his vantage point. Townsend was being led down the stairs, which meant he was inside. Having discussed their plan on the journey in, Sam had made it clear to Townsend that he needed to get underground to his wife. Handing over the documents and demanding to see Mandy was the only way to do that as efficiently as possible, and Sam moved through the trees to change his vantage point. He placed his foot on a low branch of one of the trees and hoisted himself up higher, clambering a few more feet until he could see just over the entrance way balcony. Just as Townsend had laid out, there was a vast, open room, but Sam could only see the back portion of it.

He clocked the three men sat at the table, all of them carrying the threat of elite soldiers.

There were another two patrolling the outside, with one of them shielding himself from the rain as he lit a cigarette.

Both men were holding rifles similar to his own, and Sam cursed silently to himself. Kovac had beefed up his security, no doubt in an effort to either push back against Sam or to send both Townsend and Sanders a message.

Kovac was the one with the power.

And Sam could see, through the weaponry and re-enforcements, that he intended to keep it.

Then he saw Townsend.

Clearly rattled by what Sam could only assume was a

strike, he was being shoved towards a doorway on the far wall, his hands bound behind his back and being closely followed by Luka. Sam recognised Kovac's right-hand man, who seemed more than eager as they disappeared through the wall and out of sight.

It was where Townsend had told him the stairwell was, which meant they were heading underground to Mandy.

Which meant the clock was ticking.

Sam lowered himself from the branch and then dropped the remaining foot, his boots planting firmly on the wet mud beneath. Peering through the woodland, he watched as the two guards patrolled the area, their hands gripping their rifles with the intent to fire. Having only expected a few guns pointed in his direction, opening fire would eliminate his element of surprise, but more alarmingly, it would call the cavalry.

And Sam didn't know how many men that would comprise.

As the two guards split off in opposite directions, Sam's eyes fell upon the lavish Range Rover parked on the right-hand side of the house. It was similar to the one he'd torched two nights before, and Sam's hand fell to his belt. Carefully, he unclipped one of the grenades from the loop and then, keeping to the trees, he circled round the house until he was opposite the vehicle. One of the guards was out of sight, while the other was casually walking towards the blast radius.

Sam took a breath.

He pulled the pin.

Then he rolled it towards the car. The grenade rolled along the gravel at speed; the metal clattering against the gravel and drawing the attention of the guard.

The man's eyes widened in fear and just as he turned to scream for support, a mighty explosion ripped out from under the car. The flames erupted beneath, lifting the car clean off the floor and sending it clattering into the side of the house, rocking its entire foundation. The glass windows blew out, spraying tiny shards into the courtyard, and the ferocious blast sent the guard spiralling backwards. An alarm began to ring from somewhere, and Sam could already hear the footsteps crunching across the gravel as the other guard came racing towards the mayhem.

As the man rushed towards his fallen comrade, Sam stepped out, the SA80 tight against his shoulder and his impeccable eye locked to the sight.

As the rain tried its best to battle the flames that flickered from the shell of the vehicle, Sam squeezed the trigger, sending a bullet ripping through the side of the guard's head and sending him down to the gravel. Instinctively, he lowered his sight to the man caught in the explosion and put him out of his misery with a bullet of his own.

Both men were down, but Sam turned his attention to the glass door, where he could already see the commotion of more men rushing up the stairs. Sam dropped to one knee, steadied his aim, and absorbed the full impact of the rifle as he sent another bullet out into the world with pinpoint precision.

The bullet whizzed through the air, shattering the glass of the front door, and embedding itself in the neck of the armed man who was reaching for the handle. Blood sprayed up the other glass door as the man grasped at his throat, stumbling backwards until he collided with the edge of the balcony and fell from view.

Sam could hear the fury within the house, and he fired a few more shots towards the stairwell, where an unknown number of soldiers were ready to pounce. Buying himself enough time, Sam pulled the pin on the second grenade, hoped that Townsend was locked firmly in a steel tomb under ground and then he hurled it through the shattered door.

The panicked screams of 'GRENADE' followed, before another earth rocking explosion erupted, blowing out the rest of the glass panels and extracting cries of agony from within the house. Keeping his body low, Sam approached the shattered remnants of the door and stepped over the threshold, his boot crunching down on the broken shards underfoot. He unhooked the rifle strap from his body to afford himself a better range of movement, and he scanned the entrance way as he entered. Plumes of smoke had begun to rise within the building, the explosion no doubt causing a few fires to spark to life and would most likely spread.

The clock was ticking.

With his vision skewed partially by the smoke, Sam stepped carefully towards the balcony, peering over to the destruction below. What had once been a pristine seating area had been obliterated, with the charred remains of two upturned sofas smouldering in the middle of the room. Shattered glass and wooden shards littered the floor, and on the far side, an oak table had been blown to smithereens, with some embers of it already ablaze.

Among the wreckage, Sam counted six bodies. One of them was clearly dead, the grenade blowing a large chunk out of the man's torso, and he laid motionless among the debris. The others were all in varying states of pain, groaning and slowly trying to collect themselves.

Sam raised his rifle and as he drew one of them in his sights, he was angered by the thick smoke that robbed him of his clarity.

Before he could pull the trigger, a boot crunched on the glass beside him and Sam turned, tried to whip the rifle around with him, but a clubbing blow to the side of the rifle sent it sprawling from his hands. The rifle clattered over the balcony and landed in the wreckage below. Sam raised his arms to absorb the next blow as the frenzied attacker unloaded with a barrage of ferocious fists. The man had been on the stairwell when the grenade had exploded, sending him spiralling down a few concrete steps that had resulted in a few nasty gashes down the side of his head.

Beyond that, the man showed no signs of pain, and through the smoke, Sam could see the cold, calculating eyes of a man who was trained to kill. The man ploughed a left hook into Sam's ribs and then managed to wrap one of his hands around Sam's neck. With all his might, he tried to push Sam back against the rickety barrier of the balcony. Sam planted his foot, shifting his body weight to keep himself steady and with his right hand he managed to grip the man's skull and pushed his thumb into the man's eye socket. As the pressure increased, the man howled in agony, and before Sam could blind him, he relinquished his hold, giving Sam the opportunity he needed.

Driving a solid tape kick into the man's chest, Sam sent the man back to the top of the stairwell, smoothly removed one of the Glocks from the back of his waist band, drew it up and pulled the trigger.

The gunshot echoed loudly, and the man flew backwards down the staircase, the bullet blowing a spray of blood from the back of his skull as he tumbled down the steps.

He was dead before he hit the bottom.

Sam followed the man, stepping down each step carefully, his arms outstretched, his finger itchy. Through the thickening smoke, he saw another figure stumble forward, hands wrapped around an assault rifle.

Sam eliminated him efficiently with two shots to the chest. As he stepped off the final step, Sam squinted to survey the scene, and he saw another henchman hauling himself up, blood smeared across his face. Dazed, the man stumbled out from under the broken dining table, his hands loosely gripping his rifle.

Sam wouldn't afford him the opportunity to use it, and he sent a bullet through the man's skull with expert precision.

Three down.

The smoke was becoming a problem, and Sam kept low, taking measured breaths as he carefully plotted his way through the room. Behind him, a heavy cough averted his attention, and he saw another man hunched over, trying his best to clear his lungs of the damaging smoke. Sam spun, dropped to one knee, and although the man desperately tried to raise his rifle, Sam hit him with two to the chest that sent him straight back to the ground. In the far side of the room, the oak table had set the venetian blinds ablaze, only exacerbating the fire and daring it to the consume the entire building. Sam quickened his pace, scanning from side to side as he went, hoping to find Kovac with the very real intention to put a bullet between the man's eyes.

A bullet collided with the remains of the sofa behind Sam, and instinctively, Sam dived forward, rolling away from his position before rising to one knee and drawing his weapon.

He aimed it in the direction of the bullet, and he clocked the henchman who was limping horribly, and had blood pumping from a wooden shard that hung from his stomach. The man feebly tried to raise his gun again, but Sam beat him to the punch, sending a single bullet through the smoke and snapping the man's head back as it obliterated his forehead.

The man dropped down dead, the back of his head oozing blood and brain.

It wasn't Kovac.

As Sam approached the door to the stairwell, he turned

back to the room, surveying it one more time with his finger on the trigger. As he did, he saw the jacket whizz past his eyes as it was brought down over his head, and as it was pulled tight around his throat, Sam managed to get his fingers behind it. The final henchman had taken refuge in the stairwell, avoiding the impact of the blast, and waited patiently for the shooting to stop. With his gun somewhere among the fire, the man had removed his jacket, pulled it tight, and now had it wrapped around Sam's throat.

'Die you motherfucker,' the man roared as Sam stumbled forward back into the room, his hand pressed against his neck as he tried desperately to stay alive. The man twisted the jacket, locking it tightly to the back of Sam's neck, and wrenched harder. The pressure on his neck, combined with the smoke, started to cause Sam to fade and with his energy seeping from him he dropped forward and pulled the jacket with him, flipping the man over his shoulder and both of them clattered to the floor. As they both scrambled to their feet, Sam noticed another figure limping up the stairwell to freedom, clambering over the body of the man Sam had left at the bottom. Sam went for the final gun in his waistband to stop, who he assumed was Kovac, from making a break for it, but as he held it up, a boot sent it flying from his hand and it clattered somewhere out of sight. The final henchman then sent another boot at Sam, who deflected it with his forearm, sending the man off balance. Sam stood, raised his fists, and then ducked as the man wildly threw one of his own. Sam responded with a right to the man's kidneys, followed by a hard uppercut that sent the man stumbling back. On the far side of the room, the blinds collapsed from their fixtures, sending another wave of fire across the room and ignited another piece of furniture.

The place was burning to the ground, and Sam needed to get to Jack and his wife.

The man roared with anger as he charged at Sam, and despite driving an elbow down into the man's spine, the man drove his shoulder into Sam's midsection and took both of them off the floor and into a pile of decimated furniture. A sharp piece of wood sliced Sam's right bicep, the nasty gash immediately dripping blood. Sam got to his feet first, and as the man rose, Sam stamped forward, driving his foot into the man's knee and knocking him off balance. As he dropped to one knee, Sam slapped his hand against the man's head and drove it to the side, impaling it on the broken leg of a table. The man's eyes widened as the wood penetrated his skull, and Sam stumbled back, leaving the man to his final few seconds before he fell limp.

Coughing and spluttering, Sam covered his mouth and nose with his T-shirt, squatted as low as he could and then hurried towards the stairwell, cursing the fact that he'd lost his guns.

But he was running out of time, and as he rushed down the stairs to find Townsend and Mandy, he hoped that their time hadn't run out already.

CHAPTER TWENTY-SEVEN

Sanders didn't even realise what was happening when the grenade went off, the explosion causing the entire room to erupt in a devastating avalanche of fire and broken glass. By the time he'd come too, he had been blown ten feet across the room, finding himself pinned by one of the overturned sofas. The distinct smell of burning filled his nostrils, along with the thick, dark smoke that signalled it was time to leave. But his body was too weak to move and, as he feebly attempted to push himself up, he collapsed forward on his chest once more.

Through the high-pitched squeal that had set up camp in his ear, he grit his teeth, trying to regain his composure. Through the interference, he could hear the groans of pain from the other men, all of them likely just as rattled by the explosion.

Or even worse.

After a few moments, clarity began to settle in, and he could see that his knuckles were bleeding, surrounded by darkened skin. Everything was sensitive to the touch, and he soon realised it was a minor miracle he was alive.

Then a gunshot reminded him that it might not be for long.

The blast of the handgun rang out, swiftly followed by the sound of a heavy body crumpling down the stairs. Sanders tried once again to push himself up, and this time, he managed to slide his ankle free. He could already feel the agony racing through his nervous system to his brain, telling him that there had been some serious damage to it. Somewhere in the room behind him, he heard the sound of someone scrambling to their feet, only for two more gunshots to echo loudly.

Someone was executing Kovac's men.

Sanders finally pieced it together.

It was Sam Pope.

Suddenly, the reason for Townsend arriving on his own and not in the company of Kovac's men became clear and despite the spreading fire, Sanders felt terrified by the more dangerous element in the room.

Another gunshot rang out.

Another body hit the floor.

Sam was systematically killing anything that moved. With his whole body shaking, Sanders lowered himself back to the floor, hoping that the debris and thickening smoke would provide him with enough cover. On the other side of the room, someone coughed, giving away their position, and Sam duly obliged them with two bullets.

Kovac's army was being depleted and Sanders arched his head up slightly, estimating how many steps it was to the stairs. If he kept low, and stepped as quietly as possible, he could make a break for it.

Leave everyone else to die and finally be free of the whole situation.

A bullet exploded from the opposite side of the room, clearly missing Sam before burying itself in the sofa a foot above Sanders' prone body. His entire body tightened with fear, and through the smoke, he saw the silhouette of Sam dive expertly to a new position, rise on one knee, and send a deadly bullet back from whence the first one came.

This one was accompanied by the sickening sound of a skull exploding, followed by the hard collision of a dead body on the stone floor.

Just then Sanders noticed movement near the stairwell, and sure enough, clambering slowly through the wreckage, was Slaven Kovac. His hair was wet with blood, and his entire forehead wore it like face paint. His arms were shaking as he tried to pull himself up using the metal frame of the shattered glass handrail, and Sanders knew the man was weak.

Weaker than he'd ever seen.

Weak enough for Sanders to get out.

From the stairwell where Luka had long since disappeared with Townsend, Sanders could hear the beginning of a struggled, with one of Kovac's men angrily proclaiming death upon Sam. The two men stumbled back into the room, and as they both hit the floor, Sanders pushed himself to his feet and buckled forward immediately. His ankle gave way, and without the ability to put any pressure on it, he hobbled as quickly as he could to the stairwell, where Kovac had managed to pull himself to his feet.

A few feet behind him, a pile of debris had ignited, with the flames crackling through the rubble and growing by the second. The smoke provided Sanders with enough cover, and as he approached the stairs, he took his shot.

Catching Kovac by surprise, Sanders threw his entire bodyweight into the shove, colliding with the weakened man and sending him spiralling backwards.

The last Sanders would see of Kovac was him tumbling backwards over the flames, disappearing into a fiery unknown.

Sanders didn't look back. Despite the leash the man had kept him on for years, he didn't have time to watch the man burn to death as much as he wanted to. Somewhere in the room, Sam and the final guard were fighting to the death, but the smoke made it impossible to see.

It was making it almost impossible to breathe, and with excruciating steps, Sanders managed to haul himself through the pain and the smoke until he collapsed through the shattered front door and onto the gravel outside.

His hands were sliced by the broken glass, and his ankle was most likely fractured.

But the rain washed over him, stripping him of the soot and the blood, and most importantly, the fear.

He was free from Kovac.

Taking lungfuls of fresh, brisk spring air, Sanders could feel the tears streaming down his cheeks, allowing them to camouflage with the rain and be lost forever.

It was time for him to do the same thing.

But first, he pulled his phone from his inside jacket pocket and smiled to the heavens that it wasn't damaged. As the operator connected his call to the police, Sanders finally saw the light at the end of the tunnel.

———

Townsend could hear the muffled shrieks of his wife, and as he slowly came to, the words immediately snapped into clarity.

'Jack! Jack, hurry!'

Pushing himself up onto his knees, he shook the aching in his temples and scanned the room, the blurriness slowly dissipating. His wife was still strapped to the chair, the explosion not doing enough to pull that from its fixings. A few feet to her right, Luka was lying motionless, a trickle of blood dripping from his eyebrow and onto the floor. Mandy continued yelling.

'He hit his head on the edge of the chair. Come on, get up!'

Townsend grit his teeth at her command, and he shuffled along on his knees to the overturned metal table, which had been thrown recklessly across the room by the explosion. Surrounding it, a collection of Luka's disgusting torture implements were scattered, and Townsend ignored all the agonising pain in his body as he awkwardly leant at an angle. With his hands still bound behind his back, he frantically wriggled his fingers against the floor, trying his best to lift the dangerously sharp scalpel that was at his fingertips.

The emergency lighting in the room had kicked in, offering a dull, yellow glow, but it was enough. Outside the room, the worrying stench of burning began to filter through the crack of the door, and Townsend knew it was only a matter of time before the smoke followed.

They needed to get out, or they would surely suffocate.

Gunshots boomed somewhere above them, and Mandy shrieked with fear upon each one, terrified by the unknown war above.

Townsend knew what was going on. Sam was staying true to his word and was laying siege to Kovac and his men in a brave attempt to get Townsend and his wife to safety. It was a selfless act, one which put Sam in unthinkable danger, but there was a calmness to the man that gave Townsend a shred of hope.

Kovac was known as The Man of Stone, but even the hardest rock could break under the right amount of pressure. And judging by the cacophony of gunshots that were rippling through the house, Townsend knew Sam was doing his best to apply it. To his wife's delight, Townsend scooped up the scalpel, and with an anguished groan and blood dripping down his face, he scrambled towards her, clutching the blade for dear life. Carefully, he dipped down so she could retrieve it with her own bound hand, although her restraints offered her slightly more wriggle room. As he turned around, he noticed that Luka was beginning to stir.

'Get a move on, babe,' Townsend encouraged, as Mandy began to slash at the cable tie with the blade. Luka pushed himself to his knees, dabbing at the bloodied gash on his head before he began to frantically look around the room. He saw the overturned table, the fallen instruments and then his eyes locked on Townsend.

They narrowed.

This would be to the death. Townsend knew it as well.

'You…' Luka began, pushing himself to his feet. 'It's time for you to die.'

Luka lunged at Townsend.

Mandy sliced through the plastic and Townsend's hands snapped free, and catching Luka by surprise, he rocked the ex-soldier with a vicious right hook, sending him sprawling to the side. Although Townsend hadn't been trained in the Croatian Special Forces, he'd grown up on the mean streets of Liverpool, and his boxing record during his teen days and early years in the Merseyside Police gave him a fighting chance.

Luka steadied himself, placed a hand to his jaw and looked almost impressed as he spat a dollop of blood to the ground. A trickle of smoke began to trickle underneath the steel door as the fire within the house grew and as Luka stepped towards Townsend, he sprung with incredible speed and tackled Townsend to the ground. Both men hit the concrete and Luka maintained his position on top, viciously driving his elbow down the as much venom as he could. He connected once, splitting open Townsend's other eyebrow, before the police officer was able to pull his arms up, absorbing each dangerous blow with his arms.

Behind both men, Mandy had managed to turn the scalpel around in her hand so it was facing down, and by pulling the restraint up as far as she could, she was able to bring the blade to the leather strap holding her in place. With her movement limited, she was still able to begin sawing her way through, although she had to fight against her eagerness to go too fast.

If she dropped the scalpel, it was all over.

'Give it up,' Luka shouted, as he drove his fist into Townsend's ribs, driving all the air out of his lungs and pulling his hands from his face. The window of opportunity was seized upon by Luka, who drove another powerful fist into Townsend's face, and causing his head to crack against the concrete.

Consciousness threatened to leave him, and with the smoke quickly filling the room, he gasped for air.

That was quickly cut off by Luka's powerful hands, as his murderous fingers clasped around Townsend's throat, and he squeezed. The pressure on Townsend's jugular was intense, and his eyes bulged in panic as he realised he was moments from death. Luka returned the stare, a devilish excitement sparkling in his eyes as he choked the life from the man he despised. Townsend tried to throw a few fists upwards, anything to try to survive, but they lacked any real power. Nothing to stop Luka.

Behind the hulking man, Townsend could hear his wife calling to him.

'Fight, Jack. Fight for Eve!'

Luka turned his head, looking back at Mandy, who steadied her hands to not arouse suspicion.

'When he is dead, I am going to show you what a real man is.' Luka snarled, turning back to Townsend. 'You hear that, Danny. You fucking rat. Your wife will beg for death when I am finished…'

Luka's brief lapse in concentration meant he hadn't

seen Townsend's hand grip the handle of the meat tenderiser that had fallen among the mess. With his final push of strength, Townsend swung it upward with all his might, drilling Luka in the temple with a sharp, grated edge.

The thud was sickening, and as Luka rocked backwards, Townsend gasped for air as soon as he relinquished his grip. Rolling onto his front, Townsend tried his best to keep his head low to avoid the smoke, and he drew in a few deep breaths. He kept his grip on the metal hammer, noticing the blood and skin that were stuck to the face of it, and he pushed himself up, ready to fight for his family.

Luka was on his knees, his hand pressed to the destroyed cheek, a relentless flow of blood flooding through his fingertips. He turned back to Townsend, who stood over him with the hammer, and for the first time in his life, he backed away.

He ambled backwards on his knees, his other hand held out in a desperate plea for mercy.

He didn't realise he was by the chair.

With her free hand, Mandy drove the scalpel with as much power and fury as she could muster, and it embedded deep into the side of Luka's neck. She angrily ripped it out, flicking a spray of blood across the room and Luka fell backward, his hands pressed to the hole in his throat, and he immediately began to choke. Townsend watched him for a few moments, meeting the man's desperate gaze before turning to his wife and condemning Luka to a slow and painful death.

'You look like shit,' Mandy joked, as she handed her husband the scalpel.

'I feel like it.'

They both forced a smile as Townsend cut through the rest of her restraints, before she hooked his arm over her shoulders and they both moved to the door as quickly as they could. As they approached, it flew open, and in stepped Sam. Weapon less, bloodied, and covered in soot, it looked like he'd been through the wars, and he looked at them both with a frown. He then saw the twitching body of Luka, who was entering the final few breaths of his life, and Sam nodded with approval.

'Good timing.' Townsend smirked.

'Let's get you guys out of here,' Sam commanded, ushering Mandy out of the way to support Townsend. 'Keep as low as you can and follow me.'

Townsend ignored any pain that shot through his body as Sam hauled him back up the stairs. The heat of the fire and thick smoke welcoming them to the war zone. Through the limited visibility, Townsend could see the destruction of Kovac's life, and the prone bodies of his men.

Sam had gone to war.

Just as he'd promised.

Mandy followed, her T-shirt over her face, and she tried her best to keep her eyes squarely on Sam and her husband, not wanting to commit any of the horrors to her memory. As they approached the stairs, a few rumbles emanated from below the floor. The fire had spread downstairs, no doubt making its way into the armoury and destroying the cabinets full of weapons.

All the money.

All the drugs.

All of it would be destroyed.

In a lonely hole in the ground where he'd tortured so many, Luka's final few moments would be spent in agony as the fire engulfed the room.

It was over.

As they scrambled over the final step and onto the balcony overlooking the chaos, the only thing they could see was the thick smoke and a few flickers of orange behind it. Sam relinquished his hold on Townsend and allowed Mandy the honour of walking him out of the house, the two of them safe and ready to get back to their daughter.

As Sam went to follow them, Kovac burst through the smoke and charged at him. Sam tried to move, but Kovac drove his shoulder into his stomach and kept on running.

Townsend and Mandy screamed in terror as Sam and Kovac fell over the balcony and plunged into the fiery pit below.

CHAPTER TWENTY-EIGHT

As Sam began to stir, a blinding light welcomed him, and he lifted his hand to shield his eyes. The humidity was stifling and as he pushed himself to a seated position, he looked around in complete confusion. The last thing he remembered was falling down towards a grisly end, and now, having miraculously survived, he had no clue where he was.

The run-down shack was thick with dust, and he sat up completely on the uncomfortable bed that he'd been laid up on. His body was aching, and somewhere in the echoes of his mind he felt like he'd been there before. With his head heavy from the fall, he swung his legs over the side of the bed and planted his feet on the dusty concrete.

Everything ached.

His mind was fighting through the throbbing pain, trying its best to remind him that he'd been in a mansion, putting down criminals before tumbling to a fiery demise.

But here he was.

In an old, dusty shack that someone had once called home.

A place he'd been but couldn't decipher when or where.

As he looked at the contents of the side table, he found a half-empty cup of water and a bloodied army uniform.

Was it his?

A scuttling of feet in the doorway caused him to turn sharply, and he made out the outline of a young child running away from him, giggling as he went.

'Hey,' Sam called out, to no avail. As quickly as he could, Sam limped towards the doorway, looking down at his body as he did. He was wearing a black T-shirt, jeans, and boots, and was soaked through. As if he'd been in a torrential downpour.

But once he stepped outside the shack, the relentless heat of the Middle East welcomed him, mocking his idea that it had even been raining.

Where was he?

The clink of metal hitting stone drew his attention to behind the shack, and as he rounded the modest building, he saw a man he knew, driving a shovel into the dead earth in a lame attempt to farm. He shook his head.

He'd seen this scene before, but then, there had been a fresh batch of vegetables at the man's feet, and a healthy glow to the rest of the land.

Everything before him now, as he stepped carefully forward, was grey, and the man seemed oblivious to his presence. Fifty feet away by the well, two boys were playing, chasing each other around the stone structure and ignoring the relentless heat of the sun.

It felt real.

Sam had definitely been there once, experiencing the burning heat and the dry, uncomfortable humidity that clung to the back of his throat. But he wasn't experiencing that now.

This wasn't real.

This was a fragment of his mind.

'You are lucky to be alive.' The man spoke without turning, driving the shovel down once more and hauling more dirt from the earth. The ditch he was digging had the makings of a grave, and Sam knew what the next words out of his mouth were before he spoke them.

'Is that for me?'

'It could be.' The conversation was different from how he remembered. The man was less friendly.

Cold.

Like a ghost.

Sam stepped next to the man, and for the first time in nearly fifteen years, he saw the world-weary face of Farhad Nabizada. The man hadn't aged from the day he'd rescued Sam, when he'd been blasted from the cliff face above the village. Broken shards of the event began to slide through Sam's mind. Broken pieces of a puzzle that had never been completed.

'Farhad?' Sam spoke softly in disbelief.

'There were times when this village was peaceful. When this world was peaceful.' Farhad dug further into the earth. 'When we didn't rely on violence.'

'You saved my life,' Sam began, but Farhad cut him off, as if he was relaying his own inner monologue.

'Yet there is always violence now. All people want is what they can take, and it doesn't matter who is in the way.' The shovel hauled more dirt up, and Sam realised the grave had grown at an unnatural rate. 'My boys will succumb to the violence. You may have tried to save them, but the world will swallow them up when they have nowhere left to turn. I kept you alive, but for what purpose?'

Sam could feel his eyes watering, and Farhad refused to look at him. Instead, with a frail hand, he pointed to the well where the two boys were playing. Sam had recalled

Farhad's two sons, Tahir and Masood, and not a day went by that he didn't wonder what had happened to them.

But only Masood was by the well, merrily playing with another young boy.

Jamie.

'What is this?' Sam spat angrily, and Farhad finally turned to Sam who recoiled in horror. Farhad's eyes were completely grey, the life having been ripped from his body by the bullet hole that was displayed proudly in the centre of his skull. Sam remembered that moment, watching in horror as the Taliban pinned the doctor to the ground and executed him in front of his own son.

All because he'd dared to do the right thing and keep Sam alive.

To give him a chance.

'For what purpose?' Farhad repeated.

'I don't understand…' Sam muttered, guilt-ridden tears rolling down his cheek.

'Your life.' Farhad spoke softly, as if he was beginning to fade from Sam's memory. 'What purpose?'

'To fight back. To fight for those who can't.'

A cruel smile cracked on Farhad's face, and he dropped the shovel, allowing it to fall to the ground with a loud thud. Calmly, the broken memory reached out a hand and placed it on Sam's shoulder.

'Then fight.'

Sam stepped back, looking frantically around as the landscape began to become engulfed in shadow. The world was beginning to die before his very eyes, with every detail and fragment of his surroundings being engulfed by the darkness. He turned back to Farhad, but no one was there.

Nothing but the shovel on the ground, and when Sam looked down at his hands, he was now inexplicably holding it.

Then he looked into the grave.

The crumpled, broken corpse of his son stared back at him. The same image he'd seen every time he'd closed his eyes, and the one that had haunted almost every dream since the night he lost him. Blood trickled from Jamie's ear, dripping onto the grey soil, which was slowly turning black.

Sam dropped to his knees, weeping as his boy began to fade into the darkness.

Then Jamie twisted his head to look up at his dad and he yelled.

'Dad. Wake up!'

———

Sam opened his eyes and saw the grey smoke pressing against the ceiling of Kovac's home. The heat from the surrounding fire was palpable, and as he coughed and spluttered, he knew there wasn't much time left before the entire place was an inferno. Pushing himself up, he realised he'd fallen on the remnants of a sofa, the remaining cushions absorbing most of the impact from his fall.

Most. Not all.

His body ached, and as he tried to raise his arm, he felt a searing pain from his rib cage. A few more broken ribs to add to the ever-growing collection. His spine was stiff and in sharp, jagged motions, he managed to push himself off the sofa and to his feet. The collision with the sofa had still taken its toll on his mind. His memory was hazy, and he was trying to establish what had happened.

Townsend and his wife were through the door to safety.

Kovac.

Sam instinctively shot his hand to the back of his waist band, only to find his guns were gone. They were lost to the blaze, meaning he was stood, surrounded by fire, with no weapon and no clue where Kovac was.

Wherever the man had fallen, he'd moved, as Sam couldn't see a body.

He also didn't see the fist which hurtled through the smoke and caught him flat on the cheek. Sam stumbled backwards, his feet scraping up charred embers of Kovac's life, and The Man of Stone appeared through the smoke.

His shirt was ripped, revealing charred skin and a well-toned physique. His hair was matted with blood and his stern face was littered with cuts and burns. There was no weapon in his hand, and he stared at Sam, clenched his fists and sent a silent acceptance that this was it.

Sam raised his fist to the challenge.

This would be to the death.

Kovac lunged forward, swinging a few rights which Sam evaded, before he himself ducked a retaliation from Sam. Weaving under Sam's arm, Kovac drilled his elbow into Sam's busted ribcage, and followed it up with a solid left hook that sent Sam stumbling backwards.

'You take everything from me,' Kovac moaned, his voice heavy with hatred. 'Now I will torture your body, so that your soul will beg forgiveness.'

The ominous threat was followed by a few more strikes, which Sam absorbed in the blockade he'd created with his arms, but Kovac drove his knee into Sam's gut and then quickly smashed his other knee into Sam's face. Hitting the burning floor, Sam felt the blood dripping from his mouth and for the first time in a long time, he felt outmatched.

Sam had been an elite soldier for many years. One of the best.

But so had Kovac.

As Sam tried to crawl to his feet, Kovac kicked him in the ribs again, causing Sam to howl in agony. Dropping to one knee, Kovac nailed a few hard right hands to Sam's face, trying his best to beat the life from him. Sam, ignoring the pain from his ribs, managed to use his own body weight to flip Kovac off him and both of them scrambled up at the same time. As Kovac turned, Sam rocked him with a hard right, and then in one fluid motion, drew the elbow back up and caught Kovac on the other side of the face. Shaken, Kovac tried to throw a punch of his own, but Sam hooked the man's arm in close to his body and then twisted, wrenching Kovac's shoulder until the tendons began to rip. Gasping in pain, Kovac swung his head forward, his skull catching Sam on the jaw and causing him to fall back and release his grip. As both men tried to regroup, their eyes were locked on each other. Neither man was going to back down, and both men respected the other for it.

But the smoke was thickening.

The blaze was growing.

Time was running out.

'We can end this, Sam,' Kovac barked across the noisy fire that was roaring around them. 'We could call truce and take this whole country. Together.'

'Not gonna happen,' Sam said, throwing his fists up and signalling the unofficial second round.

'What the hell do you fight for? Huh?' Kovac spat, reaching behind him to the remnants of his bar, where his fingers wrapped around a corkscrew which he clutched, with the curled spike poking between his index and middle finger. 'This had nothing to do with you. So why fight?'

'Because it's the right thing to do.'

Sam's response triggered a response from Kovac, who leapt forward and slashed wildly with his newly acquired weapon. Sam managed to dodge the first few swipes before the third one sliced across his forearm and drew blood. Ignoring the pain, Sam blocked the next attempt and caught Kovac with an elbow before swinging a clubbing forearm into the man's chest, just as he swept a foot behind Kovac's legs.

The Man of Stone left the ground, his back colliding viciously with the concrete and his head making a sickening thud on impact. Dazed and desperate, Kovac stumbled back to his feet and lunged, the corkscrew aimed for Sam's eye. But Sam weaved, but grabbed Kovac's tired arm and bent it back, redirecting the screw back at him. Flustered, Kovac tried to squirm free, but Sam pressed harder, the screw inching back closer and closer to Kovac's own face. As the two men struggled among the burning wreckage, Kovac swung his knee forward and caught Sam between the legs. Sam's knees buckled, and he dropped to the floor in pain and Kovac dived on top of him, using his bodyweight to pin Sam to the ground and with the advantage over Sam, he drove the corkscrew down towards Sam's throat. Sam got his arm up, using every fibre of his being to resist, but Kovac leant forward, rising up onto one knee and using his other hand to apply pressure, pressed down as hard as he could.

'This is my kingdom!' Kovac screamed with delirious rage.

Sam knew he wouldn't hold him off, so redirected the man's body weight to the shoulder and as he let go, Kovac rammed the curled blade into Sam's skin. Sam grit his teeth, but his focus was on the shard of wood that was an arm's length away, and as Kovac pressed the blade down, he lost his balance.

Sam drove his knee into the base of Kovac's spine and sent him falling forward, releasing Sam, who fought through the pain barrier and snatched up the sharp, broken wooden beam. Kovac returned to his knees, just as Sam did, and Kovac once again swung the corkscrew towards Sam's face.

Sam reached up and caught Kovac by the wrist, stopping him in mid-lunge and with his other hand, he rammed the wooden shard into Kovac's waist.

Kovac shuddered with pain as the wood pierced through his skin and lodged into his stomach, the warm blood flowing out over the wood and covering Sam's hand. Kovac's eyes widened with acceptance, and the force within his lunging arm dropped. Sam snatched the corkscrew from Kovac's hand and without hesitation, he drove it upwards, piercing the skin under Kovac's jawbone and he pushed it until the metal spike ripped through the man's tongue.

Blood filled his mouth, and Kovac rolled to the side, gurgling as he began to drown in his own blood.

Ten seconds later, he was dead.

The Man of Stone was no more.

Still on his knees, Sam took a moment to try to catch his breath, only to heave as the smoke became too much to bear. Spluttering, he scrambled to his feet, his woozy feet struggling to form coherent steps towards the stairs. His ribs were shaking in his chest, and his left arm was limp from the puncture wound to his shoulder. The final few grains of sand in the hourglass trickled through and although Sam could see the staircase that led to his freedom, his lungs were too beaten.

There was no air in the room.

Sam stumbled forward, his eyes closing, and as he hit the ground, he accepted that this was finally where his final race had been run. With his final moments, Sam felt his body being pulled up from the ground, and the sudden movement caused him to half open his eyes.

Townsend.

Despite the clear signs of the monstrous beating he'd taken, Townsend had returned to Sam's fiery grave, holding on to the slimmest hope of getting him out. As he hoisted Sam limply to his feet, Townsend draped Sam's arm over his shoulder.

'Fuckin' hell, Sam. How much do you weigh?'

Townsend chuckled beneath his T-shirt, which he'd pulled over his nose and mouth, hoping it would add a little bit of protection. Beams began to fall from the rooftops with mighty thumps, and fire blazed higher, roaring with unstoppable rage and with an unpredictability. Townsend heaved Sam up the first step, and as he battled against the severe lack of oxygen, Townsend thought of Eve.

He thought of everything he'd been through for his family.

To get back to them.

And as he hauled Sam's lifeless body up the final few steps, he knew he owed everything to Sam Pope. That even if he was dancing dangerously close to the devil, Townsend needed to pull Sam out. As he pulled Sam up over the final step, a large rumble beneath them echoed through home and Townsend, with his arms wrapped around Sam, fell out through the front door and onto the glass shards that surrounded it. Townsend knelt up immediately, looking down at Sam who wasn't moving.

Wasn't breathing.

'Jesus Christ, Sam. Wake up!' Townsend screamed loudly, before he immediately went into CPR. He did thirty compressions and then pulled Sam's head back, pressed his finger down on the chin to open the airway. Townsend breathed a lungful of fresh air into Sam's mouth.

Nothing.

'Fuckin' fight, Sam,' Townsend yelled, as the rain hit them hard, and he continued his compression. 'Don't you give up, you hear me?'

Townsend didn't even realise he had tears streaming down his face, and as he pressed down on his thirtieth compression, he went through the same process of mouth to mouth once more.

This time, Sam coughed.

Townsend rocked back on his knees as Sam turned to the side, spluttering wildly as the air made its way through his body and kick started his body once more. After a few seconds of realisation, he turned back to Townsend and shook his head.

'Thanks. You saved my life.'

'I'd call us even.' Townsend smiled and stood, offering his hand to Sam who took it, and very carefully made his way to his feet. His balance was off slightly, and his body needed to stabilise itself after his near-death experience. After a few deep breaths, he noticed Townsend pacing the front garden with a haunted expression on his face.

'Everything okay?' Sam asked weakly.

'Where the fuck is my wife?' Townsend said in a panic, breaking into a small jog towards the only working car on the vast gravel forecourt.

A terrified scream echoed from the woods in the other direction, and without hesitation, Townsend set off towards it, leaving Sam and the burning wreckage behind. As he passed one of the dead bodies that Sam had left in his wake, Townsend bent down and retrieved the Glock 17 from the corpse.

He'd never fired a gun before.

But as he set off into the woods to find his wife, he had no problems in experiencing it for the first time.

CHAPTER TWENTY-NINE

There was no way anyone could have survived.

Sanders was still laying on the wet gravel, soaked through by the downpour as the fire rampaged through Kovac's house. He'd heard no more gunshots after he'd managed to escape up the stairs, and the chances of anyone making it out had long gone. His stomach knotted with guilt at the thought of Townsend and Mandy on the floor, overwhelmed by the smoke as they slowly faded from the world.

At least they wouldn't feel the pain of the flames them-selves, unlike Kovac.

Sanders may have been in the pocket of the criminal, but he'd never killed someone before. But he saw his chance to escape from Kovac's grip and he took it.

Now, he was waiting for the cavalry to arrive, with his call to the police completed a few minutes ago, meaning he had a good ten to fifteen minutes before anyone would actually arrive. Kovac's home was as remote as he could get it, and Sanders was happy to wait.

He'd already figured out what he was going to say.

When Sam Pope had orchestrated an attack on Kovac's

home base, Sanders rushed to try to pull Townsend out, along with his wife. Unfortunately, everything escalated, and Sanders was the only one who survived.

All evidence of his association with Kovac would have been eradicated by the fire, and anyone who could ever point the finger at him was burning beside it.

He was a free man.

Despite the rain, Sanders was kept warm by the searing heat emanating from the house, and as he waited for the boys in blue, he wondered what his next step would be. With Kovac's operation gone, along with Sam Pope and regrettably, Townsend, he was in the position to write his own narrative. Perhaps he could spin it to make it seem more deliberate, that maybe Townsend had gone too far across the divide and Sanders had bravely tried to bring him back?

As the ideas began to formulate in his head, Sanders heard what sounded like the crunching of footsteps on glass, but he shook the notion from his mind.

There was no way anyone was getting out alive.

Another crunch.

Sanders sat up, agitated, as he tried to peer through the smoke. Sure enough, he saw the figures of two people shuffling towards the door.

'What the fuck?' Sanders uttered to himself, and he hobbled to his feet. His ankle was next to useless, and as the people got closer to the door, Sanders shuffled as quickly as he could to the side of the house, passing one of the dead bodies that Sam had left to the elements. As Sanders disappeared from view, he listened intently as he heard the footsteps drag across the gravel before someone collapsed onto the stones.

Carefully, he peered round the side of the house and his eyes widened with horror.

It was Townsend and Mandy.

Despite his restraints and being locked underground with the murderous Luka, somehow Townsend had survived. As he watched Townsend rock forward on his knees, his body and face covered in blood, he soon realised what the feeling was that was bubbling inside of him. It wasn't guilt.

It wasn't self-hatred.

It was jealousy.

Sanders was jealous of the man that Townsend clearly was. A man who was willing to fight for and die for his family. A man who was compelled to do the right thing. And by being that man, despite the absence and the borderline drinking problem, he still had a wife and child who loved him.

The man had courage.

He had integrity.

All the things Sanders knew he lacked, and watching Townsend struggle to his feet, despite his wife's best attempts to keep him down, Sanders understood that the world was a better place for people like Townsend.

Except now, it meant that his narrative was no longer his own to write.

As Sanders raced through his options in his mind, Townsend pushed past Mandy and stumbled back into the fire, his wife howling in horror as her husband disappeared into the smoke. She screamed out his name, begging him to turn back, but there was no response.

Having just been reunited, Mandy dropped to her knees in the rain, her eyes flooded with tears as she wept in terror.

Sanders saw his opportunity and disguised by the audible damage of the fire that was rampaging through the building, Mandy didn't hear him shuffle to the dead body between them. Mandy only realised she wasn't alone when she saw Sanders lift the handgun from the dead body and aim it directly at her. With her jaw open in shock, Mandy raised her hands and slowly got to her feet.

'Reece. What are you doing?'

'I'm sorry, Mandy. I really am.'

'It's over, Reece.' Mandy shook her head. 'Everyone's dead.'

'Where's Jack? Huh? Why did he run back in?'

'Kovac took Sam over the balcony. They're dead, but Jack needed to be sure. The fool.' Mandy took a deep, comforting breath. 'He said he owed Sam. Please put the gun down.'

Sanders was crying, and he scolded himself for being so pathetic.

'I'm sorry, Mandy. But I can't go to prison. I just can't.'

'You messed up, Reece. But you don't have to do anymore damage. Just put the gun down and…'

From inside the house, something heavy collapsed under the duress of the fire, and Mandy startled. Sanders realised that at any moment, Townsend could fall back through the door, and even with a gun in his hand, he had no fear of Sanders. Not after everything he'd done.

What he'd put him through.

Put Mandy through.

Keeping his gun trained on Mandy, he nodded beyond her to the trees at the perimeter of the forecourt. Despite the wall that ran through the woods, there was enough of a woodland within Kovac's ground for them to disappear, at least until the police arrived. Hopefully, Townsend didn't make it back through the door, and then the only thing standing in the way of Sanders and complete freedom was the woman staring down the barrel of his gun.

Sanders had been to enough crime scenes to know how to make it look like he had nothing to do with it.

There was already blood on his hands. A little more, despite how innocent, was the price to pay for his freedom.

With a hard, reluctant sigh, he directed Mandy towards the trees with the gun.

'Move. Quickly.'

With her hands still raised, Mandy obliged, and Sanders limped heavily behind her, leaving a few feet of space to ensure she didn't try anything brave. As they passed the first tree of the threshold, a large clatter echoed behind them and they both turned to witness Townsend collapse onto the gravel just outside the door, with the life-less body of Sam Pope rolling off his shoulder and into a limp sprawl.

Mandy tried to scream, but Sanders stuck the gun directly to her head and she caught her tongue. Angrily, he yanked an arm around her neck and held his hand over her mouth to keep quiet. Now and then, as he uncomfortably dragged her further into the woods, he pressed the gun to her head to remind her of the consequences.

But Mandy was a fighter.

Just like her husband.

And realising the inevitable if she did nothing, Mandy stamped down as hard as she could on Sanders's injured ankle, and then at the top of her voice, she screamed for her husband.

———

Townsend rushed into the woods in a panic, his feet taking him in the rough direction of his wife's terrified call. His feet slid in the wet mud and he nearly fell, before steadying himself against a tree. Although the adrenaline was doing a fine job of keeping him going, the moment he stopped, the pain of his beating rushed to the surface.

'Mandy?' Townsend called, looking in every direction. The downpour and the thick woodland crowded his vision, and he cursed under his breath with worry. Somewhere to his left, he heard a crash, and with his gun raised, Townsend pushed off in the direction of the noise. As he rounded a large tree, he saw her.

Mandy.

She was on her knees, refusing to move, as the detestable Sanders pulled at her arm in frustration. Seeing the man's hand on his wife caused Townsend's blood to boil, and he yelled with fury as he rushed into the opening. Instinctively, Mandy turned, her face morphing into a smile. But that loss of focus was enough for Sanders to wrap his arm around her neck and hoist her to her feet. With the barrel of his gun pressed against her head, he shook his head at Townsend.

'It was never meant to be this way, Jack. You have to believe me.'

'I don't believe anything that comes out of your damn mouth.' Townsend took a step forward, causing Sanders to tighten his grip. 'All of this, Reece. Everything. For this?'

'I had no other choice.'

'There is always a choice. A better choice.' Townsend could feel his voice breaking, the emotion of the betrayal and his wife's abduction threatening to derail him. 'You should have told me what the hell was going on. What you were getting me into.'

Sirens wailed in the distance, meaning the police were nearly there. Whatever plan Sanders had constructed would now be rendered pointless. There were survivors who knew what he'd done. There was no walking away from it now.

'Just walk away, Jack.' Sanders took an uncomfortable step backwards. 'Let me go, and I swear I will release her when I'm far enough away. I can't go to prison…'

Out of nowhere, Mandy lifted her foot and drove it down as hard as she could on Sander's already damaged ankle. Sanders howled with agony, relinquishing his grip of her and his gun as his ankle gave out beneath him. He could feel the shattered bone within his skin and on his knees. There was a sense of finality to everything.

All of it had come to the only conclusion he could now hope for.

He was on his knees. In the dark woods under a torrential downpour. On the outskirts of the property, the police were fast approaching, ready to send him away to a life of solitary confinement for his own safety.

There was only one way to end this.

And as Townsend stepped forward, lifting the gun in his hand, Sanders could see that he agreed.

'You won't be going to prison.' Townsend spat through gritted teeth, lining the pistol up with Sanders' forehead as he stood roughly four feet away from him.

Mandy begged her husband to put the gun down.

Sanders closed his eyes in acceptance.

'Don't do it, Jack.' Townsend and Mandy spun round at the sound of the voice, and Sanders opened his eyes. Through the trees, walking gingerly and with his hand pressed over his own punctured shoulder, Sam ambled into view. He coughed a few times, still battling the smoke inhalation but he was standing. He stopped next to Jack and reached out for the gun. 'Give me the gun, Jack.'

'This man deserves to die,' Townsend cried, his eyes watering.

'Listen to him, babe.' Mandy pressed her hand to Townsend's cheek to calm him.

'Come on, Jack. Kill me,' Sanders begged, trying to run from his fate. 'Look at what I did to you. To your family.'

'Shut up,' Townsend yelled, stepping forward and pressing the barrel of the gun against Sanders' forehead.

'Give me the gun, Jack,' Sam repeated.

'Think of your daughter,' Sanders goaded. 'Three years without you…'

'Look at me, Jack. Look at me. Give me the gun.'

'Everyone shut the fuck up!' Townsend lifted the gun into the air and pulled the trigger, blasting a bullet into the night sky and shaking the trees with the gunshot. Sanders and Mandy startled, but Sam didn't flinch. Stepping forward, Sam placed his hand on top of the gun, which Townsend had redirected at Sanders.

'Be the better man, Jack,' Sam said calmly. 'Be better than him. Be better than me.'

'After everything he did…' Townsend stammered, a tear rolling down his face as he struggled with his conscious. Sanders leant forward, pressing his own forehead against the barrel.

'Come on, Jack. I deserve it.'

Townsend lifted the gun, causing Sanders to fall flat on his front with a grunt.

'No, you deserve to rot in prison.'

As Sanders pushed himself up to respond, Townsend drilled him with a kick to the jaw, knocking him back into the mud. The front of the burning house was now intermittently lit up in blue, as the police cars flooded the forecourt. Instantly, an officer called for the fire service and ambulance, as the blazing house was accompanied by a few dead bodies. With the reports of who was inside, they suspected there would be plenty more.

Townsend draped his arm over Mandy's shoulder as they watched on from the protection of the trees, before he turned to Sam who offered him a smile.

'Thank you, Sam.' Townsend extended his hand. 'For everything.'

Sam shook it firmly.

'Don't mention it.' He then looked at the increasing

number of police officers, who were beginning to spread across the premises. 'I better be going.'

Mandy stepped forward and wrapped her arms around Sam, drawing a slight grimace from him when she touched his ribs. She hugged him gently and then rested her hand on the side of Sam's face. The rain was doing its best to wash the blood from it, but he still wore the scars of his brutal conflict with Kovac.

Mandy was crying.

'Thank you for bringing him back to me.'

Sam smiled, patting her hand with his own. He nodded before turning on his heel and hobbling off as quickly as he could, his hand pressed against the wound on his shoulder and his lungs still struggling under the relentless assault of that smoke.

But Townsend was alive. So was Mandy.

Kovac had been stopped.

As Sam Pope disappeared among the trees, he knew that whatever lay ahead, he'd done the right thing.

Townsend and Mandy watched for a few more moments, until Sam had merged with the woods, and then turned towards the police officers, ready to put everything behind them and get their life back.

CHAPTER THIRTY

'We're here.'

Mandy's voice infiltrated Townsend's dream and pulled him from his slumber. For a split second, he had no idea of his surroundings, but he quickly collected himself. His face was a tapestry of pain, with stitches, cuts, and bruises holding the whole thing together like a crude jigsaw puzzle. The painkillers he'd been prescribed were especially strong and given what he'd been through the night before, Mandy felt it was best to let him get some rest.

After Sam had disappeared into the night, Mandy had taken her husband to the police, revealing his identity and requesting medical assistance. As he was treated at the scene, Townsend relayed everything to the officer in charge, ensuring that they arrested Sanders for his role in it all.

Despite his assurances to Kovac, Townsend had made back-up copies of his files and was willing to share them with the police to ensure everything was handled properly.

The only thing he and Mandy omitted was their associ-ation with Sam Pope.

When questioned about it, they both claimed ignorance, stating they'd been kidnapped and were just fortunate enough that Sam was there to give them the opportunity to get out.

The whole situation was a mess.

The fire fighters eventually brought the blaze under control, but the damage to the building was so significant that it made it a death trap to venture in to. They would eventually retrieve body after body, all of them charred to the bone. Dental records would be pulled, but Townsend wondered if they would even exist.

Kovac was a careful man, and there was every chance that his body would remain unidentified. It would keep his name out there, haunting the local criminals and hopefully closing a gap that Townsend and Sam had created.

Someone was always willing to sit on the throne.

Even more satisfying for Townsend was that it was a certainty that all Kovac's arsenal and stock would have been destroyed. Millions of pounds, in cash, drugs, and guns lost to the devastating fire.

It may not have been the way he'd envisaged, and it was considerably more painful, but Townsend had done what he'd set out to do.

Kovac and his guns and drugs were off the street.

Mandy pulled the car to a stop, and Townsend rubbed the sleep from his eyes. It was a little before lunchtime, and the car park to the office block was reasonably full. He didn't doubt that that many people required therapy, but as a shared office, he knew there was multiple business inside. Gingerly, he followed Mandy to the glass door, and they approached the receptionist who looked at Townsend's beaten face with horror. She lifted the phone.

'I assume you're here for Mercer and Gibbons?'

'Huh?' Townsend shrugged. Mandy looked at the chrome sign behind the receptionist that listed every business that was based within. Mercer and Gibson were lawyers, and Mandy chuckled.

'We aren't here for a lawyer.'

'Oh, right.' The woman placed the phone back down. 'You sure?'

'Yeah, I'm pretty sure.' Townsend rolled his eyes.

'We're here to see Amy Devereux…' Mandy could feel her voice cracking. 'She's expecting us.'

The receptionist directed them to the lifts and then scurried back to her desk, leaving Townsend and Mandy to ascend in the lift. Once the doors pinged and they stepped out, Townsend recalled the route they'd taken the day before, and this time they were greeted by a friendly receptionist and a busier waiting room. Before Townsend even spoke, Deesha knew who he was, and she raised a finger to them, lifted her phone, and pressed a button.

'He's here,' Deesha said politely. She nodded and hung up the phone. 'Go right through.'

A few waiting patients scowled at a perceived jumping of the queue, but Mandy didn't care. She marched as quickly as she could through the waiting room and to the door that was embossed with Amy's name. Impatiently, she pounded on the door, and it was quickly pulled open by a frowning Amy.

'Please. I have a headache.'

'Sorry,' Mandy said as she stepped in. She pointed at Amy's stomach. 'Better get used to them, eh?'

'So I hear.' Amy chuckled and extended her hand. 'I'm Amy.'

'MUMMY!'

Mandy's attention was taken away by the bounding steps of her daughter as an excited Eve rushed across the office and leapt into her arms. Mandy fell to her knees to embrace her, and she welcomed the floods of tears that rushed down her face and into her daughter's hair.

'My girl,' Mandy whispered quietly. 'My girl. My girl.'

Townsend walked in behind Mandy, and he offered Amy a sheepish grin. He looked like hell, with two bandages holding his stitches in place, a clearly broken nose and bruising around his eyes. Amy felt immense sympathy for the trials the man had clearly gone through, but it was balanced with respect. The man had fought valiantly for what he loved, and now, as he watched his wife hug their daughter, she saw the pride that beamed from him like a lighthouse.

'Thank you, Amy,' Townsend said quietly, reaching out and patting her shoulder. 'How can we ever repay you?'

'Don't be silly. We had fun, didn't we, Evie?'

'Yup. I was a doctor,' Eve stated proudly, her back straight.

'Were you?' Mandy faked her excitement. 'Did you help Dr Amy?'

'Mmmm hmmm.' Townsend felt his heart race at how adorable she was. 'Daddy, do you need a doctor?'

'I've already been, pickle.' He lowered himself down, so he was next to Mandy, and Eve stepped forward and looked at him, inspecting the remnants of battle that covered his face.

'Can we go home now?' Eve asked.

'We sure can, kiddo,' Mandy chimed in before looking lovingly at her husband. 'All of us. Together.'

'Together,' Townsend repeated, feeling his bottom lip wobble. Eve gave a cheer and then buried herself in her father's arms. Townsend absorbed the blow and ignored the agony shooting through his body.

It was worth it.

She was worth it.

After a few moments, she let go and then, taking her mother's hand, she led her to the door. As she opened it, Eve turned back to Amy, who was smiling at her.

'Bye, Doctor Amy.'

'Bye, Doctor Evie.' Amy waved. She then looked at Mandy and smiled. 'You take care of her.'

'We will. Thank you.'

Amy nodded and watched as Mandy was led from her office by their eager child. Townsend followed her gaze and then turned to her. His eyes were watering, and he extended his arms for a hug.

'Thank you, Amy.' She stepped in and embraced him. 'You didn't have to do that.'

'I wasn't given much choice.' She joked. 'Plus, it's kind of hard to turn down doing the right thing. Especially with Sam about.'

'I hear that.'

Amy stepped back and anxiously bit her lip.

'Is he…'

'Alive?' Townsend nodded. 'Yeah. He's alive. Funnily enough, I saved him. And then, when I was so sure I was going to do something I regret, he stepped in and saved me.'

'Like I said. A difference between a bad man and a broken one.'

'And there is a difference between a broken man and a good one, as well.'

Amy raised her eyebrows, as if she was impressed. She stepped back to her desk as Townsend headed to the door. As he pulled it open, he looked back at her.

'Take care of yourself, Amy.'

'You too, Jack.' Amy lowered herself uncomfortably into her chair. 'Now go and be with your family.'

Townsend stepped through the door and back across the waiting room to his two girls who were waiting by the glass door. Without saying a word, he lifted Eve off her feet, wrapped his other arm around his wife, and buried himself among them. Holding them as tight as he could, and he knew that he would never let them go.

Never again.

———

Sam had slept until midday, and when he awoke, the first thing he did was hunt for the paracetamol. After scaling the wall of Kovac's land and making his way through the woods to freedom, Sam had made his long, arduous way back to Lowestoft and to the Airbnb he'd used as a base since the beginning. He smirked, thinking about the owner having no clue what they'd helped him to accomplish.

On his way home, he'd stopped at the twenty-four-hour Asda megastore, and raided the pharmacy for painkillers, antiseptic, and high-quality medical bandages. When he'd arrived home, Sam had treated the stab wound in his shoulder, cleaning it through gritted teeth before bandaging it up. There was little he could do about the broken ribs, and after an awkward shower where he kept his bandaged arm out of the cubicle, he felt a little better.

He collapsed on the bed in his towel and didn't move until he naturally woke.

The painkillers went down well, and he carefully got dressed, sliding his broken body into another plain black T-shirt with as little pain as possible. He'd been through the wars, and his body had another chapter of scars to add to the others, in the ongoing story of his life.

He may have lost some of the weapons he'd taken, but he'd still significantly increased his arsenal, ready to take on whatever else he could find that was rotting his country from within.

Kovac had been killed, and Sam didn't feel a shred of remorse. He'd long since made peace with the fact that he'd broken the promise to his son, and when the time came for them to be reunited, he hoped his son would understand why Sam's path was so necessary.

The ripple effects of Kovac's empire would have destroyed thousands of lives and probably ended hundreds. It's not just those who get hooked on the drugs, or those who take the bullets that are the ones effected.

It's those who loved them.

Those who cared.

The ripple effect might lessen the further it goes, but make no mistake, Kovac was responsible for so much damage that watching him die had filled Sam with pride.

And affirmation.

He'd tried to run from who he was and live a quiet and peaceful life surrounded by good friends and trying his best to do good the right way. But after what happened to Sean Wiseman, Sam knew that he was made for one path.

Seeing the damage Kovac had done and witnessing the corruption of Sanders who was willing to throw a good man and his family to the wolves, only served to confirm to Sam that he was needed.

That there was a fight.

His stomach rumbled, and Sam packed up his remaining possessions, which all fit in a second sports bag. In the other, Sam packed away his remaining assault rifles and handguns, ready for another venture into the belly of the criminal underworld. He hadn't seen any of the news yet, but there was no doubt that Kovac's murder and the destruction of his empire would be all over it. By burning it all to the ground, Sam had successfully decimated any resource that Kovac's benefactor may have still had.

The supply line was cut.

The stock was destroyed.

Whoever was pulling the budgetary strings behind Kovac had nothing left.

Along with that news, Sam Pope would undoubtedly be

the story. After what he'd done to Bowker a few weeks prior, the papers were speculating on his return. Lynsey Beckett, the BBC reporter he'd saved, had decided not to re-introduce him to the world, instead giving him as much of a head start as possible.

But they would piece together the evidence. Two weeks after Sam supposedly rose from the dead, one of the most dangerous criminals in the UK is brutally slain in his own home.

Along with his whole empire reduced to rubble.

Every police department in the UK would be on high alert, and every major criminal would be arming his men for war.

Sam marched out of the Airbnb for the final time and dumped both sports bags into the boot of the car before dropping into the driver's seat. He had no idea where he was heading, nor what his next move or target was.

Besides getting something to eat.

He at least knew that.

Sam brought the car to life, and pulled away, heading off to fill his stomach and walk the next journey of his life.

And if that meant he was going to war, then so be it.

EPILOGUE

'*Buvaj.*'

On a brisk evening in Kyiv, Uri Zubov hung up his phone and neatly slotted it back into his blazer. The dark grey suit, worn over a crisp, well-fitted black shirt, clung to his hulking frame, one that was forged by the Burket through years of service.

Now, just the sight of him made sure everyone stayed in line.

In his previous role, he would need to use his physical attributes to more devastating effect. But in the new line of work, all it took was a glare to quieten down the most belligerent of clientele.

Nearly three years ago, he used to run the door of *Ешелон*, known as 'Echelon', one of the busiest and most frequented night clubs in the city. The police were paid to stay away, and punters paid to have their wishes fulfilled.

Drink.

Drugs.

Sex.

Everything was on the table, and for years, Uri watched as the punters rolled in and the cash piled up.

When someone stepped out of line, he had carte blanche to deal with them as he saw fit, which usually resulted in broken bones and missing teeth.

All in a night's work.

But that all crumbled to the ground on the fateful night Sam Pope arrived holding that fat, pathetic Burrows at gun point. Uri had always hated Burrows, even though the man had been loyal as a dog to Uri's boss, Sergei Kovalenko. The slimy politician had used his connections to facilitate Kovalenko's operation in the UK, where his nephew, Andrei, was placed in charge and made it thrive. Armed with his dangerous brother, Oleg, and feisty sister, Dana, Andrei soon became one of the most powerful crime lords in London.

But then he crossed Sam Pope.

And Sam Pope killed him. Oleg, too.

Then, to finally put a lock on Kovalenko, he arrived in Kyiv, blew *Ешелон* to pieces and left Sergei on his knees, his insides hanging from the slash across his gut. Uri's two friends, Artem and Vlad, were executed and somehow, through the ensuing gunfight, Uri survived.

As did Sam.

Until he was killed in America over two years ago.

That was it.

The opening Uri's new boss needed to return to Kyiv and reclaim the dilapidated building that Sergei Kovalenko had so proudly owned. With the world watching on, *Ешелон* was transformed into a day and health spa, offering the finest quality skin and health treatments. The entire place was reimagined, even winning an award within its second year of operation for exceptional service.

The world finally looked the other way.

Which allowed Dana Kovalenko to finally take her rightful place atop the Kovalenko empire and rebuild. With the fortune left behind Sergei's only living relative,

Dana had secured Uri's loyalty with a hefty pay rise and the promise of a role by her side.

He was as loyal to her as any dog would be to their master. Through his Berkut connections, she was placed in contact with Slaven Kovac, a man who reminded her a little too much of her brother, only this time there was no taboo about them getting physical.

It was all about power to her.

Looking down upon these naked, pathetic men as she sat atop of them, using her own body to render them helpless.

Kovac had more of a backbone than Uri, and she set him and his crew up with a base operation in a different part of the UK and he quickly took control of most of East Anglia.

But then the rumours arrived of Sam Pope being alive.

A few weeks later, Kovac was dead.

His whole crew, along with her operation, had gone up in smoke.

Uri walked into Dana's office and relayed the entire situation to her, although he made little effort to hide his enjoyment at Kovac's demise. But all the drugs and the money were gone.

Over half her empire had existed within that safe which had been burnt to the ground.

Another nail in the Kovalenko coffin, hammered in by Sam Pope.

Dana's eyes narrowed, and she gave Uri the order.

'*Put the word out.*' She spoke in her native tongue. '*Five million alive. Three million dead.*'

'*Of course,*' Uri replied.

'*Then start making the necessary arrangements.*' A cruel smile spread across Dana Kovalenko's face. '*We're heading to England.*'

GET EXCLUSIVE ROBERT ENRIGHT MATERIAL

Hey there,

I really hope you enjoyed the book and hopefully, you will want to continue following Sam Pope's war on crime. If so, then why not sign up to my reader group? I send out regular updates, polls and special offers as well as some cool free stuff. Sound good?

Well, if you do sign up to the reader group I'll send you FREE copies of THE RIGHT REASON and RAIN-FALL, two thrilling Sam Pope prequel novellas. (RRP: 1.99)

You can get your FREE books by signing up at www.robertenright.co.uk

SAM POPE NOVELS

For more information about the Sam Pope series, please visit:

www.robertenright.co.uk

ABOUT THE AUTHOR

Robert lives in Buckinghamshire with his family, writing books and dreaming of getting a dog.

For more information:
www.robertenright.co.uk
robert@robertenright.co.uk

You can also connect with Robert on Social Media:

 facebook.com/robenrightauthor

 twitter.com/REnright_Author

 instagram.com/robenrightauthor

Printed in Great Britain
by Amazon